SPELLBOUND STATUES

SPELLBOUND STATUES

REG RAWLINS, PSYCHIC INVESTIGATOR
BOOK TWENTY-THREE

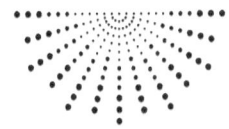

P.D. WORKMAN

PD WORKMAN

ISBN: 9781774687512 (KDP Paperback)
ISBN: 9781774687529 (KDP Hardcover)
ISBN: 9781774687543 (Lulu Paperback)
ISBN: 9781774687536 (Large Print)
ISBN: 9781774687550 (Digital)
ISBN: 9781774687567 (Auto-narrated audiobook)

ALSO BY P.D. WORKMAN

MYSTERY/SUSPENSE:

Reg Rawlins, Psychic Detective
Paranormal Mystery & Adventure

What the Cat Knew

A Psychic with Catitude

A Catastrophic Theft

Night of Nine Tails

The Immortal's Key

Yule's Sinister Spell

Fairy Blade Unmade

Web of Nightmares

A Whisker's Breadth

Skunk Man Swamp

Magic Ain't A Game

Without Foresight

Careful of Thy Wishes

Time to Your Elf

Undiscovered Tomb

Missing Powers

Thrice Spared

Cloaked Campaign

Sleepwalker's Sanctuary

Cat Tales in the Swamp (Short Story)

Tainted Truffle Treachery

A Fowl Play on Christmas Day (Christmas crossover story)

Lunar Lies

X Marks the Past (Coming Soon)

Spellbound Statues (Coming Soon)

Fur and Fury (Coming Soon)

Kenzie Kirsch Medical Thrillers

Unlawful Harvest

Doctored Death

Dosed to Death

Gentle Angel

Rushin' Death

Posed for Death

Death of a Corpse

Endowed with Death

Shattered to Death

Captured in Death

Currying Death (Coming Soon)

Healed to Death (Coming Soon)

Death's Charm (Coming Soon)

A Bleeding Hearts Valley Thriller

An Abrupt Departure (Coming Soon)

AND MORE AT PDWORKMAN.COM

To all those willing to join hands
and save the world.

* * *

CHAPTER ONE

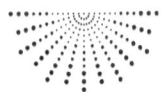

*G*ideon Darkwood crept through the trees, taking the well-worn pathway to the temple in the orange grove. The moonlight filtered through the dense canopy of orange trees, casting eerie shadows that danced around him as he moved stealthily along the path. The citrusy aroma of oranges lingered in the air, but Gideon's thoughts were far removed from their sweetness.

Though Gideon had traversed this way many times before, it was not he who had worn the path through grass and dirt. That had been formed by the feet of the warlock coven that met there regularly.

It was hard to believe that Corvin now led the coven. Back when they had been young warlocks together, it was unimaginable that a power drinker would ever be allowed to hold such a position in the coven. Back then, Corvin had been barred from even being a member of an established coven. How things had changed since then.

Corvin's leadership of the coven had not been as successful as he had hoped. He had promised the coven members that he would share some of his accumulated powers and gifts with them if elected. And to his credit, he had followed through and tried to do that.

But things had gone awry.

What Corvin had done to merit the attack by the werewolves, Gideon didn't know. And he probably didn't want to know. He'd seen enough of Corvin's nature in the past. They had worked together to maintain the spell of the Temple Orange Grove for decades. Centuries, now. He had seen many of Corvin's highs and lows.

The warlock might have good intentions, but his inborn nature, which he could not change no matter what he willed, always twisted those good intentions into something else.

Since the attack, Corvin had cloistered himself within the walls of his home and would take no visitors. Gideon's attempts to communicate with him had been rebuffed. Corvin said he needed some recovery time and would get back to Gideon when he was feeling better. Many rumors were flying around about the injuries Corvin had received, but Gideon assumed most of the rumors were false. He wouldn't believe any story unless it came from Corvin's own lips, and probably not even then.

He might approach a few of the members of the coven who had been there during the attack to get the whole story. He wasn't sure whether any of them would talk to him. And there might be little they could tell him about the attack. Something like that, an ambush during the spring equinox ritual, must have shocked them. Completely unexpected, as far as he knew. Equinox was supposed to be a time of peace and balance. Most practitioners carefully avoided any offense or conflict that day.

Gideon followed the stones in the ground that had once been the foundations of the temple. It had stood there proudly many years before but, over time, it had fallen into disrepair, and relic hunters had removed many of the stones that had built the walls.

But Gideon was not looking for the stones of the walls.

There was another stone he sought.

Few knew of its existence, but its safety and integrity were vital for the welfare of the people of Black Sands. During the years before the stone had been laid there, life in Black Sands had been chaotic and dangerous. It had not been the sleepy little town it was now, sitting back quietly in contemplation. A place where magical practitioners had free commerce with one another. One of the safest places for psychics and witches to openly practice their craft. It had flourished for many years as the social center for all practitioners for hundreds of miles around.

Yet they were all ignorant of why Black Sands had become the magical mecca it was. That secret was shared by a select few, Gideon among them.

He found the altar stone the warlocks had placed at the central point of the temple. The herbs placed upon it were withered and dry, looking almost as if they had burned in the sunlight.

A faintly familiar smell rose to his nostrils. Pungent and earthy.

He heard a noise and startled, whirled around to look behind him. He pulled his cloak close to him in an effort to blend in to the darkness. A cloak of invisibility it was not, but the hood shadowed his face and kept it in darkness and the capacious sleeves covered his white, wrinkled hands.

Had someone followed him here? He had not seen anyone else on the road. He had watched carefully to make sure that no one could follow him. But he was not immune to mistakes.

The leaves of the orange trees rustled in the wind, and the fruit's smell once again covered the subtle scent from the altar a moment earlier.

After standing frozen for several long minutes and seeing no movement around him, Gideon decided he had imagined it. He was being paranoid. Corvin had been injured in a werewolf attack, but that had clearly been planned for when the coven was meeting and was at their most vulnerable. No one knew that Gideon was coming here tonight. The wolves would be far away. They had reportedly left Black Sands and perhaps even Florida. They were not eager to face retribution for what they had done. Cowardly dogs that they were, they hoped that if they just disappeared for a while, people would forget what they had done, and they would not have to pay for it.

Gideon leaned closer to the altar, trying to pick up the scent he had detected a moment earlier. What was it? As old as he was, his sniffer wasn't quite as sensitive or reliable as it had once been. He inhaled deeply, thinking he would only smell the sage and other herbs placed on the altar.

But once again, he detected the pungent smell of another herb —mandrake.

What would they have been using mandrake for in their equinox ritual?

Had Corvin incorporated it into an empowerment ritual? He had promised to share some of his powers with the coven.

Or had it been brought by the wolves? What spell could they have performed? What had they hoped to achieve with the attack on the coven, and on Corvin in particular?

Gideon bent down and brushed the dried herbs from the flat stone of the altar to examine the symbols carved into it. They were rough under his fingertips.

His heart thudded hard in his chest.

The altar stone was broken in half.

He straightened and looked around, the rustling of the leaves again raising goosebumps on his skin. Who was there? Who had followed him? Or had someone already been there, waiting for him? Had someone or something known that he would be coming there?

It was not his first foray there. He had come to the temple grove regularly over the years but had not followed a predictable schedule. He did not want people to know when to expect him there. He came and went quietly without telling anyone of his visits. He would inform Corvin after he was gone, confirming that everything still appeared to be in order and they did not have anything to worry about.

No one could have known he was coming.

"Who's there?" he demanded, his voice cracking and sounding way too tentative for a warlock of his stature. "Show yourself."

No one spoke or moved. Was it all just in his imagination?

Paranoia because of the attack and the broken altar? Just the rustling of the wind and night animals?

"*Appare et ostende te!*" he again commanded the intruder to show himself. But there was still no response, and Gideon did not want to use any magic against whoever was there with him.

It was, of course, against his covenants to use magic to harm a creature who had done nothing to him. He had no idea what kind of entity might be there with him. It could be a natural ally or someone who had no intention of interfering with what he was there to do.

Not to mention the possibility of triggering an attack on himself by a more powerful practitioner. As strong as his powers had once been, they were starting to wane. He had used much of his strength over the years in this task, even though the brunt of it was supposed to be borne by Corvin.

And last but not least, he was on sacred ground. The walls of the ancient temple might be long since gone, but its magic was still there. The temple existed there still, even if it had no physical form. Even without the rocks in the foundation that remained. For him to initiate an attack on these grounds might have serious consequences. Just as the wolves now faced the possibility of war with the warlock coven, as well as the witch's coven and several other organizations who had been offended by the attack on the warlocks and sworn retribution.

Gideon did not want to find himself in the same circumstances.

He stood there for a long time, his heart pounding hard in his ears, before he finally decided that the noises he was hearing were just the usual night sounds, like Gideon had heard every time he had come here before. The broken altar had spooked him, that was all.

He held his hands above the altar, beginning his incantation. The gem in the large ring on his finger began to heat and glow. He could feel the power of the words he spoke. He reached out, through the soil beneath his feat, to what he knew lay buried there.

A rumble sounded in the distance. At first, Gideon thought it was thunder, then realized the sky was clear, and it came not from above but from the ground. And it was growing. He could smell sulfur and felt a heaviness in the air. He had never experienced this reaction before. He raised his voice louder, growling out the words. His old hands shook. His breath came in shortened gasps.

The rumble grew into a crescendo, and the glow of the gem in his ring was extinguished.

CHAPTER TWO

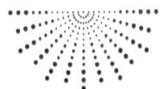

*W*hen Reg wandered out to the kitchen in response to her tuxedo cat Starlight's imperious meows and insistence that he would starve to death if she did not remedy the situation forthwith, she found a note on the coffee machine.

Sarah, the pleasant, gray-haired witch who rented her the guest cottage, knew very well that Reg could not function upon awakening until she'd had at least one cup of coffee. Preferably more. So it was a good place to put a note where Reg would see it as soon as she got up. Reg didn't generally look at the appointment book that lived on the island in the kitchen until later in the day when she was considerably more wide awake.

Come see me and Davyn in the house

Reg yawned and scrubbed at her eyes. She wasn't really ready for company. She needed coffee, a shower, and fresh clothing. And maybe an hour or two to get her engine running.

But she knew she wasn't going to get all that. Sarah would expect her to be there right away, as soon as she was up. Sarah already thought Reg was a slacker for sleeping so late in the morning, regardless of how late Reg worked into the small hours of the morning.

"What do you think all this is about?" Reg asked Starlight as he noisily chowed down on the stew she'd found in the fridge. The stew that, of course, Sarah had intended for Reg to eat. "Sarah and Davyn… I hope this isn't anything to do with the werewolf-warlock war."

Starlight didn't even look up from his feast. Reg shook her head. "They aren't going to find October. He and the others knew well enough to get out of town. They won't be sticking around to face whatever the witches and warlocks have in store for them. Do you think that the warlocks and witches would try to track them? Like, into the wilderness?"

Starlight paused in his meal and glared at Reg with one green and one blue eye. She was bothering him with her chatter. He wasn't interested in the wars of humans. Or he already knew the answers to Reg's questions and didn't want to be bothered by her inane chatter.

But it helped Reg to work things out if she could say them out loud. And it helped to say things out loud if she had a cat, so people didn't think she was just crazy.

She had been talking to the voices in her head for years, but there was no need for the general populace to know that.

"It must be something else," Reg concluded. She hit the button on the coffee machine and waited like one of Pavlov's dogs, her mouth watering, until her coffee cup began to fill.

Maybe she would only need one cup. Sarah would be bound to have coffee on. Or tea. And maybe some muffins or something suitable for breakfast, even if it was Sarah's lunchtime by now.

Starlight had finished eating his breakfast by the time Reg's cup of coffee was ready. He sat on the floor, licking his lips for a few minutes, then his front paws and face, then his back paws, one at a time, with his little bean toes spread wide apart.

Reg watched his ablutions as she took the first few swallows of her piping hot coffee, wincing at the burn. She'd better start her own morning routine if she were going to get over to Sarah's before it was officially afternoon.

* * *

With a fresh, long, colorful skirt and blouse on and her red box braids neatly arranged under a head scarf, Reg was ready to face the day. Or at least ready to face Sarah and Davyn. She gave Starlight a few scratches around his black ears, a quick kiss on the short fur on top of his head, and headed down the stone path across the yard from the guest house to the big house where Sarah was waiting.

Reg raised her hand to knock on the door, even though she knew Sarah always told her to just go right in.

"We're in the living room," Sarah called out before she had the chance to decide. "Come on in."

Sarah must have seen her coming up from the guest cottage. Reg opened the door and let herself in. She crossed through the kitchen and joined Sarah and Davyn at the front of the house.

Reg was relieved to see it was only Sarah and Davyn. She had been worried about finding a whole council or coven waiting for her.

Davyn was not quite as handsome as was Corvin, Reg's nemesis. He was leaner, his features sharper. Dark hair and eyes like Corvin, but clean-shaven. His youthful appearance gave no hint of his actual age, as the magical practitioners tended to look much younger than they really were.

But surely if it had been urgent or there were that many people waiting for her, Sarah would have woken Reg up instead of just leaving a note on the coffee maker.

"Hi," Reg smiled and greeted her mentor and her landlady. "What's going on?"

"Sit down and have some refreshments," Sarah invited.

Reg had been right with her prediction of tea. But with quarter sandwiches rather than muffins. It was apparently too late in the day for muffins. Already past noon, despite Reg's best intentions.

She sat down, chose a tea bag, and poured the steaming hot water from the teapot into her cup. Sarah must have just been in the kitchen pouring boiling water from the kettle. That was how she had seen Reg approaching the house. Reg picked out a couple of sandwiches that she hoped would not bother her stomach so early in the morn— in the day.

"So, are we just having tea? Or is there an occasion?"

"Well… there has been a very unfortunate development," Sarah admitted.

Reg tried to breathe through the immediate tightening of her stomach muscles and the twisting of her intestines. Something unfortunate? She hoped it wasn't something unfortunate to do with the werewolves. Especially not any of the cubs. She was very fond of the little furballs. She was sure that the witches and warlocks would not target puppies but, if they happened to get in the way when they went after October or one of the other wolves who had attacked Corvin's coven…

"What is it? What happened?"

Davyn and Sarah looked at each other as if measuring what to tell Reg. Surely they'd already had enough time to thoroughly discuss what to tell her.

"There was… an attack last night," Davyn said carefully.

"An incident," Sarah corrected.

Davyn looked at her but did not amend his statement.

"We don't know if he was attacked or… if something else happened," Sarah insisted.

"Who?" Reg asked. She didn't really care what they called it. She needed to find out what had happened and see what she was expected to do about it, if anything. She was supposed to be staying out of the way of the war, not taking sides.

"A warlock named Gideon," Davyn told her. "I know that you do not know him. He doesn't live in Black Sands. He has been away for many years. But he is known here."

"Where was he attacked? How did you hear about it?"

"In the Temple Orange Grove."

Reg put her hand over her mouth. The same place as Davyn,

Corvin, and the rest of the coven had been when they had been attacked by the wolves.

"What happened?"

"That is a harder question to answer. He has been cursed…"

"Like Corvin?" Reg had seen Corvin several times since he had been attacked, and maybe understood his injury better than anyone else. Her psychic connection with Corvin meant that she could feel it when he tried to use his powers and was afflicted with excruciating pain.

He did not try to use his magic while she was there, but it was like a new paper cut or canker sore that was constantly irritated by incidental movements throughout the day. Corvin was not accustomed to functioning without magic and kept accessing his powers by accident.

Even just charming Reg, something that came to him so naturally that he didn't even think of it, was enough to make him jolt and groan, and she could feel both his hunger and his pain.

Corvin was a power drinker and, unlike a regular warlock, he was cursed with a hunger for the powers and gifts of other magical practitioners. He could suck the powers from another person, but was required to abide by certain laws and pacts made by his ancestors, requiring that he only take them in exchange for something else of value, and that the victim had to yield to him voluntarily.

Those practices had been warped and twisted over time until the supposed rules that Corvin followed had become meaningless. He had stolen Reg's powers from her once, supposedly following the rules, but she had no clue that she had been agreeing to give them to him. He had returned them to her, something that was never done, in order to save her life. But he had tried to take them many times since, both by force and by utilizing his magical charms.

"Not like Corvin," Davyn said, recalling Reg to the conversation. "He was… turned into stone."

Reg stared at Davyn. "Turned into stone? Like he was frozen? Paralyzed?"

"More than that. He is actually stone. Like a statue. But no one knows who did this or why."

Sarah shook her head. "It is very strange. Who would do that? And in the Temple Orange Grove. All these things happening at that sacred site..."

"All these things? You mean the wolf attack? And now this petrifaction thing?"

"Yes. It is a special place. Many sacred rites have been performed there. The magic of the ancient temple still exists. That is why the warlock coven often meets there."

"I know," Reg agreed. She had been there only once, when she had been trying to find Davyn. She had been able to see the temple as it had once been, in shining silver and gold light that rose from the ground up into the air in ethereal beauty. It had been breathtaking, but she had been the only one able to see it.

"We are going to go over there to have a look," Davyn said. "See if we can find any clues to who did this terrible thing and why."

"Yeah," Reg nodded. "That makes sense."

They would want to put a stop to whatever was happening in the Temple Orange Grove making it the center of an apparent outbreak of magical violence. Was it just a coincidence that Gideon had been attacked there after the attack by the werewolves on the coven? Was something attracting them there? Was there a connection between the attacks?

Reg didn't think there was any connection, but it was impossible to know without investigating. Corvin wasn't likely to tell her anything she didn't already know. From what she knew, October and the other wolves had attacked Corvin and the coven to stop Corvin from doing Reg or October any harm, as October had believed that he had harmed them in past lives. But the person who had been guilty of those attacks had not been Corvin.

That didn't mean Corvin wasn't dangerous. Reg had wished many times that something could be done to make him stop hunting her. The banishment that he had received as a punishment for trying to take her powers by force had not prevented him from pursuing her again. And again, and again. It had proven not to be a deterrent at all.

But October's attack and the curse he had placed on Corvin had stopped Corvin cold, and Reg was grateful to him for that. Confused, because she no longer knew how to view Corvin or whether he would regain his abilities and overcome the curse. Confused because the charms that had drawn her to Corvin so many times in the past were gone, but she still found him attractive.

Sarah leaned forward, meeting Reg's eyes. "We thought you would like to come with us."

CHAPTER THREE

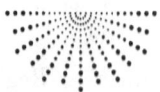

*R*eg searched Sarah's eyes. "You want me to come with you? Why? What for?"

"You are the only one who has seen the temple in centuries. You may be able to see other things there that no one else is able to. You might be able to solve this mystery for us."

"I doubt there is anything that I'll be able to do that you and Davyn couldn't," Reg said uncomfortably. They were experienced witches. They had been practicing for decades before Reg had even been thought of.

"You are a powerful practitioner in your own right," Sarah said firmly. "Don't sell yourself short. You have talents which are very rare, which many of us have not seen in years. You may be able to provide us with some insight."

"Well… I'm happy to come if you want me to. I just don't know if I'll be of any help. Don't get your hopes up too much."

"All right, we won't," Davyn agreed, smiling wryly. "We'll just see what happens. We will all go together and use our own talents and gifts and see what we can discover."

Reg nodded her agreement. "Okay. Yes. Of course, I'll come and help if I can. When are you going?"

"Now would be a good time,"

"Oh… okay."

"You don't have anything to do now, do you?" Sarah asked. "There wasn't anything on your appointment calendar, and you usually schedule things for later in the day. Early afternoon seemed like it should work. You've showered and dressed, you've had your coffee, or your tea at least. A bite to eat. Now… we could go to the grove and see what we can see."

"Yeah, yeah, of course. No, I don't have anything else planned."

"Good. Shall we all go in my car?" Sarah suggested.

Davyn looked alarmed. "We could take mine…" he suggested.

Reg nodded. "Let's take Davyn's," she agreed quickly. She had been in a vehicle driven by Sarah in the past and wasn't eager to repeat the experience. Reg's car was too small to fit all of them comfortably. Not much leg room in the back of the sporty little car.

"There's lots of room in the van," Sarah encouraged.

Both Davyn and Reg shook their heads. Sarah sighed. "Men are so controlling," she complained. "They always have to hold the remote and drive the car. Have you ever noticed that, Reg?"

"Well, yes," Reg admitted. "That is true." She nodded and gave Davyn a wink. "But we'd best just let him do it."

Sarah nodded sagely. "Have another sandwich for the road," she suggested. "And we'll be on our way."

* * *

Reg didn't remember much from her previous trip to the Temple Orange Grove. But she did remember the sight of the edifice of light rising from the ruined foundations of the ancient temple. It would be hard to forget.

She walked around it in reverence before daring to go inside with Sarah and Davyn. She was afraid that when she went inside, it would all disappear or that she would be punished for entering such a sacred place unworthily. She wondered if there were some sort of cleansing ritual she should go through before entering. But Sarah and Davyn simply walked in ahead of her, and nothing happened to them.

But they also walked through the interior walls of the temple, which Reg could not make herself do. She navigated her way through the halls and rooms of the temple to reach the inner sanctum where Sarah and Davyn waited. Even though her behavior must have seemed odd to them, insisting on a meandering route through what to them seemed to be an open space, neither of them said anything or made fun of her for it. Reg cleared her throat and looked around, wondering whether she would be able to find anything helpful.

"What should I be looking for?" she asked in a whisper.

Davyn nodded to a statue and Reg walked up to it curiously, expecting it to be in the shape of one of the gods. But the man who stood before her did not belong to any of the pantheons she was familiar with.

"Who is it?" Reg asked, studying the face creased with deep wrinkles, the long, knobby fingers, and the big ring carved of the same gray stone that the rest of him had been carved from. His deep frown behind a scraggly, old-man beard and bushy eyebrows was foreboding.

"Gideon."

"Gideon... oh," Reg took a step back from the statue, realizing that it was a real person. The warlock they had come to see. The victim of a petrifaction spell. "Oh, I didn't realize. I'm sorry."

"No need to apologize to him," Sarah said with a chuckle. "He is past hearing you."

Reg wasn't so sure. She directed her thoughts into the deepest heart of the statue, where there was still a living, thinking soul. He was buried too deep for coherent conversation, but he was still there. Reg was reminded of when she had first come to Black Sands and had been in contact with a man who was supposed to be dead, yet had only been in a coma.

"He is still there," she told Sarah.

Sarah looked at her, wide-eyed. Reg turned her gaze to Davyn. "He is still there," she insisted. "He is still... a thinking, feeling person."

Davyn laid a hand on the stone as if this might help him to feel the man's aura himself. He closed his eyes for a few seconds, then shook his head.

"Are you sure, Reg?" Sarah asked in a hushed tone.

"Yes, of course I'm sure. I don't feel souls where there aren't any."

"No, I don't doubt you. Of course not," Sarah quickly backtracked. "I am just so shocked. How could he still be living, thinking and feeling when turned to stone?"

Reg shook her head. "I don't know. Magic, I guess!"

Sarah gave her a small smile and looked at Davyn. "If he is still there, living, frozen in the stone, then... perhaps the curse is reversible. He is not lost forever."

"Maybe," Davyn allowed. "We will have to research the matter... we will have to be very careful not to do any damage while we are here, to avoid anything that may cause him harm."

Reg stayed a few steps back from him. She didn't want to take the chance of doing anything that might change the state that Gideon was in for the worse. Worse would be dead, or lost in the stone statue for eternity. She didn't want to inflict either one on him.

"The altar is broken," Sarah observed after looking around for a few minutes.

Reg walked up to where Sarah was and looked down at the flat stone with some symbols engraved upon it. It was cracked down the center, split into two tablets of roughly equal size.

CHAPTER FOUR

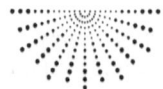

*H*ow was it broken?" Reg asked. It looked like a strong enough rock, yet it had been cracked down the middle. But there were no markings on it that hinted at the fact it had been struck by a sledgehammer or other similar object. It hadn't been dropped from a great height. What else could do that? Heat?

Sarah looked at Davyn. "The last time I was here, it was whole," she said. "What can you tell us?"

"The night of the werewolf attack," Davyn said slowly. "I didn't see it being broken, but… I do remember October throwing a vial on the altar stone, smashing it."

"Smashing the stone?" Reg asked in disbelief. It didn't seem very likely that a fragile vial would be able to do anything to hurt the large, flat rock. Unless it contained nitroglycerin.

Or magic.

"No, he smashed the vial," Davyn corrected. "Like I said, I didn't see the altar broken. But that is probably when it happened. I didn't stop to examine it… things were in chaos that night. But it contained oils infused with herbs, I assume. Part of a larger spell designed to cause confusion and destruction."

Reg had only heard bits and pieces about what had transpired that night. But Davyn had been there. He was the former leader of the coven and had been with them for the spring solstice ceremony, of course. Reg had no idea what the ritual involved, but she assumed it was something to do with a transfer of Corvin's power, since he had been elected on the platform that he would be able to share some of his vast storehouse of powers with the other members of the coven. From what Sarah and Marta Jessup, a detective with the Black Sands police department, had said, spring solstice was a particularly favorable time to perform such a ritual.

From what Reg knew of spring solstice, it was supposed to be a time of balance and drawing together as a community. So it made sense on that level that it would be a good time for Corvin to share his power with his fellow warlocks and for them to draw closer as a coven.

"What exactly happened?" Reg asked Davyn. She looked around the temple for some sign of it, something that would tell the story of the attack. But it was all either stone or the ethereal temple composed of light, which had both been unaffected by the attack.

Davyn looked around. Reg imagined it looked quite a bit different to him. He could not see the vision of the temple so, for him, it was just the old stone foundation overgrown with the wild flora of the grove, the fragrant orange trees that surrounded the temple site, leaves rustling in the wind, and his memories of that night.

"Everything was normal, as we had planned it, as I had expected it to be. The sky was clear, so all the stars and moon were visible. The full coven was assembled. Corvin was leading the ritual. He had placed the herbs on the altar and was chanting."

There were no herbs on the altar anymore. Any loose leaves would have blown away. Reg tried to envision the ceremony that had taken place. All the warlocks standing in a circle in their black cloaks. At least, she assumed it was not a sky-clad ritual. She preferred not to envision them in their altogether. So, in her mind, they were dressed in their long, black cloaks.

Stars twinkled in the sky. It was peaceful. She could imagine the balance and good feelings that Sarah had previously described to her as the essence of spring equinox. A brotherhood of warlocks, gathered as one. Together for a singular purpose. Looking forward to receiving a part of the powerful gifts that Corvin had to offer.

That thought disrupted the feeling of peace. Warlocks hungry for power and excited to be able to receive what Corvin had promised. The envy and desire for power didn't quite align with brotherhood, balance, and serenity in Reg's mind. But she didn't say anything, not wanting to disrupt Davyn's description of that night. She needed to hear the details to picture what had happened.

Was the werewolf attack related in any way to the petrifaction of Gideon, the ancient-looking warlock? Had a second attack taken place and, if so, was it related to the first or something new? Or had the spell the werewolves had cast that day, the disruption and the curse placed on Corvin, had other, perhaps unforeseeable, consequences?

"It was shortly after Corvin had begun the ritual," Davyn told her. "We were suddenly assailed on all sides by a coordinated attack. It was very sudden, and we were all... engrossed in the ritual. It wasn't easy to separate from it immediately, take in what was happening, and react to it. I stood there like a statue, just like everyone else."

Davyn's eyes flicked toward the petrified warlock, and perhaps he regretted his choice of words, but he didn't try to change it.

"They were all in wolf form except for October. I saw him throw something on the altar, felt the... impact or shock waves when the vial shattered. There was a definite disruption of the spell Corvin had been weaving. It hit like a blow, stunning us even further. October transformed into wolf form after throwing the vial. He must have stayed in human form until then to allow him to carry and handle the vials. As a wolf, he slashed Corvin's arm. He had a second vial between his teeth, which he broke over the wound."

Davyn stared off into the distance, replaying the scene in his mind. It was probably hard for him to keep it all straight when he had been startled out of the ritual like everyone else.

"It happened so fast. Corvin was hurt. I could see the blood and hear him yelling. I expected him to fight back, but he collapsed. The rest of us were starting to... come out of our trance... to start to react. At that point, it was too late; they had already done what they had come to do. There were a few clashes between wolves and warlocks... a few superficial injuries, and then they were retreating, disappearing into the darkness of the grove."

"Who was hurt?"

"John Saunders's was the worst wound, aside from Corvin's. A more serious physical injury, but he was not cursed like Corvin had been. I did what I could to help him and the others. Wilf. Hershel."

Like Reg, Davyn was a firecaster and had some healing powers as part of that gift. As Reg's mentor, he had far better control than she did and was training her to manage her gift. Firecasting was a volatile power, and practitioners who could not control it eventually came to a fiery end.

"Corvin was October's target," Reg confirmed. "Probably anyone else who was injured was just reacting to the wolves. Except maybe John... he might have been a secondary target."

John was Corvin's son and had the same ability as Corvin to take the powers from others. He had not been raised to follow the rules they were supposed to be bound by, so he was perhaps even more dangerous to the public than Corvin. Though as far as Reg and October knew, John had not targeted either of them. Reg still feared John, not only because of his ability and his lawless upbringing, but also because Reg had been indirectly responsible for Verity, John's mother, being killed. He had been very attached to his mother. In fact, he was *still* attached to Verity. Reg could hear Verity's ghost whispering in John's ear whenever she was near him. Either that or John was recreating her voice himself, unhinged by his loss.

Davyn surveyed the area, inhaling deeply before letting out a long sigh. Clearly, it was causing him some anxiety to be there remembering the attack. Asking him further questions about the werewolf attack would just cause him more stress, and would probably not reveal anything else to them about what had happened to

Gideon. Reg suspected there was no real link between the two attacks. Gideon had not even been a member of the coven.

"So, did you know him?" Reg nodded toward the statue. "If he didn't live here or belong to the coven, what was he doing here?"

"Mystic tourism?" Davyn suggested with a shrug. "People do like to visit sacred or mystical sites. Gideon was no stranger to Black Sands or the Temple Orange Grove. He hasn't lived here for many years, but he may have before my time. A lot of people in the magical community know him."

"So he came back here just to be in the temple again? To pray or see if any damage had been done by the werewolf attack?"

"Probably. It might have been a scheduled visit, but I have no way of knowing his plans. I don't know… maybe you can ask him." Davyn looked at the statue.

Reg fidgeted with her box braids, smoothing and wrapping a few around her fingers. She could sense Gideon's consciousness, but she didn't think he was present enough to answer questions.

She looked around her at the walls of light, the broken altar stone, and the weeds growing around the ruins under her feet. Sarah and Davyn had asked her to come along to see if there were anything she could sense there that they could not, something that might help them figure out what had happened to Gideon and whether it had any connection with the werewolf attack.

She closed her eyes and was as still as she could be, reaching out all her senses to the temple, the grove, and the planes above and below the ground. She felt for any presence other than her little group and Gideon himself. She was not interested in animal and insect life unless they were capable of and interested in direct communication. Most of the creatures of the forest were happy to go about their own business without any communication or interaction with humans.

She didn't find anything surprising until she sank her consciousness deep down into the earth. Then she stopped, holding the images and feelings in her mind and analyzing them.

"There is something here."

Davyn and Sarah hovered nearby. They were careful to stay out of her way and not upset any fragile connections she might be able to make.

"What do you mean, *something*?" Sarah asked.

"I don't know." Reg explored it with her mind, though her consciousness really wanted to flit off and explore more interesting and exciting things.

She thought her firecasting meditation training was making a difference in her ability to keep her focus on the object, and she was proud of her improvement.

"If feels… like a stone," she said slowly. She had communed with stones before, the gemstones she had received from the fairies. She had been able to sense which of them were safe and which had been cursed and, even with the cursed stones, had been able to discover their origins and in some cases, to cleanse them by returning them to their source or rightful owner.

Few people other than dwarfs had any affinity for stones. Humans might be able to appreciate their beauty or, in some cases to feel whether they were imbued with power or were darkened by trafficking or a curse, but to actually sense how the stone *felt* or its personality was something usually reserved for the children of the mountains.

"It is a stone," she confirmed. "But… not like anything I've ever encountered before. It has… power."

"Like a gemstone?" Sarah asked.

"No… maybe it also has innate power, it is very precious… but it was imbued with power. A great deal of power. It has been here for many years, hidden in the ground. It has been…" Reg looked at Sarah and Davyn, "It has been protected by other ward stones and spells."

Sarah and Davyn exchanged a look. Reg wasn't sure what it meant. Had they already known about this stone or suspected its presence? Did they know what it all meant?

"An ancient treasure?" Davyn asked eventually. "How long has it been there? Has it been… dormant? Maybe it was part of the original temple. Maybe that is what gave the temple its power, and why it is still such a powerful site even after being ruined for so many years."

Reg was good, but not that good. She shook her head. "I can't answer all that. I would just be guessing."

It was tempting to make up a story and see how it was received. Reg had always enjoyed spinning a tale, making it more elaborate and detailed as she went along.

"Should we retrieve it?" Sarah asked. "If it is an important part of this place... maybe it holds the key to why Gideon was turned to stone. Maybe something he did triggered a protection spell, backfiring on him."

"If he was cursed because he was trying to retrieve it, I'm not going to try to dig it up," Reg declared.

"Well, no, that is a good point. But if it holds the key to recovering Gideon... to reversing the curse and getting him back..."

CHAPTER FIVE

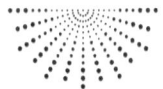

*R*eg considered whether there was a way for her to get her hands on the stone or find out more about it without digging it up or disturbing any of the wards or spells that secured it.

Sweat trickled down her back.

It wasn't even that hot out. The grove was shady, and a light breeze rustled the leaves of the trees almost constantly. Distant bird calls echoed through the grove.

Reg rubbed her hands together briskly as if warming them up, but it was just an exercise to help focus her attention and sensitize them to the magical influences around her. She took a deep breath and let it out slowly. The effort was wearing her out, even though she hadn't actually *done* anything.

"It's one of those rocks that looks normal on the outside, but it has crystals inside," she told Davyn and Sarah. "What are those called?"

"Geodes," Davyn suggested.

Reg nodded. "Geodes. They're really pretty, sometimes. And… there are six other stones around it, ward stones to protect it. It has been enchanted… but I don't know how or why."

"There must be a reason it's there," Sarah observed. "Maybe it was part of the original temple treasure."

Reg nodded. "Maybe. I feel like it's been there for a long time, but..." She shook her head. "I don't know. I can't tell how long or why."

"Where is it?" Davyn asked.

Reg pointed. "Under the altar. But it is buried quite deep. No one would know it was there if they weren't looking for it."

They all looked at each other, wondering what to do next. Reg was the least experienced of them all; she had no idea how to proceed. Sarah bit her lip.

"Well, we know it is there. We will keep that to ourselves for the time being. We will not disturb it or tell anyone about it. Perhaps after we have investigated a little more, we will know whether it has a direct bearing on this situation and whether it is something we need to reverse the curse on poor Gideon."

They all nodded, agreeing to proceed as Sarah had suggested.

Sarah sighed. "There is something else we are going to need you to do. I hate to suggest it, but..."

CHAPTER SIX

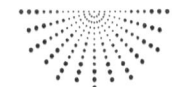

*N*othing seemed to have changed since Reg's last visit to
Corvin's house. It was a large house, like Sarah's, but
nothing remarkable. Nothing that said "a dangerous warlock lives
here" or even that it was occupied by an old, magical being. The
magical population did a good job of blending in or assimilating
with the nonmagical culture. Nothing made the house stand out
from the rest of the neighborhood.

A number of flyers were on the porch and stuffed in the mail-
box. Reg collected them before ringing the doorbell. When Corvin
came to the door, she handed them to him. "Throw those in your
recycle bin, at least."

He scowled and took them from her. "What are you doing
here?"

This time, Reg had not bothered to bring a bottle of Jack
Daniels with her, so maybe he was worried about his supply drying
up. Though she suspected he probably had quite an extensive wine
cellar somewhere in the house, even if there weren't a basement.
The high-water table in Florida made basements impractical.

"Invite me in," Reg told him.

If he recognized that he had once given Reg the same instruction, he did not give any indication of it. He stood there for a

moment, then nodded and backed out of the doorway to let her in, swinging the door wide.

Reg stepped into the house.

Though Corvin didn't smell sour and sweaty or have unkempt, oily hair, she doubted he had been out of the house since the last time she had seen him. As far as she knew, he had not been out of the house since being injured in the werewolf attack.

She couldn't blame him for preferring to stay at home to recover from the attack, but the timeline was stretching out, and she would have expected him to be out and about again by now. He had always been a fairly social person, not someone likely to be kept down by an injury for long. The flyers on the porch suggested he was not even stepping out of his door to pick them up.

"How is it going?" she asked him.

"About the same."

"Are you in a lot of pain?"

He shrugged. "As long as I do not try to use any of my gifts... no. Thanks to you," he acknowledged with a nod, "the physical wound is healing well."

The faint ticking of an old grandfather clock filled the silence as they walked through the hallway. They entered the well-appointed living room and Reg took her customary armchair, sinking into the soft upholstery.

"But of course, getting along without any gifts is a challenge," Corvin went on. "Not because life is so difficult without them, but because... I am so accustomed to using them that I do it without thinking. It's like... trying to speak without using any word with the letter A in it. It is possible, but you have to think through every word of every sentence..."

Reg nodded. Even though she had only recently discovered that she had gifts, she had unknowingly been using them her whole life. She thought she was good at cold-reading people, when mostly she was using her psychic power. She had been told that the voices in her head were her imagination or psychosis, and she had suppressed them the best she could, but even at her most repressed, she had never been able to completely get rid of them. Not even with antipsychotics. She stopped talking about them or to them, and the doctors declared her cured. But the voices had still been there. Until the day that Corvin had stolen her gifts, when Reg was suddenly confronted with silence for the first time.

Loud, echoing silence.

She never wanted to face that again, so she tolerated the voices in her head and thanked heaven for them even when they became too unruly.

"It's not exactly like a vacation, is it?" Reg asked Corvin.

He gave a bitter chuckle. "No, it is not."

"Remember that is what you have consigned so many people to over the years when you have taken their gifts from them. Living with that... flatness. That emptiness. For the rest of their lives."

"Not everyone is like you, Reg. Some people barely even notice the difference. And some actually desire it. To have all the chaos taken away and just live their flat, ordinary lives."

He poured himself a drink from a decanter on the sideboard and automatically poured one for Reg. She took it, had a small sip, and put it on the side table.

"Besides," Corvin said, "it isn't the same thing. I never caused anyone pain by taking the gifts they offered me. My gifts are not gone, but I am in excruciating pain whenever I accidentally use them."

Reg nodded, conceding the point. She had found it painful when he had taken her gifts, but it was not in the same way as he felt it, so she wasn't going to argue about it. She was there seeking his help. It wouldn't do to get him riled up over some pointless argument.

"So what are you doing here?" Corvin asked after another sip of his drink. "I wasn't expecting to see you again so soon."

"Something happened last night at the Temple Orange Grove," Reg told him, going straight to the point rather than trying to tell him that she was just there to visit him and make sure he was recovering from the attack. She didn't see the point in pretending she was there for his welfare when she wasn't.

"Oh?" Corvin straightened and looked interested. "What happened?"

"Do you know a warlock named Gideon?" Reg tried to remember if they had told her his last name, but couldn't think of it. "He's quite old—or he looks old, anyway. I know you're old, but you don't look it."

"Gideon Darkwood? Certainly. We have known each other for many years."

"He was attacked there last night. Or Sarah and Davyn think it was an attack, anyway. It's possible that it was just some kind of accident..."

"What do you mean he was attacked?" Corvin leaned forward. His face was animated, unlike the last few times she had seen him when he had acted uninterested in much of anything she'd had to say. "Attacked how? It wasn't the werewolves again, surely."

"No. We don't know that anyone attacked him, for sure..."

Corvin made an impatient motion. "Well, go on! Tell me about it. What happened?"

"He was petrified. Turned into a stone statue. A living stone statue."

"Living?" Corvin demanded.

Reg nodded. "He was... I could still sense him there. Feel him there."

"He is aware?"

"Yes... at some level."

"Can you communicate with him?"

"I don't know... if I can *talk* with him. Communicate in words and sentences and complex thoughts. But I can... sense him and try to send him reassuring thoughts."

"And nobody knows how this happened? If he was attacked or it was some... phenomenon?"

"No. Sarah and Davyn were hoping that you could do some research, or that you might already know something. What could have caused it, and how can we get him back? If anything can get him back."

"What did he look like? Can you describe it?"

"Like he was turned into a stone statue. He was... gray, and hard as rock. Just like he was a carved out of stone."

"And yet you could still sense him. His... life force."

Reg nodded. "Sarah and Davyn were surprised. They didn't know that he was still in there. They said that as long as he was, maybe it was reversible and they could get him back again."

Corvin nodded thoughtfully. "Perhaps," he agreed. "Gideon. What was he doing in the grove?"

"They don't know. Gideon was there alone, so... unless he had an assistant or understudy or something, no one knows."

"An apprentice."

"What?"

"Not an understudy. That is for the theater. An apprentice. Someone studying under him."

"Oh. Yeah. Like in that cartoon. Did Gideon have an apprentice?"

"Not as far as I am aware. But we were not in contact often."

"So you don't know why he was here in Black Sands or why he would be visiting the grove?"

Corvin didn't answer immediately, which made Reg wonder whether he was composing a somewhat misleading answer.

"There could be many reasons he was here. He didn't contact me to say that he was in touch. Perhaps he would have reached out to me when he was finished there or if he needed my help. But he didn't." Corvin shrugged. "So I guess I can't answer that."

Reg considered his answer and decided he wasn't really telling her anything; he was just trying to make it sound like he was being open and honest with her, which he might or might not be doing.

"Did he used to live in Black Sands? It sounded like it from what Sarah said, but neither of them had much to say about him."

"Yes, he lived here a very long time ago." Corvin thought back and gave Reg a brief smile. "Back in wilder, more chaotic times."

"The two of you were friends?"

"Yes. We did things together. Talked. Exchanged... 'hopes and dreams' sounds too cliche. Philosophies. The ways we hoped to change the world. We were young and idealistic. Full of vision and… energy. A will to effect real changes and shape how the world would look in the future."

"That sounds pretty heavy."

"It was. And exciting at the same time. A lot of the stuff that we dreamed up *has* become a reality. The world has changed a lot in the past few centuries. This has gone from being a wild, untamed country to something quite civilized. And we have many opportunities and conveniences that we would never have even imagined."

"I guess so."

Reg had seen movies about the Wild West. She had thought of it more as fiction than anything. Stories people told for entertainment. Her life was so different from anything she had seen on TV that she assumed it was mostly made-up junk. But of course, the country had gone from being populated with Indigenous people connected to the land and nature to settlers from other countries and cultures and, eventually, to people who were more connected to their screens than anything else. That wasn't just imagination.

"So, what did you guys want to change?"

"Everything. We wanted… wealth and power, but also all those things other people valued—family, love, houses that were more than just windbreaks. Stability. The ability to… be who we really were. We were both on the outside, looking in, and we wanted to partake in it all." He sat back, chuckling at the memory. "It was a long time ago."

"You were both on the outside?" Reg asked. "What do you mean? Because you didn't have money and power?"

"Well, you know about my situation. My kind have been outcasts from society for generations. It is only recently that we have been allowed to even live near other practitioners, much less to participate in covens."

"Or to lead them."

"Yes," Corvin gave a small, self-satisfied smile. "That is a *very* recent development. I would not have ever guessed that I would see this day when I was a young man."

"So Gideon… was he your kind too?"

"Oh, no. There are not very many of us around, and we generally do not… congregate. In order to fly under the radar, it is best if there is not more than one in a close community. John being here has… complicated things significantly for me."

"What was he, then?"

"Gideon was…" Corvin considered this, "…we both lacked wealth and power. Gideon was very outspoken. He did not have tact or a sense of propriety. People did not particularly appreciate ideas about how the world should change. Or how he intended to acquire the money and power he deserved."

"Well, I can see how that might make people a little uncomfortable around him."

Corvin laughed. "Yes. People do not appreciate being told how you are going to change their world and flip society on its head. The elite and ruling classes do not like hearing of revolution."

"And I guess… he eventually accumulated what he hoped to."

"When you have a few hundred years to work your plan… that helps."

"I guess so." When Reg considered the few decades she had been on the earth, it seemed like a drop in the bucket compared to Corvin, Gideon, and the immortals. If she had that much time to work her plan, maybe she would eventually be able to achieve what Corvin and Gideon had. While Reg enjoyed her current life, it would be nice to have a house of her own instead of renting from someone else. And to have figured out who she was and what exactly she wanted to do with her life, rather than being blown from one thing to the next.

Corvin grimaced, and his hand went to his head, body rigid. Reg had seen this before and waited it out. Corvin took a few deep breaths and relaxed his body. He rubbed his head and dropped his hand again. Neither of them commented on this "slip," using his powers and suffering the consequences of it.

"You have done very well in your life," Corvin told Reg. "You may not see it, but you have been told you have some significant powers. Far from being 'just' a psychic with some natural ability to read faces and body language. What you can do now, the gifts that you can manage, compared to what you could do when you first came to Black Sands... you don't see how far you have come?"

"I guess so. But it doesn't seem like so much compared to those of you who are more... experienced."

"Trust me. You have come far and will continue to progress. And as far as wealth goes... you have enough for your needs and could afford to leave Sarah's guest cottage if you desired."

"Well..." Reg shrugged. He was right. She had a number of gemstones she could liquidate that could buy her quite a nice house without any need for a mortgage. But she was comfortable where she was and enjoyed the way Sarah helped look out for her. She didn't really have any motivation to move. Not yet. "I guess so, yeah. Someday."

He smiled and nodded. "Or perhaps... you are waiting for an invitation to move in with someone else." He leaned toward her, looking sly. "Is that what you are waiting for, Regina?"

CHAPTER SEVEN

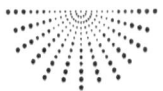

A wave of heat went over Reg's face. She had always been attracted to Corvin, but she had thought that was simply because of his charms. Like the scent of the Venus fly trap that lures insects into its predatory traps, Corvin's appearance, scent, and magnetism were all part of the magic that he used to lure women to him so that he could steal their powers. They would voluntarily give up what was most precious to them for a taste of his offerings.

But even without Corvin using his powers, she couldn't help but feel drawn toward him. He wasn't trying to steal her powers this time. That would only hurt him more. But he was still interested in her, and she couldn't help responding to his proximity and flirting.

She pulled back from Corvin slightly, turning her eyes to the rest of the room so that she wouldn't be tempted by him. She was there on a mission. Not to help Corvin by healing the physical wound or to keep him company with a visit this time. She was there because they needed him.

"We were hoping that you might be able to help with Gideon," she told him bluntly. "You have a lot of knowledge about ancient spells and magic, and you probably know more about the temple than anyone else. So we were hoping you could help us to figure out how or why Gideon was petrified and how to reverse the spell."

Corvin mirrored Reg's movements, leaning back in his chair. He took another sip of his drink.

"So even without my powers, you need my help."

Reg nodded. It was true and, even if it weren't, she would use whatever flattery necessary to convince him to help them with the investigation into what had happened to Gideon. "Sarah and Davyn couldn't think of anyone with more knowledge about these things. They said you are the guy. You're the one who would have this knowledge or know where to find it."

Corvin seemed pleased with this. He had probably been brooding since the attack, thinking he was no longer useful to anyone. What was he without his magic? How could he continue to contribute to his community? Or, since he was more likely to be concerned with himself than anyone else, how could he build himself up? How could he amass more wealth and rare ancient relics? How could he keep his reputation if he couldn't perform?

"We need you," she encouraged him. "Gideon needs you."

"Yes." A shadow passed over his face. "It is strange that he would fall prey to another practitioner. He had a great deal of knowledge and power. He was a careful man, or he would not have survived this long."

"He could have been ambushed, just like you were during the spring equinox ritual."

"Yes. You are right, of course. It is difficult to be on alert at all times. He probably thought that he was alone in the grove. Perhaps he was followed there. Or maybe there are still wolves around watching it. They could hide in the wilderness surrounding the grove and be undetected. Even if he was looking for an enemy, he might be unaware of an animal lurking nearby."

"I'm sure there aren't any wolves hanging around there anymore," Reg objected. She knew for certain there had not been any there when she had been in the grove with Davyn and Sarah. "Why would they still be hanging around after the attack? They've gone away to avoid retribution."

"Perhaps they became aware of something there... something they hadn't been aware of before. It has been a long time since there were any wolves in Florida. During the attack, they might have become aware of something... some power, artifact, or secret that didn't mean anything to the coven but would to the wolves."

The stone, perhaps? Would a werewolf have been aware of it, buried so deep in the earth? Reg had not known about the stone until she had searched the ground with her psychic powers and, as far as she knew, none of the werewolves in October's pack shared those powers. She couldn't think of any reason a werewolf would have an affinity for a magical stone.

But maybe there had been an inscription in the temple she had been unaware of that one of them had been able to decipher. If the stone had been buried beneath the temple for hundreds of years, there might have been some runes explaining to future generations its power or why it was there. There had been symbols on the altar stone that she had been unable to read.

"Is there something there?" she asked Corvin. "Some artifact that they would be interested in? I thought it was just old ruins. The foundations."

His eyes glittered. *Did he know?* Reg probed at the edges of his mind, which wasn't really fair since he could not use his powers to push her away as he normally would. Even detecting her there might cause him pain.

He knew about the temple. He had been meeting there with the coven for years. He had explored it hundreds of years before with Gideon when they had been young men.

"Why is it that Gideon looked like an old man, but you don't look like you have aged?"

"My kind does not age quickly, and I have... taken pains to slow the aging process as much as possible. It is easier to attract someone if... you are attractive."

"But he didn't care if he looked old?"

"It wasn't his priority. But he was still in good physical shape. Vigorous. He would not have been easy prey."

"But someone attacked him. Or he triggered some kind of defensive spell."

"What makes you say that?"

Reg shrugged and chose not to tell him about the stone. It was best to keep that secret to herself if he didn't know about it. And Sarah and Davyn. "Just a thought. We can't assume that someone was there. He might have just... wandered into some kind of a trap."

Corvin nodded. "I suppose so. Maybe something the wolves left behind. They cursed me; perhaps they cursed the ground or the altar. I remember October smashing a vial on the altar stone. Perhaps he cursed the altar and then Gideon attempted to use it."

"If he didn't know about the attack, he wouldn't have known to be careful of it."

"He knew—I expect that he knew about the werewolf attack. Word has spread throughout the magical communities across the country. It would have been hard for him not to have heard something about it."

"Did you talk to him about it?"

Corvin's eyes moved around the living room as if he weren't sure what to look at. He cleared his throat. "He had planned a visit before the attack. Much of what has happened in the last couple of weeks is not clear in my mind. Between the pain and... the painkillers... I confess to being in a fog much of the time."

Too much Jack Daniels, a problem that Reg had contributed to rather than directing him toward healthier ways to handle his pain and distress. She shifted uncomfortably.

Did Corvin really not remember whether he had told Gideon about the attack? It seemed unlikely. If they were old friends and Corvin knew that Gideon was coming to Black Sands, he would undoubtedly have told him what had happened at the temple. Would it have made Gideon wary? Would he have been watching for werewolves? Would he have been aware of a spell cast on the altar stone?

"Do you think you will be able to help Sarah and Davyn to figure out what happened to Gideon?"

"You are no longer saying 'us.' Have you decided to remove yourself from the case?"

"No... I just mean... they're the ones who are in charge. They know much more about this kind of thing than I do and are leaders in the community. I'm... too new to be in such a position."

"But you are still helping with the investigation?"

"Yes, I'll help out if I can."

He nodded and took another sip of his drink. "Then I will help you."

CHAPTER EIGHT

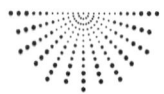

*R*eg let out her breath.

"Thank you."

He nodded. "I should be thanking you for trying to help an old friend of mine."

She got the distinct impression that Corvin's relationship with Gideon was less as an "old friend" and more as someone he had been involved with and needed to keep an eye on. Why had Gideon left Black Sands? Did that reason have something to do with Corvin?

Corvin watched her with bright, glittering eyes. Even without his powers, he could probably read her better than anyone else. He had been inside her brain. He had held her powers. He probably had a pretty good idea of where her thought processes would take her.

"I wonder… if there is something you could do for me," he suggested.

Reg nodded. It was much easier to agree to do something for him when she knew that the result would not be his taking control of her and stealing her powers. "Sure, if I can."

"In the past, there have been times when you have tapped into my power when you needed extra strength."

Reg shifted uncomfortably. There had been times when she had taken power from Corvin or others. Sometimes without permission. Other times, Corvin had offered her strength for healing or to boost her power as she performed a difficult task.

"You have given me your power," she rephrased his suggestion.

Corvin smiled wryly. "Okay, then, I have given you power."

Reg nodded.

"I would like to give you power now. Let's say... it is to help you with this investigation into what happened to my old friend, Gideon. In addition to delving into my ancient tomes to see if I can figure out what happened to him and how to reverse the process."

Reg frowned, trying to follow his suggestion. If he tried to transfer power to her, it would cause him pain. What strength did he think she needed for her part in the investigation that he was willing to make such a sacrifice?

"In this case, I cannot *give* it to you. But you could *take* it from me."

"Oh... I guess so."

"It would be a great help to me if you could do so."

Reg wasn't sure that was a good idea. "Won't that... increase your hunger? So that you will need to replenish it sooner?"

And, of course, he could not just steal power from her or another gifted individual or from an artifact imbued with power. Doing so would cause him more pain. It didn't seem like a wise course of action.

"Would you just do it?" Corvin asked, an edge to his voice. "Can't you just do what I ask and believe I know what is best for me?"

"I just want to be sure," Reg told him, resisting the urge to snap back at him. He was in pain. Everyone got irritable when they were in pain. And the fact that his pain was wrapped up in his not being able to be the person that he was had to make it even worse. He had lost his identity. "I don't want to do something that will harm you."

"An' it harm none," Corvin intoned.

The phrase didn't make sense to Reg, but she knew it meant

that a magical practitioner should not do anything to harm anyone else. The acid test of whether an action was right or wrong. If it harmed someone, it was wrong.

She questioned whether the absence of apparent harm meant that something was right. But then, she'd lived with so many different families with varying rules of what was right and what was wrong. She was pretty screwed up. She *did* believe that harming someone was usually wrong but, if it were a case where she had to choose between harming someone else and protecting herself, she would protect herself. And the same might apply to protecting someone else. On the other hand, there were times she believed that a course of action was wrong even if it didn't harm anyone.

It made defining her own ethics a little difficult. Not having a defined set of ethics made some decisions difficult or impossible.

"You are not going to harm me by doing what I ask," Corvin assured her. "I agreed that I would help your cause. You won't do this thing for me in return? Even when it benefits you?"

"I didn't say I wouldn't. I just want to be sure that it isn't going to hurt you or make things worse."

"You are not going to hurt me."

"Okay..." Reg raised her hands slightly, pointing her palms toward him. "So what exactly do you want me to do? How do I know I'm not doing too much?"

"I will guide you."

He waited. Reg reached out, feeling his aura and his power. In the past, she had only taken power from others when she had needed it, when she had been desperate to shore up her strength in order to complete a task. Taking from him when she was feeling fine was a strange feeling.

Did it make her a power drinker? Was it wrong even if Corvin said it was what he wanted her to do?

"Relax," Corvin urged. "It will come naturally. You've done it before."

"Not when I didn't need to."

"It will come."

She tried to relax. Davyn had tried to teach Reg meditation, and she was getting better at it but, normally, when she meditated with him, it was with a flame, and that helped her focus and stay on track.

She looked at Corvin. "Do you mind…?"

"Do I mind what?"

Reg was used to him knowing what she was talking about. "Do you mind if I use fire? Just a small one."

"By all means."

She breathed slowly and kindled a flame between her palms. She held a ball of fire there and focused her attention on it, trying to get rid of all the tics and twitches of her body and the random thoughts pinballing through her head. She tried to quiet the voices and let them know she was busy with other things. They would have their chance when she did her next seance. For now, she needed them to fade into the background. She focused on the fire.

She was aware of Corvin's power and used it to feed the fire and then to transfer from the fire to her so that it didn't grow too large or hot. There seemed to be great force propelling it, and she tried to bleed it off slowly, not to let the pressure get away from her. She needed to stay in control and not take all Corvin's power.

Not that she ever could take all of it. Corvin was very powerful, especially with the gifts he had taken from the Witch Doctor, and she could never pull all that into herself. She imagined herself exploding like an overfilled balloon. Not the way she wanted to depart this life.

After a while, she encountered some resistance and tried to pull back. Her fire flared.

"Enough," Reg murmured. "That's enough."

She brought her fire down in size, squeezed her hands together, and extinguished the flame. Her body still wanted to pull more power from Corvin, but she looked away from him, focused on the window, and stared outside, trying to divert her attention.

Corvin was quiet. Eventually, Reg looked back at him. He was sitting in his chair, chin to chest, with his eyes closed and his chest rising and falling slowly.

"Corvin?" she asked worriedly. If she had taken too much and harmed him… "Are you okay?"

He didn't open his eyes. "Good now," he murmured. "Now I can sleep."

She wanted to ask him more questions about what was happening and why he wanted her to take his power. But he clearly wanted to rest now, and she hadn't seen him so relaxed since the attack. Or after a siren's kiss, when he was sedated by the venom. It was not the time to be asking him anything.

She rose from her chair and headed for the door. She didn't even bother to tell him goodbye, not wanting to do anything that might rouse him. Sleep was what he needed right now. When he woke up, he could study the questions they had put to him. And then she could ask him more questions.

CHAPTER NINE

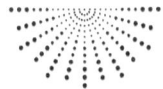

*R*eg went home practically walking on air. She was full of energy. Her anxiety had melted away. She felt like she was on top of the world, like she had accomplished something amazing, even though she had done nothing but visit with Corvin and help to bleed off some of his excess power. She had a high that a drug could never have provided.

In the back of her mind, she knew the high was not natural and that she would not be able to replicate it again. Taking Corvin's energy had been a one-time thing and could not become a regular occurrence. She was not a power drinker. She did not want to become like Verity, John's mother, who had fed off of his powers even though she had not been a power drinker and, in the beginning, had only had minor powers. From the time he was a child, Verity had trained John to feed her the gifts he took from others, so she had grown massively in her powers. And she had not been the good kind of witch. She had wanted nothing but more power for herself and her son and, in the end, had signed her own death warrant.

Reg did not want to be another Verity. She had just done a small favor for a friend. Or an *acquaintance*, since she couldn't quite bring herself to consider Corvin a friend, even when he had no powers.

Reg returned home and strengthened all the wards in the garden and inside the cottage. She had cleaned the cottage, sorting much of the miscellany that had been shoved into the second bedroom, her "office" until she had the time to deal with it. And she cleaned out the fridge and got rid of most of the stuff that she and Starlight would not eat.

Starlight watched this whirlwind of activity with concern but, eventually, it was too much for him, and he retired to the bedroom to sleep on the bed, curled up in a ball.

When her first evening appointment arrived, Reg was ready and waiting. She had several good consultations before the seance scheduled for midnight, and the seance itself had gone well, the spirits more orderly and well-mannered than usual, as if an army drill sergeant had whipped them into shape.

When her clients were gone, Reg had a drink to relax before bed and watched a few short videos on her phone. Then, she closed her eyes and waited for sleep. She was afraid that after such an energetic afternoon and evening, she would not be able to sleep, but she did not toss and turn. In a few minutes, she had drifted peacefully off.

* * *

And then she was awake. Reg sat up in bed. Something was happening. Something was wrong, and she wasn't sure what it was. She reached out her senses to all corners of the cottage until she was certain that no one was there—no unexpected visitors. Then she stretched her consciousness out farther and farther, knowing that something physical had woken her up.

There was a fire burning.

Not just a fire. A huge forest fire, burning out of control.

She knew that forest fires happened, even in Florida, where she would have expected it to be too wet for an uncontrolled burn. But it was the first time she had been so close to one, and the flames drew her.

Reg called Davyn. She couldn't imagine he would still be asleep with a fire so large burning that close.

He sounded foggy when he answered the phone. "Mmm. Reg? What is it?"

"The fire. Can you feel it?"

He cleared his throat, but otherwise was silent for a moment. Reg could hear Julian asking him something in the background. Who it was and why she was waking them up, Reg assumed.

"Yes," Davyn said eventually. He sounded more awake now. "It's not that far away... around Fort Walker."

"We should go there."

"What for, Reg? You know you could end up in trouble walking into a massive fire like that. You are not prepared. Maintaining control in the face of an out-of-control forest fire is almost impossible, even for an experienced firecaster. Much stronger practitioners than you have lost their lives, or cost the lives of others, by getting too close to a fire of that size."

"But it is moving in this direction."

"Yes. But we are still safe for now. Why do you want to get closer to it?"

Davyn had to know how thrilling it would be to feel the power of a fire like that. What kind of a boost it would give them. If they could feed off of its power without succumbing to its uncontrolled nature, it would be incredible.

And they could use the power they got from the fire to keep it in check. To keep it from getting too close to Black Sands and harming anyone. Of course they would want to do that.

"If it is coming this way, we could protect the town. Prevent anyone from having to evacuate."

"I don't know if that is a good idea, Reg. I know this is exciting, but you need to think. You know how hard fire is to control. You know how close you came to being killed in the fire at the conference center."

"But that was before I was trained. I managed to save Damon

and that family. Without any help or training. I know how to fight fires."

"Not this kind of fire."

Reg was frustrated. She had seen it on TV. She'd watched plenty of firefighter shows and those old nature movies about forest fires, and she'd learned about how fires behaved from foster families who'd had to deal with firebugs. And she'd been training with Davyn for over a year, and he was the foremost expert on firecasting in the region. She didn't even know any firecasters other than the two of them. If they couldn't fight a fire together, who could?

"You can't leave it to volunteer firefighters to try to get this thing under control," Reg told Davyn sternly, as if she were the more experienced one. "You and I know more about fire than they ever will. We can fight it. We know all the strategies. And plenty of stuff they don't know."

"Reg…"

"There are people out there," Reg warned. "I can sense them. There are people in the forest who don't even know the danger the fire poses. They are right there in the path of the fire and don't know a thing. We need to do something."

"Come over here," Davyn said finally. "We'll talk."

"Okay."

"And Reg?"

Reg had been reaching for the hang-up button on the screen, and paused.

"Yeah?"

"Don't drive. We don't have the time. Just… transport yourself here."

Reg's heart sped. She was thrilled with the chance to show off her skills and maybe to be able to do something to fight the fire. She disconnected and slid the phone into the pocket of her shorts. Starlight was lying on the windowsill and trilled a query at her, wanting to know what she was doing.

"There is a fire," she told him. "I'm going to Davyn. We'll see what we can do about it."

Starlight rose to his feet and stretched. He yawned and quivered from toes to tail, stretching all his muscles out. Then he sat down on his haunches and looked at her. Reg took a minute to scratch the super-soft fur behind his ears, and he bumped his forehead against hers. She felt the blessing he extended to her, sending her on her way with whatever special power and gifts he could extend to her.

She kissed him on the top of the head. "Thank you, Star."

She closed her eyes and pictured herself in Davyn's living room, standing in front of the big fireplace that was central to the house. Big enough to throw a party in, with man-size doors to allow access to build an indoor bonfire.

"Good," Davyn said. "You're here."

CHAPTER TEN

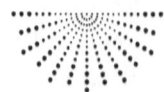

*R*eg opened her eyes and smiled at him. She looked around the living room, proud of herself for how smoothly she was able to travel now. In the beginning, it had been a very bumpy ride. Now, it was smooth as silk. Most of the time, anyway.

Davyn motioned for her to sit on the couch, and he sat at the other end, turning to face her.

"How did you know about the fire?"

"It woke me up."

He shook his head. "How could it have woken you up? You aren't anywhere close to it."

Davyn was closer, and it hadn't woken him up. Even with his affinity for fire, he would have slept right through everything. Until perhaps the emergency personnel knocked on his door to evacuate him. How *would* they manage to evacuate people like Davyn, who lived in the wilderness area, away from the populated centers? They wouldn't be able to go door to door with the speed at which the fire was moving. Would they drop water bombs on the area? Did they have any strategies that would be effective?

"I woke up. I could feel that something was out there. I reached out, and I could feel it." She rubbed her arms. Her skin was tingling. "It's a lot closer to you. And it's coming closer."

Davyn looked her up and down. "You're *glowing*."

Reg looked at herself. She couldn't usually see her own aura. But she could see a faint glow around her skin.

"You can feel it too, can't you?" she asked him. But he wasn't glowing. His aura didn't seem to be any brighter than usual.

"Is there any reason you would be extra sensitive right now?" Davyn asked.

Reg thought about taking powers from Corvin. Had he anticipated this? Had he known that she would need extra powers to sense the presence of the fire and to fight it? Had he had a feeling about it? Or had he had entirely selfish reasons? Just to ease his pain?

"I don't know. But I think we should do something about the fire, don't you?" Reg asked. "Before it gets to the house?"

"What do you think we should do?" Davyn turned and looked outside. The big floor-to-ceiling windows were dark. There was no sign of the fire yet. No brightening of the horizon to show that it was coming. No helicopters.

Reg outlined her plan. "I think... we should start a backburn. Burn the area ahead of the fire, so it doesn't have any fuel when it gets there."

"Have you ever done that before?"

"Well... no, but I've—" Reg stopped herself from saying she'd seen it on TV. "But that's what they do. And we could do that. It wouldn't be so hard."

"With the speed that fire is moving, you think that a second fire would be easy to control? There's obviously enough dry fuel for it to really get hold and burn hot and fast."

"But you and I together could do it. And Ember, he could help too."

"I wouldn't recommend using a dragon for a controlled burn."

"I could show him what we wanted him to do."

Davyn shook his head. "I don't think a dragon can... judge something like that. He can start a fire, yes. But a specific kind of fire meant to burn in a certain way in a certain place? I don't think so. And he has no control over it once the vegetation is on fire. Not like a firecaster."

"Okay, so... what do you think? Can we start a backburn?"

"What are the firefighters going to think when they get to it? We're not exactly trained professionals, as far as they are concerned."

Reg shrugged. "What do we care what they think?"

"There might be some awkward questions about how we anticipated the fire would get here and how we knew to do a backburn."

"Because I watched a lot of TV coverage of forest fires. Like I said, who cares? You're not going to let your house burn to the ground because you're afraid of what other people will think, are you?"

"No... of course not. But maybe they will extinguish it before it reaches us."

"Then they won't even see the backburn."

"All right," Davyn said finally, letting out a sigh. "We'll give it a try."

CHAPTER ELEVEN

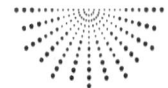

*R*eg tried to tamp down her excitement and show Davyn that she could be a professional. This time, it was more than just "playing with fire" as she had during her training sessions with Davyn. She was actually going to do something important, something that could save people and their properties.

She could sense people in the forest near the fire, which worried her. The fire was moving so rapidly that she didn't know whether the emergency personnel would be able to warn people about the danger in time. Some people were so isolated.

But she could do something about it. She and Davyn could establish the backburn and stop the fire in its tracks. They had an advantage over the firefighters in that they could actually control the flames and where they went. The firefighters could light it and try to predict where it would go, but the wind could change or the fire could take an unexpected leap, and then it got out of control.

Davyn brought up satellite pictures of maps on his computer and they discussed where the fire was burning and where it was likely to go, and where the best position for the backburn was. They would drive out to the location on Davyn's ATV. Reg had never ridden an ATV before, so this only added to her excitement.

"We need to be careful," Davyn reiterated to Reg. "We'll take water with us, but there is always the danger of getting dehydrated working with fire, especially one of this size. Drink more than you think you need to."

"But not enough to suppress my fire."

Reg had learned the previous year during the Spring Games that drinking large quantities of water could prevent her from unintentionally igniting a fire when drawn by something like fireworks. She did not enjoy the waterlogged feeling of drinking that much, but it did prevent her from burning the stadium down.

"I don't think that is going to be a problem here," Davyn told her. "I doubt you could drink water fast enough to get to that point." He added his supplies to the ATV, tying everything down. "You're going to need to listen to and obey me even if you think you know better. I am more experienced and, if you go off on your own plan of action, you could make things much worse."

Reg nodded. "Of course. Yes."

"I mean it. Even if you think you know better." He held her gaze, his eyes steady and his expression stern. "You are going to think that I'm being too strict or too cautious or that I am not aware of the danger. You need to listen anyway."

Reg let out her breath slowly and repeated these words to herself, trying to impress them on her brain so they would still be there when she was in the middle of the action. She would think she knew better, but she didn't. She needed to listen. "Okay."

He nodded. He climbed onto the ATV and motioned for Reg to get on behind him. He turned the key in the ignition and it roared to life. Reg hung on to Davyn as he put it into gear and started to drive, heart pounding with excitement.

It didn't take long to get to the location they had picked to start the firebreak. Reg was surprised that it was so close to the house. With the speed at which the fire was moving, if the backburn didn't work, they wouldn't have much of a chance to do anything else before it reached Davyn's house.

Davyn dismounted from the ATV, looking back toward the house, even though it was not visible from where they were. Reg sensed that he was also second-guessing how close they were to the house. He met her eyes.

"It was built to be fire resistant," Davyn commented. "Lots of stone and metal work. Very little in the way of wood or textiles. The structure of the house itself will survive."

Reg nodded. It made sense for a firecaster to consider these things when building a home. Davyn would know that there were things that could set a firecaster off so that he ignited a fire without intending to. Like having a firedrake in the vicinity. Reg had unintentionally started a couple of fires in her sleep after Ember had hatched in her garden before Davyn learned what was setting her off. Stress, nightmares, or other fires in the area could all set an untrained firecaster off. Maybe even an experienced one like Davyn.

"Where is Julian?" Reg asked, realizing that Davyn's partner had not greeted her at the house, even though she had heard him on the phone when she had called.

"I sent him away."

Of course, Davyn wanted Julian out of the way in case they were unable to stop the forest fire or if their backburn got out of control. It was one thing for firecasters like Davyn and Reg to be exposed to the fire. They had natural defenses. But a human without an affinity for fire was another story. He was very vulnerable. And they were much closer to the fire now than when Reg had first sensed it.

"We'll start here." Davyn gestured to the invisible line they would follow. "It will need to be fifty to a hundred yards wide, and we will extend in either direction until we reach a body of water, either the river or the lake." He looked around him, clearly anxious. "The biggest problem will be keeping it from getting out of control. If it does, you need to keep it from spreading east toward the house and Black Sands. West is toward the existing fire, and it will hopefully burn up all the fuel on the way there, so there is nowhere else for it to go. North and south are water."

Reg nodded. "Keep it from going east."

"It is easy to get disoriented in a fire. Do you have a compass?"

"There's an app on my phone."

"Not good enough." Davyn dug a couple of compasses out of his pack and hung one around Reg's neck. "Show me you know how to use it."

Reg held the compass horizontally and lined up the red pointer with the big N. "North. So that way is east," she gestured back toward the house. "And that is west."

Davyn nodded. "We will start together and move apart." He handed her a yellow walkie-talkie and attached one to his own belt. He looked over Reg's shorts and t-shirt. "I appreciate that you're not wearing one of your long skirts that could easily catch fire, but I'm not sure this is the best outfit to wear to a forest fire."

Reg looked down at herself, heat rising to her cheeks. "I didn't think. I just... got out of bed."

"I suppose we should be grateful you don't sleep in the nude. You'll need to get some fire-resistant clothing if this is going to become a thing."

Reg laughed. "I don't think it will be a regular occurrence."

"I hope not. Not sure my heart could take it."

They each drank a bottle of water in silence, then Reg followed Davyn's instructions as they started the burn. She had been through many training sessions with him, following his directions to create various kinds of fire in a variety of different settings. She was grateful for the detailed training they had done on different kinds of fuel, how to control a fire in the underbrush versus one in the tops of the trees, and the various types of terrain they had practiced in. She had often been bored and impatient with what seemed like tedious, unnecessary instruction, discussion, and practice. Now, she was thankful Davyn had taken the time and not given in to her complaints.

They worked mostly in silence, occasionally shouting some-thing out. They started working side by side but moved apart and, after a while, they were too far apart to yell to each other. They switched to the walkies as they needed them.

The flames glowed bright orange and red, crackling through the underbrush like some hungry beast. Waves of heat poured off of the fire. If she had not been a firecaster, she would not have been able to withstand it. Smoke filled her eyes, but she was able to blink it away and still see where she was going. Another firecaster skill.

Reg thought she was doing pretty well. They were getting a nice, controlled thirty-yard strip burned clean of vegetation. Much neater than anything the Florida Forest Service could have accomplished. Reg was keeping her focus, though she was monitoring the progress of the forest fire moving toward them as well as the backburn they were creating.

She was still worried about the residents of the area. They were taking care not to trap anyone between the two fire lines, but fires and people could both move in unexpected directions. She could sense the movements of humans as they became aware of the fire and tried to move out of its path. At least emergency services seemed to be making contact with them. They didn't seem to be doing much to stop the spread of the fire. She supposed it took time to get the specialized equipment and people in place to fight the fire. It wasn't like sending a fire engine to a single house. It might take days for them to get everybody in place with an effective plan.

Reg sensed Ember flying overhead, though she couldn't see him yet through the billowing clouds of smoke. She hadn't expected him to take long to became aware of the fire or her presence.

Her mind filled with pictures as Ember communicated his excitement about the fire and her activities. She tried to work steadily while feeding pictures back to him about what they were doing and how it would stop the fire from reaching the house, his lair.

Ember landed next to Reg with a whoosh. He was eager to help with the project. Despite what Davyn had said, Reg was sure he understood what she was doing and would be able to help. They worked in tandem, with Ember moving ahead of her and starting fire in strategic positions, and Reg guiding and directing the fire along the swath they wanted to burn.

A sudden wind picked up burning embers and fanned the flames west. Reg kept her focus, not panicking. They had expected this. Fires didn't just burn in neat lines. Changes in terrain and the wind would affect it. She directed the fire farther north, trying to funnel it along the path she and Davyn had determined. Ember took wing and flew over the section of burning brush to the other side. Reg had to move to the east to navigate along that border. She could walk through the fire if necessary, but that would deplete her powers and onboard water faster. She was in it for the long haul, so she needed to exercise caution, as Davyn had warned her.

She used the walkie-talkie to update Davyn on the behavior of the fire and what she was doing. He had experienced a similar reaction to the wind and confirmed her actions. Reg said nothing about having been joined in her work by a juvenile dragon.

When she reached the other side of the fire, she found Ember on the other side watching it and waiting for her.

Ember sent Reg a mental picture of herself in dragon form, the one time she had transformed. He wanted her to transform now, to work with him as a dragon. She would still have the ability to control the fire as she was doing, but would also be able to create fire through her breath rather than psychically, and would be able to fly as Ember was rather than having to walk around or through the fire, trudging at slow human speeds.

I don't know, she told him. *We'll see.*

He sent her the picture more urgently. Did he know something about the fire that she didn't? He had just flown over it, so she suspected he probably did.

Show me, she told him.

Ember sent an aerial view of the fire, and she saw that one part of the backburn she had thought was completely burned out had still been alive and had reignited the trees behind her. The fire was curling around as if it intended to trap her. There was still enough room for Reg to walk out, so she immediately started walking toward the opening, reaching out to the stray leg of the fire to send it back upon itself and burn out.

She felt immediate resistance.

CHAPTER TWELVE

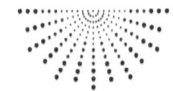

*R*eg jolted.

It wasn't the reluctance she was used to feeling from a fire, the tug to go on and find more fuel and keep burning. The hunger that led the first from one place to another, consuming everything combustible in its path.

Instead, it was like running into a brick wall. As if the fire had said "No!" and pushed back against her. She had never felt that sense of will from a fire before.

It seemed as if it did have intent. It wasn't just a coincidence that it was curling around behind her. It *wanted* to trap her. It wanted to stop this firecaster from interfering with its course and to be allowed to burn wildly in whatever direction it wanted.

How could that be?

Reg clicked her walkie-talkie. "Davyn?"

He didn't respond immediately. That was understandable. What they were doing was not a walk in the park. It was hard work and took effort, will, and focus. Reg kept working her end of the fire, keeping an eye open for the other end of that curl of fire to come into view as she worked. Ember let out a cry that sounded like the shrill call of a falcon or hawk overhead, and she looked up at him. He continued to circle, watching her with concern.

"Reg?" Davyn's voice came over the walkie-talkie. "What is it? What's going on?"

"There's something weird about this fire," Reg said. "Have you noticed anything?"

"It is difficult," Davyn admitted. "I told you it might be too much for us to take on."

But it wasn't that. It wasn't that it was too hard or that the fire was too big or too hot for them. There was something else at work here.

"The fire is… resisting," she told Davyn. "I don't know how else to explain it. It… doesn't want to be stopped or manipulated. It wants to trap us. To trap me."

"What do you mean?"

His voice was difficult to hear over the crackling of the fire and the static of the walkie-talkie. Reg was used to talking on a phone, where the signal was nice and clear, not on a two-way radio.

"It's… sentient," Reg tried.

There was no reply from Davyn. Reg continued to battle the fire, but she could see the other end now, starting to surround her and close in. Ember gave another warning call.

Reg needed an answer from Davyn. Some clue as to what he thought she should do.

"Reg," his voice came over a loud crackle. Was the heat from the fire affecting the walkie-talkie? Reg could feel how hot it was on her face. It didn't burn her, because she was a firecaster and she was prepared for it. She was well-hydrated, awake, and charged up with Corvin's power. To be burned, she would have had to be taken off guard. "Reg?"

"Go ahead."

"Reg…" his voice was distant and faint, "Get out of there."

Reg looked around for the best way to extract herself from the situation. The curl of fire reached around to join with the backburn she had created, but the backburn had not yet burned up all the fuel. It burned hotter when joined by the rogue leg of the fire. She felt its strength and the fire's exultation at trapping Reg inside the snare.

Despite the heat she could feel pouring off the fire, she could walk through it. It would not be hard to just walk through the flames to safety.

Except that she wasn't sure of the nature of what seemed to be sentient fire. She could walk through normal fire. She could absorb its heat and be energized by it. But this new fire? Was she willing to take the chance that it had the same nature and composition as a regular fire?

Ember sent her his memory of Reg as a dragon soaring above the earth. Reg focused on it, trying to feel how it felt to be in that form again. She felt the wings that would lift her, the strong legs and muscles, the lung capacity, and the ability to breathe in pure air and breathe out fire—bright, beautiful fire.

She kicked off the ground without even a thought, soaring up to meet Ember, who shrieked a greeting. They flew around each other, playing on the updrafts from the fire, enjoying the total freedom of flight. Below her, she could feel the fury of the fire, rising up to chase her, but unable to reach her.

How about that, fire?

She flew loops with Ember for a few minutes before recalling her task and turning her attention back to the fire. It was her job to ensure it did not get back to the house, however much it wanted to destroy her. She could not allow it to spread east.

But it did not appear to be trying to make its way in that direction. Instead, it was pressing westward, to meet the main fire. While they had intended to only burn the portion of the forest that they needed to stop the advance and to wait for it to reach the backburn, if the backburn burned west and the original fire burned east so they eventually met in the middle, the effect was the same. The fire would burn out when there was no more fuel.

Reg circled, watching the backburn and its progress. She could see the other end of the line of fire they had created, where Davyn was. He did not seem to be contending with the same stubborn flames as she had. Or maybe he was just better at it and she had imagined the active resistance of the fire, had personified it when it had been challenging to control.

She reached her senses down into the forest and spread them out, looking for any conscious thought—the fire itself or residents who had not made it out of the path of the fire in time.

And they were there. She could sense someone down there, more than one mind, terrified and trapped by the inferno.

CHAPTER THIRTEEN

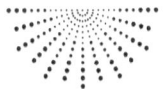

*R*eg spiraled down from the sky, searching the forest below for the minds she could feel there. She saw no sign of movement and heard no cries for help.

But they were still there, and they were afraid. They were trapped. There was no way for them to move, no way they could escape the fire that was closing in around them.

Reg wheeled around, trying to pinpoint them, but she could only see flames closing in, shadows under the trees, rocks, and dark underbrush. She tried to get Ember to help her look for them, communicating their fear, and Ember joined her in circling, trying to find the refugees from the fire.

The fire burned hotter. The distance between the two fires grew narrower and narrower. Reg was frantic, but she could not find them. Were they hiding in a stream? Under an outcropping of rock? She could see no shelters that hadn't been consumed by the fire. Wherever they had come from, their homes were now part of the inferno. And they would be, too, if Reg couldn't find them.

She worked north and south along the line of fire, looking for anyone who had made it to the edge of the backburn and then found themselves trapped. No one.

No one.

She saw Davyn standing by the river, watching to see if their plan worked. If the fire got too close to him, he would retreat into the water if necessary. As a firecaster, he should not need to take that precaution unless he had become dehydrated.

She circled overhead. Davyn looked up and waved at her, his face turned toward her so she could see he was happy to see her, relieved that she was okay. She had stopped responding to him on the walkie-talkie, and he wouldn't know that she had escaped the malevolent fire until he saw her overhead in her dragon form.

Reg watched the forest fire raging below her. It was enthralling for her as a firecaster; it made her heart speed—at least when she was in human form—and her muscles tense in anticipation. She wanted to be a part of it, playing with the fire, diving into it. But even as a dragon, that probably wasn't recommended. Especially when she didn't know what she was dealing with as far as the rogue fire went.

The big forest fire and the backburn they had set eventually ran into each other and while, for a few minutes, there was a flare-up as the two joined into one massive fire, suddenly, there was nowhere for the fire to go, no more fuel to burn. It got smaller and smaller, burning down to the ground to glowing embers.

Reg and Ember wheeled around the sky, getting lower over the charred trunks of trees, looking at the destruction.

Reg reached out her senses tentatively, not expecting to find anything more of the fire that had spoken to her or the people it had trapped. She had a fleeting sense of the fire's voice, as if it were far away—muted because it had burned down to almost nothing, she assumed. A voice on the wind.

But she also sensed something else. Humans. Still trapped. Still frightened and trying to escape.

CHAPTER FOURTEEN

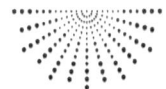

*R*eg wheeled in the sky over the trees, searching for the source of the fear. She couldn't believe anything could have survived the devastation of the forest she saw below. But perhaps they had sheltered deep in a cave or a stream or pond, somewhere that had escaped the wrath of the fire but had still left them trapped and frightened.

At first, Ember was curious about what Reg was doing, then snorted when she fed him a mental picture of the people hiding in a pond to escape the fire. He wasn't too impressed with anyone who would run away from a fire. He and his people went toward fire. Played with fire. Used it as a tool. A weapon. But he stayed with her as she searched for the survivors.

Davyn followed on the ground but, of course, could not move very fast. There were many obstacles, even where the forest floor had been burned clear of brush and undergrowth. And he didn't want to trip and fall and wreck his clothes.

Reg homed in on the fear she could feel. Eventually, she saw forms in the trees. They appeared at first glance to be stones, but she knew from the emotion that they were not.

She landed on the ground and approached them on foot.

A man and a woman stood in front of her. Or, rather than

standing, they appeared to be mid-stride, running or walking. But like Gideon, they were petrified. The once-living humans had been turned to rock.

Ember landed with Reg and approached the statues, nudging them with his nose. Reg would have told him not to do that, but supposed it didn't make any difference to the statues whether he touched them or not. They couldn't feel anything that was happening to them. Only the emotions they had been feeling when they were petrified, or what they felt upon discovering that they had been petrified.

Terror at being trapped inside the unyielding forms.

Dragon Reg stalked around the statues, sniffing at their feet and in every direction to determine where they had come from and what had happened to them.

Davyn came tramping through the blackened, smoking forest. He saw the statues and approached them, frowning.

"What's this? More petrifaction? What happened here?"

He looked at Reg and Ember as if they might know the answer and communicate it to him. But neither of them could tell him, even if they knew. Reg looked at Davyn.

"Do you know what happened here?" Davyn asked.

Reg swung her head back and forth to indicate that she did not. Davyn touched one of the statues uncertainly.

"Can you still feel them? Like Gideon? Are their minds still in there?"

Reg nodded.

"What is causing this? A curse? The fire? It couldn't be the fire; there was no fire at the temple. What ties these people to Gideon?"

Reg looked at him. She didn't even know who the couple was; she didn't know how she was supposed to know anything about how they were connected.

"They're... neighbors," Davyn explained. He shrugged help-lessly. "I know little about them. They seem like nice enough people. Mostly keep to themselves, but it isn't like they are hermits. I don't think they are practitioners; I haven't seen them at any magical gatherings."

So what would they have to do with Gideon, an ancient warlock who had been worshiping at the temple?

Reg sniffed the air. It was difficult to smell anything but the smoke. She couldn't smell anyone else who had been in that part of the forest. With this powerful magic afoot, it would have made sense for her to smell John Saunders or some other powerful warlock or witch nearby. Then she would know who had done this thing. But she couldn't sense anyone else.

She flapped her wings and rose up in the air, a few feet off the ground. She smelled the wind higher up where it was not so laden with smoke. She looked back in the direction that the forest fire had come from. Where had it originated? If it were connected with what had happened at the temple, perhaps they would find something at the fire's origin that would give them a clue. She looked over the trees far into the distance and saw the ruins of some old settlement. She sent a picture of it to Ember, and he rose up to look at it himself. He went up higher and closer.

Reg stayed close to Davyn. She didn't want to abandon her mentor there, especially if there were something evil in the woods igniting malevolent fires and turning people into stone.

She returned to the ground, where Davyn was still looking around. Like Reg, he had been unable to find anything to indicate another presence there or who might have turned his neighbors into garden decorations.

"Where is Ember going?"

Reg tried to send him pictures as she did to Ember, but Davyn was not on the right wavelength to receive them. She pointed her nose toward the source of the fire's ignition and kept it in that position for a few seconds before turning back to look at him. She hoped he could understand it to mean more than "he went that way."

Davyn was smart, a quick thinker, and he nodded after thinking about it for a moment. "To see where it started."

Reg gave a nod.

"Good idea. How far is it? Can I walk to it? Go back and get the ATV?"

Reg considered. It was pretty far to go on foot, and for him to go back to get the ATV would also be quite a distance, and she didn't know how well it would go through the forest with all the newly fallen burnt timber. She didn't think it was very conducive to transportation of any kind.

She crouched as low as she could, which wasn't easy with her massive, muscled legs. Davyn shook his head, unsure what she wanted at first.

"You want me to climb on?" he asked, a note of disbelief in his voice. "Are you thinking you can fly me there? There isn't exactly... a saddle or anything to hold on to back there."

Reg rolled her head slightly to the side to look at him. Was he going to try it or not? She didn't plan to drop him. But it was up to him to decide if he were willing to try it.

She could pick him up in her claws. But she wasn't sure how comfortable that would be for Davyn or how quickly she would tire of carrying him that way.

"Well... let me see what it feels like," Davyn said grudgingly. "Just... hold still. Don't take off; I just want to see how it feels before you do anything."

Reg stayed as still as she could. *Like a statue.* Davyn used her knee to boost himself onto her back, then slid around, trying to find a comfortable space between her wings and her head to settle. He wrapped his arms around her neck and just held on for a moment. It wasn't uncomfortable for Reg. But she didn't know how it felt to him.

"Okay," Davyn said after staying still there for a few minutes. "Can you try... just lifting off the ground a few feet? Not far. Just to see how your wing movement affects everything..."

CHAPTER FIFTEEN

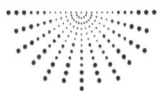

*R*eg flapped her wings gently a couple of times to lift her just above the ground. Davyn's grip tightened around her neck, but then he relaxed. Reg flapped a few more times to rise higher, just to the tops of the charred tree trunks.

Davyn shouted in her ear. "I think this will work. It actually feels a lot more stable than I thought it would. As long as you don't go too fast or... try any loops or anything like that."

Reg winced at the volume of his voice. But she couldn't do anything to tell him he didn't need to shout when he was positioned right beside her ear. She gave a few more powerful flaps to get them up to the clouds, and she headed toward the ruins.

Davyn kept a tight grip on her, but not enough to feel like he was going to strangle her. He just wanted to ensure that he kept his seat. It would not be good if he fell from that height. Reg might be able to catch him, but she didn't want to have to try. It would be pretty devastating if she were unable to catch him and saw him plummet to his death. As a dragon, she understood that was the way of the world. Regrettable things sometimes happened. She also knew that back in her human form, her emotions about the loss of her mentor would be much stronger.

It only took a few minutes to fly across the forest to the ruins she had seen in the distance. Walking or on the ATV would probably have taken all day. Transportation on a dragon was far better than an all-terrain vehicle.

When she reached the ruins, Reg circled a few times, studying the layout of the stone structures.

From a distance, she had thought that it was an old town, maybe one of the old Spanish settlements that still dotted the southern states but, looking down at the foundations that remained, she found it to be well-fortified with a strong outer wall.

Ember was still circling. One thing that Reg had not acquired from her dragon transformation was the genetic memory that Ember had. That would have been really handy. But as the two of them soared over the battlements, Ember fed images to Reg of other sites he could find in his memory with similar features. Castles with solid stone walls; long, low buildings for army barracks; and watchtowers. They were close to what Reg and Ember were looking at, but not quite the same.

"It's the old fort," Davyn shouted into Reg's ear. "Fort Walker."

A fort, not a castle. Reg nodded her understanding and agreement. That made perfect sense. There were several similar structures throughout Florida. Sarah had wanted to take Reg to the Fort San Marcos de Apalache when she was going there with some of the witches in her coven, but Reg had not been interested and made excuses. Maybe she should have gone and learned more about the features of forts in the area. Reg assumed this fort was of the same vintage as the Fort San Marcos de Apalache but, since she had not chosen to go with Sarah, she knew less than she should about it. She had barely even glanced at the brochures and booklets Sarah had brought back with her and left on Reg's kitchen counter.

Reg glided lower and lower in a gentle spiral until she landed on her toes and came to a stop. She crouched down again for Davyn to dismount. He slid from her neck and wiped his face, smeared with sweat and soot from the fire.

"Wow, that was quite the ride. Thank you."

Ember dive-bombed from high up in the clouds, coming to an

abrupt halt just an inch or two off the ground. Davyn jumped, as he always did when Ember showed off that maneuver. He laughed.

"And thank you for not landing like *that*!"

Ember's tongue lolled out in a dragon laugh, and he rubbed up against Davyn to get ear scratches and praise.

"Yes," Davyn told him, obligingly scratching the fine, smooth scales around Ember's ears. "You're a very smart dragon. And you helped Reg with the fire?"

Reg nodded and shared memories with Ember of the two of them working together to tame the fire and keep it burning in the right direction. Ember bumped his head against Reg's neck and head, and she nuzzled him back.

They had landed in a large, flat area that would have been in the inner court of the fort. Reg had observed several layers of security around the outside. What would have been a moat and draw-bridge, an outer court, the barracks, with the inner court behind another thick stone wall. She didn't know what kind of weaponry the enemies of the Spanish traders would have had. It seemed like the fort had been intended to protect them against more than just the bows and arrows she imagined the indigenous people had.

Maybe they'd had to defend against other factions of traders with canons, muskets, and other old-style weaponry.

Maybe they'd had to worry about the forest people, swamp goblins, or other magical species.

Maybe there had been dragons.

Ember had not shared any memories of his ancestors attacking the fort, so maybe not.

"Well, let's take a look around," Davyn suggested. "Reg, why don't you transform back so we can talk properly and explore the place? If this was the source of the forest fire... we'll want to know whether there are any similarities between the fort and the temple. They were built by two different peoples at two different times, so I'm not sure what similarities they will share besides being old ruins. But any connection might be significant. Especially with the petrifactions. I can't think what would connect them and how the fire would be related."

Reg did not take his suggestion. He stood there waiting for her to transform, eventually figuring out she wasn't going to.

"Why not?" he asked. He stared into her dragon eyes.

Reg wondered whether he could sense anything of what she was thinking and feeling. She had difficulty imagining what it was like for other people to discern each other's thoughts and emotions. Growing up, she had assumed that everybody could see and feel the same things she did. Most people's emotions were painfully obvious, and it could be difficult for Reg to keep her own emotions from whoever she was with. She had quick, intuitive insights into snippets of their thoughts. And the voices of others, which sometimes gave her profound insights.

But for someone who was not psychic like Reg, what was it like? Was it all guesswork? Did they logically tally up the facial expressions, body language, tone of voice, and historical knowledge of the person to come to a conclusion or series of conclusions about their feelings and thoughts? Did the feelings come easily, and the thoughts were more challenging, or vice versa? Some people seemed very empathic or intuitive, and others appeared to have no idea what others around them were thinking and feeling.

"Are you afraid that you won't be able to transform back into a dragon again afterward?" Davyn suggested.

Reg nodded.

She was a little more confident now that she could transform into her dragon form at will, but she was not one hundred percent sure she would be able to do it if she were not in danger, as she had been the only two times she had transformed into a dragon so far. Ember would probably help her, but he couldn't guarantee she could find her dragon form.

Davyn gazed out over the forest that stretched between the fort and his house or where the ATV was parked. It would be a long way if they had to walk. He sighed and nodded.

"You might be right. I have no idea if there are even roads from here. Battling our way back through the bush would be a major undertaking, and we are both tired already."

Reg was feeling anything but tired, but that might change when she reverted to her human form. She didn't relish the idea of fighting her way through the blackened remains of the forest in a t-shirt, shorts, and flimsy sneakers after a long day of firecasting, transforming, flying, and exploring an ancient fort.

"Okay," Davyn conceded. "If you're not sure you could transform back again, you're probably right. We don't want to eliminate the easiest way home. You could probably teleport us too... but only if you had enough energy."

Reg thought that she still had plenty of Corvin's power and what she had gained from the fires, but she didn't have enough experience with transformation and flight to be sure how they would leave her feeling.

"Well, let's take a look around," Davyn invited. "Hopefully, there won't be any doorways you can't fit through."

Reg had never been too fat to fit through a doorway before, so this wasn't something she had considered. But most of the ruins appeared to just be walls and foundations. She didn't think there were any buildings still fully intact.

They walked together, Reg looking at and smelling everything. She tried to picture how everything would have looked when the fort was still functional but, unlike with the temple, she could not see the bright outlines of the original structure.

As they navigated through the long lines of foundation walls and into a few low stone buildings, Reg reached out all her senses to test for old magic there.

What she found astounded her.

CHAPTER SIXTEEN

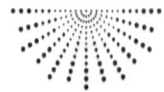

*A*t first Reg just stopped, frozen in place. Davyn kept walking and looking around, but when she didn't keep up or rejoin him, he looked back and studied her curiously.

"Reg? Did you find something? What is it?"

Reg could not communicate her find to him. Nor was she sure how to get to it or whether that were even possible. She looked for a stairway or tunnel leading down to the hidden chamber.

Davyn looked around with her but, of course, he was not sure what she was looking for. He found nothing of any particular interest.

Reg looked down, deep down where she could sense the object, and maintained this gaze for a few long seconds so that he would understand.

"There is something here?" Davyn asked. "What is it?"

She couldn't explain it to him while in her dragon form. She could try to send a picture to his mind, but she knew from experience that he probably would not be able to sense it.

Davyn looked at her. He looked down at the ground in the direction she was looking. "Something down there. Buried? Like at the temple?"

Reg thought of the geode she had been able to sense at the

74

temple. There were similarities between the two artifacts. What she could sense here was not buried in the dirt, but was somewhere in a chamber far below them.

She continued to search for a passageway down to the chamber but could not find a doorway or stairway that might lead to it. She was not surprised. If there had been an obvious way down, tourists or scavengers would have found it years ago and pillaged it.

Eventually, they had searched all they could, and Reg could see that Davyn's energy was seriously depleted. It wouldn't do them much good if he passed out during the flight back, so she decided they had better get on their way. She led Davyn back to an open area where they could take flight, and crouched down for him to mount.

Ember was bored with wandering over the ruin without finding anything interesting to eat or hoard, so he was eagerly waiting for them to say they were ready to go home. Of course, he could have just left any time he wanted to, but he liked spending time with Reg and particularly liked it when she was in dragon form. He had been bugging her to take it on again a number of times since the first time she had transformed, but Reg didn't want to do it solely for recreational purposes and didn't know how easy it would be to transform without a particular need.

Davyn climbed onto Reg's back more confidently than he had the first time, but she could tell he was tired. She looked over her shoulder at him to make sure that he was going to hold on tight. She didn't want to lose him.

"Just a short jaunt," Davyn told her. "I'll be fine. Don't worry."

She eyed him for a moment longer, then gave a nod. She flapped her wings and rose into the air slowly and gently. Davyn held on firmly and gave no indication that he was too weak or emotionally distressed for the ride. Nevertheless, she stayed low and glided most of the way back, only giving her wings the occasional flap.

She circled the ATV and looked back at Davyn to see whether he wanted to stop there or fly all the way back to the house.

"Let's just go home," Davyn said, "I can get the ATV later."

Reg nodded and glided the rest of the way back to the house. She landed gently and Davyn slid off her back. "Nice smooth ride," he told her. "The hardest part was not falling asleep!"

Her tongue lolled out in a dragon grin at that.

"Now, if you don't mind, I'd like to be able to talk with you…"

Which meant he wanted her to transform back to human form. Reg hesitated. She looked up at Ember, who was still hanging in the air, making little jiggles and loops, trying to entice Reg to join him. She gave Davyn a nod, then flew up to meet Ember.

They played for a while, doing aerial acrobatics, roughhousing, and teasing each other. Eventually, though, Reg knew she had to get back to Davyn and try to work out what was happening with him. There were lives at stake. Gideon and the others were in a state of suspended animation, but no one knew how long that state could last. Hours? Days? Years? They needed to figure out what was causing the petrifaction and how to reverse it before it was too late, and they had no idea when "too late" would be.

She did a few more maneuvers with Ember, then dropped to the ground, trying to replicate Ember's dive-bombing technique without burying herself in three feet of dirt. She was able to stop herself above the ground, but too unsure of her own abilities yet to get as close to the ground as Ember before stopping.

Ember laughed at her.

Reg set her feet on the ground and thought about her human shape and how it felt to be human again. She opened her eyes and saw that she was, once again, her human self.

"Well, it's about time," Davyn said with a smile. He handed her a bottle of water he had just taken out of the fridge.

Reg took it, cracked the top, and drank down the top third. "Thanks." She let out a sigh and evaluated her condition.

The physical activity she had done in dragon form did not seem to have affected her human form. She wasn't exhausted by flying around, searching the ruins, and playing with Ember. Instead, she was still energized, just as she had been when she had left Corvin's house. She could feel that she was a little dehydrated by the amount of firecasting she had done before turning into a dragon, but she had also topped up before starting the backburn, so she hadn't suffered too much for her fire "work."

"How are you doing?" Davyn asked.

"Good. I'm just fine. How about you? Better?"

He'd had time to drink and rest while she played with Ember, who now hung overhead, pouting at the loss of his playmate.

"Yes, thanks. Let's go inside."

Reg nodded, and the two of them headed for the door. Ember dropped down and buzzed past them, landing on the doorstep ahead of them. For a moment, it looked like he would block them from going in, but then he just pulled the door open and shouldered his way in ahead of them. Reg watched him squeeze his rump in through the front door. Before long, he would not be able to fit in anymore. Or Davyn would have to get wider doors. Plane hangar doors.

She and Davyn exchanged smiles and followed the young dragon into the house. Davyn gave him permission to start a fire in the fireplace and, since Julian was not home, Ember was allowed to make it a large bonfire, which seemed to improve his mood.

CHAPTER SEVENTEEN

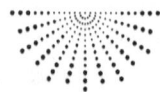

S o…" Davyn and Reg sat down on the couch, watching
Ember set up the fuel for the fire, poking it in through
the man-size doors. "What did you find in the fort? I'm afraid I
couldn't interpret what you were telling me."

"Yeah… it was a gemstone."

"A gemstone." Davyn nodded slowly. "Okay… I guess something like that could still be hidden or buried in the fort after so
long. You don't know who may have lived there over time or what
they might have stored there."

"It wasn't just something that was hidden or lost."

"How do you know that?"

"It isn't a gemstone like you would find in a ring or something
like that. It is a huge ruby, bigger than any I've ever seen. It is cut in
the shape of a heart, and it…" Reg struggled to explain the feelings
she'd had. "It was very important. It was deliberately placed there
for safekeeping."

"Like the geode that was buried in the temple."

"Maybe, yes. But it wasn't buried."

"Where was it, then? I know you were looking for something,
but I don't know what."

"There is a room in the fort, a chamber underneath, but I couldn't find a stairway or passage anywhere."

"It is just stored in a room?"

"No, there is... some kind of protection around it."

Davyn nodded. They watched as Ember blew a blast of fire into the fireplace, lighting the fuel ablaze. The room was immediately like a furnace, but neither of them minded. Reg enjoyed the heat that penetrated her body.

"Any idea what kind of protection?" he asked. "More ward stones like at the temple?" His brows came down in a frown. "Who would have put these stones into these sites? And why?"

"Not ward stones. Something... like it's electrical? I don't know. The ruins don't have electricity."

"Electricity can come from other sources, not just generators."

"Yeah, maybe. Like lightning rods or something." She nodded. "Maybe that's it. Lightning rods."

"I've noticed that we do tend to get a lot of lightning out that direction. I didn't see anything like that built into the ruins, but it could be somewhere we couldn't see, somewhere it wasn't obvious."

"Yeah. Maybe a weather vane or iron reinforcing a roof seam."

"But who?" Davyn asked meditatively. "And why?"

"It connects the two sites, but I have no idea why or what it means."

"Yes," Davyn agreed. "It's a puzzle. What do they have in common?"

"The temple and the fort are... both old."

Davyn rolled his eyes. "Yes, obviously. But not of the same era."

"They're both ruins."

"Yes, but is that different and distinct from being old?"

Reg considered and then nodded. "Well, yes. The sites are still preserved, even though the original buildings are gone. People still visit them to look at them. Was there anything magical about the fort? Sarah went to look at a different one. Is there some kind of magical or spiritual significance about them?"

"No. They were both places of protection. I suppose that is similar to the temple. But the purpose of a fort is not for worship;

it is… tied to violence, not peace. To worldly treasure, not spiritual. I don't see a lot of parallels between the two buildings."

"Both made of stone. Both here, close to Black Sands."

"Close to Black Sands," Davyn repeated.

Reg nodded. "Well… yeah."

"Hmm. So the stones were put there by someone local. More than likely."

Because if someone were hiding valuable artifacts in random protected places around the country or around the world, there would not be two so close to Black Sands. They would be spread out widely.

"I guess so," Reg agreed.

"How about the stones themselves? What do they have in common?"

Reg scratched the back of her neck, thinking back about it.

"Not much. Both are *powerful*. The geode… it's not a cut gemstone like the ruby. It's got crystals in it… green like emeralds, and gold. The ruby, if that's what it is… it's big, and it's cut and shaped. One is buried in the earth; the other is protected by… electricity. I don't know. Other than the fact that they are both stones, there's not that much that is the same about them."

"Are they protected by curses? Is that why Gideon was petrified? Because he was trying to find it or access it?"

"So it was like a booby trap?"

"Maybe."

"But the people in the forest… your neighbors… they weren't trying to get the gemstone at the fort. They weren't anywhere near it. They were trying to run away from the fire."

"Right." Davyn sighed. "The fire."

He stared into the fireplace, where Ember was sitting in the middle of the fire he had ignited, the cozy red glow enveloping him. His eyes were closed, and he snoozed like a cat lying in a sunbeam.

"What's wrong?" Reg asked. "What about the fire?"

She knew he was talking about the forest fire, not the fire he was looking at now. She had thought that he would be happy about it. They had managed to avoid disaster. The backburn had worked. The firefighters would have to look for hot spots and make sure it didn't spring up again from some embers being blown to new fuel but, as long as they were careful, there was nothing to worry about. It had been a fun adventure. Reg had enjoyed herself.

Other than when she was being stalked and trapped by sentient, malevolent flames.

"How did you know about the fire?" Davyn asked.

Reg shrugged. "I told you. I woke up. I could feel it. So I called you. Then we went and took care of it." She smiled, gathered her box braids in both hands and let them go behind her shoulders.

"How did you feel it when it was so far away? What was it about the fire that attracted your attention? That's not something you normally do, is it? Identifying the location of forest fires?"

"I don't know. I guess I was just… more sensitive. I had…" Reg trailed off.

Davyn waited. Reg didn't know why his expression made her feel so guilty. She hadn't done anything wrong. He might disapprove of her seeing Corvin or having anything to do with him, but the man was injured. She was just helping him. How could it be wrong for her to help someone?

"What's that?" Davyn prodded. "You were more sensitive because…"

"I just… I was feeling good. I cleaned the house and everything. Lots of energy. I felt like I had accomplished something."

"You cleaned the house?"

He sounded like he didn't believe her for some reason. Like maybe she didn't usually touch the housework and just let Sarah do it, and let all her junk slowly accumulate in the spare room that was supposed to be her office.

What would he know about that?

"Yes, I cleaned," she told him evenly. "Sorted out a bunch of stuff that has needed to be done for a while. I told you. I felt good. Had a lot of energy, and put it to good use."

"Where did this burst of energy come from?"

"You make it sound like you think I was on drugs or something. Just because I cleaned, that doesn't mean I did something wrong."

"I didn't say you did. But you're not answering my question, making me wonder even more."

"I'm not avoiding the question," Reg insisted.

He just looked at her, waiting. Reg couldn't think of what else to say to avoid answering the question. Why did he have to focus on that? There was nothing wrong with her taking the energy from Corvin. Corvin had asked her to; she had only done what he had wanted. And that made it perfectly legal.

"I... I saw Corvin during the day, and he asked if I would take some of his excess power. Because, you know, it causes him pain when he uses his magic, so he wanted to deplete it a little bit so it wasn't so hard to avoid using it."

"You're taking Corvin's gifts," Davyn said in a tone of disbelief.

Reg shook her head. "Just some power. Some energy," she clarified. "Not like his actual gifts, the things that he can do. I don't think I could take those."

"You think that you can take his power without taking any of his gifts? They are the same thing; they are not just intertwined; they are one and the same. An integral package. The same... substance."

"Well, I'm not a power drinker like he is, and I couldn't become one just by taking some of his extra energy."

"No, you cannot change what you are," Davyn agreed. "You are still not the same... subspecies as he is. You are what you are. But the powers that you acquire from him... that he has taken from others... that is not insignificant. It's not like... borrowing his car."

Reg stared at Davyn, trying to make sense of what he was saying.

"So you think that—what? I'm trafficking in stolen goods? I'm in illegal possession of something that he stole?"

"Corvin assures me that he follows the rules," Davyn said, avoiding grimacing or rolling his eyes. They both knew how likely Corvin was to stay on the right side of the law when he had broken it before. You didn't reform a power drinker. "If so, then those powers are not stolen, and you are not involved in any kind of magical crime by taking them when offered. But… this is very risky behavior. You are opening yourself up to being taken advantage of by him. You don't want to become a consort to him like Verity was to John Saunders, growing in strength and success from his… unsavory practices."

"I'm not. I did this once. To help Corvin. Because of the werewolf curse."

"And what sort of powers did you acquire from him? Because make no mistake: You cannot take his strength without taking something of the nature of the gifts."

"Well… I don't know, then. Nothing definable. Is there a gift for cleaning your house? Honestly, I did a really good job. I stayed focused and I sorted stuff and found places to put them away. I could never organize like that before. When I got the energy and motivation for a project like that, I would take everything out…. get half done… and shove it all back away again, telling myself that I would finish it later, and never get back to it again."

"But this time, you had Corvin's powers to help you."

Reg scowled at this. Had she only succeeded because she had used Corvin's gifts? She knew that he was a professor, that he could research and teach and write and all sorts of things that she dreaded having to do. She never could succeed in those things at school or in her own life once she was living alone.

But then she had. Reg slapped the arm of the couch and swore, making Ember open one eye to check on her and see what she was doing before going back to sleep again.

"I'm not worried about you using Corvin's powers to tidy your spare room," Davyn said. "I think you know that. I'm more concerned about what other effects this exchange of powers might have had."

"Like what?"

"Like… sensing this fire. Waking out of a sound sleep and knowing about it, even though it was nowhere near you. It was much closer to me than to you, and I should have sensed it first."

"Well, maybe you were just really sound asleep."

"That's worrisome in itself. What else happened that was different from usual? How did you feel when you were creating the backburn? What exactly happened out there when you were trapped? You said that the fire was sentient."

Reg swallowed and cleared her throat. "Well... yeah. It... kind of talked back to me. It was really resistant, and then it deliberately encircled me, tried to trap me."

"Why would it do that? You're a firecaster. You know the way fire usually responds to you. Why would this fire behave any differently?"

"I don't know. Maybe that is why you didn't sense it. Or why I got trapped. It was just... different than usual. It really didn't want me to stop it, even if I was feeding it more first. I wanted the chance to have a little fun, but I never had a fire stalk me like that before."

Davyn rubbed his forehead, wincing in pain. "We need to talk to Sarah. And maybe to Corvin. See if they can help us figure out how this second site and artifact might be related to what happened to Gideon."

CHAPTER EIGHTEEN

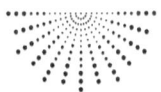

*A*lthough Davyn wanted to talk to Sarah to bring her up to speed on what had happened since they had last spoken, he was clearly exhausted by their late night/early morning firefighting and exploration of the fort. His eyelids were drooping as he watched the flames flickering in his fireplace. Ember was happy and relaxed, curled up in the fire.

"I'll talk to Sarah," Reg promised. "You need to get some rest."

"This is important," Davyn argued. "We don't know how long we have, and we don't know what the danger is to the rest of the population. How many other people are at risk? What happened to my neighbors could happen to others. If someone like Gideon, a powerful and experienced warlock, could fall victim to this force, then anyone is vulnerable."

"I know. But you're tired. You need to get your energy back. I'm fine. I can tell Sarah what happened. Then, when you've had a rest, the two of you can talk if there's anything I missed. But she can do research or make a plan while you're sleeping. So we keep moving this forward."

"I am not that tired," Davyn protested. "I used to pull all-nighters in college…"

"You're not in college anymore. You're…" Reg trailed off. "I have no idea how old you are."

Davyn smiled. "It is probably best not to get into that. Old enough to know better." He smothered a yawn. "I can make a wake-up potion, give myself enough energy to make it through the rest of the day…"

"Or you could have what your body needs. A nap. What would you tell me? That I should take caffeine or uppers to keep myself awake? Have one of Sarah's teas or let her do an incantation?"

"Or take power from Corvin," Davyn suggested, his lips twisting into a smirk.

"Yeah. Is that what you would tell me to do?"

"No," Davyn admitted. "I would tell you to get the rest you need to regenerate rather than forcing your body into a worse state of exhaustion or using other artificial means that will just result in a crash later."

Reg raised her eyebrow and nodded at him.

* * *

As Davyn dozed off on the couch, Reg transported herself back to the cottage. With all the energy she had received from Corvin and from the fire itself, she wasn't interested in going back to sleep herself.

Starlight was sitting on the kitchen island and gave her the stink eye when she apparated into the house.

"What?" Reg demanded. "I had to help stop a forest fire. What did you expect me to do?"

He stared at her balefully, clearly not pleased with her choice.

"I don't know what else I could have done," Reg said. "You like Davyn, don't you? Did you want me to just let his house burn down? And all the other houses that might have been in the path of the fire?"

Starlight jumped down from the counter with a grunt and a cross meow, ordering her to fill his dish with something suitable for breakfast.

"I'm not your servant, you know," Reg pointed out.

But he didn't give any indication that he believed this or intended to apologize for his demands. Cats never did.

She knew what it was he was upset about. Not with her seeing Davyn and helping with the forest fire. It was Ember. Reg didn't know if all dragons and cats had the same animosity between them or whether Starlight was just jealous because of the way Reg had let Ember into the house as a hatchling—which had been entirely unintentional. Either way, Starlight was grumpy whenever Reg returned from a firecasting session with Davyn and he knew she had been visiting with Ember.

She imagined she probably smelled strongly of dragon after playing with him after returning from the fort. And she had transformed into a dragon herself, which probably didn't help. The last time she had transformed into a dragon, she had been helping the cats and he hadn't minded. But this time, it had nothing to do with him, and he disapproved.

Reg looked through the fridge to find the best possible treat for him, making him a breakfast buffet of three different kinds of fish.

While he gobbled the meal noisily, Reg left him to it and headed across the yard to the big house to chat with Sarah.

The kitchen was fragrant with the smell of orange pekoe tea and cinnamon. Sarah had tea in the morning rather than coffee, claiming that, as she got older, her body did not respond to coffee the same way it used to and it was best avoided. Reg had known her to break this rule and hadn't thought to bring a mug of coffee over from the guest cottage. But unlike Davyn, she didn't need the caffeine to stay awake this morning. She would manage with just tea.

"There are some muffins," Sarah said unnecessarily, pointing Reg toward the freshly baked cinnamon streusel muffins on the counter next to the stove. "I was going to bring some over to you."

"They smell great. I'm famished."

Reg helped herself unselfconsciously to two muffins, not even waiting until a decent interval had elapsed after eating one. She'd burned plenty of calories fighting the fire and exploring the castle, though the calories burned as a dragon probably didn't count.

Sarah nodded her approval, and they sat down at the kitchen table to drink tea, eat muffins, and catch up on what had happened since they had last met.

Reg related her meeting with Corvin at Sarah's suggestion, glossing over taking energy from Corvin, then described the fire and what they had discovered in the forest and the fort.

"We were hoping you might know more about the fort, its history, and whether… there is anything you can tell us about the ruby that is hidden there. Have you ever heard about it before?"

Sarah frowned, pondering this. "Yes… I do recall a stone of that description many years ago. What happened to it, I cannot say. If it was secreted at the fort… I believe that happened since it was decommissioned. I do not believe it was there while the fort was in use."

"Why would someone put it there *after* the fort closed?"

"That is the question," Sarah agreed meditatively. "That is a very good question."

"It isn't used like the temple, is it? For rituals or prayer?"

"No, certainly not. It isn't at any sacred site, as far as I know, and it has nothing of historical or astrological significance. It was in an important position for trade and defense. The location was practical."

"And no one lives there and uses it… to defend this stone?"

"Not that I am aware of. It is not a very hospitable location. Not somewhere that attracts squatters. It is too far away from town to be convenient. It is windy and stormy because of the way it stands on its own, not sheltered by the terrain."

"So whoever hid the ruby there… they just left it unprotected?"

"Well, not personally guarded, which I don't think is the same thing. It could have all kinds of protections in place. Didn't you sense anything?"

Reg nodded and explained the sense she had of an electrical field around the gemstone, maybe powered by hidden lightning rods that attracted strikes during storms.

"Ingenious," Sarah observed. "It's very smart to use natural features to help keep the artifacts protected. The geode being buried within the temple and protected by ward stones and the altar. The ruby in a hidden chamber in the fort, protected by lightning. Some thought went into protecting them without someone guarding them."

"But I would expect there to be magical spells there to protect them as well, wouldn't you? If it was you... wouldn't you weave protective spells as well?"

"Of course I would, but not everyone has the same abilities. We must each work with what we have."

"Whoever put it there must have had power. How did they get into the chamber? We looked for a door or passageway to access it and couldn't find a way in."

"And it was too dangerous just to transport yourself into an unfamiliar room with unknown hazards."

Reg nodded. Transporting herself into the middle of a magically created electrical field did not seem like the smartest course of action. Not without finding out a lot more about it first.

"That was probably wise," Sarah agreed.

"I didn't want to end up zapped or petrified."

Sarah sipped her tea and broke a piece off of her muffin. Frown lines creased her forehead as she chewed.

"Tell me again about the statues in the forest. These... unfortunate souls."

"Davyn said they were neighbors. It looked like they were trying to run away from the fire. Their expressions were afraid."

"And like with Gideon, you could feel their presence? They were still aware?"

"Yes, just the same."

"Then they have to be connected. It isn't just some weird coincidence."

Reg nodded her agreement. She had never seen anyone petrified before, and then suddenly, multiple statues were being created. They had to all be connected.

"I guess I should find out whether Corvin has figured anything out. He was going to look into it like you asked. Do you want me to give him a call?"

"No… I think we should play this close to our chests for a while. I was hoping that, having been friends with Gideon and an expert in the history of the area and magical artifacts, he might have an immediate answer. Since he didn't, I have to wonder whether he is being honest or if he has something to hide."

"Corvin isn't involved in this."

"You don't know that."

"He's not. He couldn't be. He isn't able to use his powers right now. He couldn't be the one who petrified Gideon."

"He *can* still use his powers. It just causes him pain. You don't know whether he could withstand the pain enough to ensorcel Gideon."

Reg opened her mouth to object. She had seen how serious Corvin's pain was when he had accidentally exercised just a bit of his powers. With something big like that… she wasn't sure whether he would even be able to survive it. There had to be a certain point at which the human body just gave in. Even for someone with Corvin's abilities.

But she didn't know for sure. She didn't think that he would have been able to do anything like that, but she couldn't swear it.

"Besides, what happened to Gideon might also have been from a trap previously set. It might not have required any current exercise of power by Corvin."

Reg nodded. "So you think… Corvin could have had something to do with this? Gideon was his friend."

"One thing I have learned during my long life is that you can never be sure how a relationship will change over time. What seems like a devoted, stable relationship can quickly sour, and best friends or lovers become enemies. Or," she raised her brows at Reg, "enemies become friends. Just because Gideon and Corvin were friends a couple of centuries ago, that doesn't mean they still are. Something could have happened between them. Jealousies, lovers, insults, or even just drifting apart. Gideon could have been envious of Corvin's place as the leader of the coven. Many people were not happy with him being elected to that position. That could be true even of a friend."

"Corvin said… he wasn't sure whether he had told Gideon of the werewolf attack."

"That seems unlikely."

"Yeah. I thought so, too. But he has been drinking a lot."

"Ah." Sarah nodded. "Maybe not so strange, then. They had seen each other recently?"

"Or at least talked."

"Did Corvin have any insight into why Gideon was at the temple?"

"He didn't say. He didn't think it was odd."

"Nor do I," Sarah said quickly. "It's completely natural for any witch or warlock in this region to visit it. Whether they are seeing it for the first time or visit it regularly. But this petrifaction… that has never happened here before in my memory."

"And no one knows about the geode?"

Sarah patted her lips with a napkin. "I couldn't say no one does. But I am unaware of any lore about it. Neither Davyn nor I had ever heard anything about it, and Davyn has been the leader of the coven that has met there for centuries. If there had been rumor of the existence of the geode, then surely he would have heard about it."

Reg was inclined to think so, too.

"Then it isn't strange that Corvin didn't know anything about it? It makes sense that he would have to research it, to dig down into ancient records to see if he could find out anything about it."

"Except that Corvin… has a sense for magical artifacts. If a powerful stone was buried where he was attending regularly, he should have sensed it, don't you think?"

"It is buried very deep. And surrounded by wards."

"Yes. Still…"

Reg could understand Sarah's reluctance to accept that Corvin hadn't known about the geode. But she'd had to reach deep to find it herself. Reg had been to the temple a couple of times without being aware of its presence. And she had a certain affinity for stones, developed while learning to cleanse the cursed gemstones in her possession.

"If Corvin doesn't know anything about it and hasn't come up with anything in his research, then how are we going to find anything about it?"

Sarah pressed her lips together. "I wish I had an easy answer. There are some repositories of ancient knowledge... but many of them have passed on in recent years. I will have to make some inquiries."

Something twinged in the back of Reg's brain. Ancient knowledge. *She* had a source for ancient knowledge.

CHAPTER NINETEEN

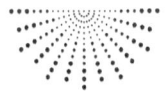

*W*hat is it?" Sarah asked, obviously reading something in Reg's face.

"I know... I know something... someone... who may be able to help."

"Who?"

"I... do you remember that witch, Sma Firea?"

"The one who was trying to poison the mayor? Certainly, I remember her."

"She had a lot of ancient knowledge. Old books and scrolls, stuff that went back hundreds of years, maybe longer."

"And you managed to acquire these books?" Sarah shook her head, frowning. "There isn't anything in the cottage."

"Yeah... I kind of... went a different direction." Reg had been keeping her project a secret, not just from Sarah but from everyone, not sure how it would turn out or what others would think of it. She thought it had worked pretty well so far but knew that things could turn sour quickly.

She cleared her throat and went on. "You know how they have those computer programs now that they feed a whole bunch of information to, and then you can ask it questions, and it will give you mostly good answers?"

"Large Language Models?" Sarah asked brightly. "Yes, they are so cool. I have a young warlock friend who is setting up a custom GPT that will—"

"I kind of had all those ancient records that Sma had converted into a format where you can... you know, ask it your questions, and instead of having to read through all of that old stuff, it will answer in normal, modern language that you can—that someone like me can understand."

"You put Sma's records into an LLM?"

"Uh, sort of."

Sarah looked at her, blinking, waiting for the rest of the story. Reg cleared her throat again. "Maybe we should go out to the garden."

"*What* is in the garden?" Sarah asked, disapproval in her voice even though she had no idea yet what Reg had done.

"It's better if I show you."

Sarah raised her brows. Reg squirmed in her seat as if she were pinned by the glare of the principal at one of the schools she had attended as a child. She hated the scrutiny of an adult who knew what she had done and was trying to squeeze it out of her or make her choose her own punishment.

Principals could be diabolical.

Rather than trying to explain, Reg stood up and headed out the back door. She went around to the garden beside and behind the cottage, which Forst, the garden gnome, had done such a great job of restoring and nurturing after many of the plants had been destroyed by a certain witch in a rage.

Sarah followed a few steps behind. Reg gazed into the pond with its tinkling waterfall for a moment, remembering the day she had found the dragon hatchling in the garden and, before that, when she had seen elves there. It was a tranquil, magical place, and she could stay calm and relaxed there even with Sarah hovering nearby waiting to see what Reg had done.

Reg bent down and picked up a handful of the rich, loamy earth, regularly turned and tended by Forst.

"From soil and stone, by magic spin,
  Theodore reform, our work begin."

She tossed the earth back into the garden. It swirled around in a mini dust devil, growing darker and more dense until, eventually, it formed the shape of a child standing before her. He had a dirty face and tattered clothes like a pixie, but he was clearly not one of that clan. His cheeks were pale rather than rosy, and he had the flat, black eyes of a shark.

"Reg Rawlins, what have you done?" Sarah demanded in a whisper.

"This is Theodore. He is a—"

"He is a homunculus."

Reg nodded. Sarah made that sound like a bad thing but, as far as Reg was concerned, a homunculus was a really handy kind of entity to have around.

"Yes. He was Sma's homunculus. And when she died…"

"Then he should have been released and ceased to exist."

"But he didn't. Her spirit refused to leave, so he was tied to her there. And I… well, I managed to straighten things out and get him attached to me, and he has all Sma's ancient wisdom…"

"You have a stolen homunculus with a library full of ancient wisdom in his head. In my garden."

"Well, he's only here when I form him…"

"Reg…" Sarah said helplessly.

"But he's helpful," Reg insisted. "You can ask him all kinds of questions about stuff that is only found in ancient books that no one reads anymore, and he can tell you the answers."

"This is not a good idea."

"No, it's a great idea," Reg insisted. "Better than Wikipedia!"

Wikipedia often failed her in answering questions about myth and magic. Even YouTube fell short on some topics.

"Theodore," Reg addressed the homunculus, "People are being petrified. Gideon, a powerful warlock, was turned into a living stone statue at the Temple Orange Grove. How are they being turned into stone?"

Theodore made a clicking sound, his head twitching for a moment as he analyzed the question and searched through his repository to form an answer.

"Corvin's woes brought cracks unseen,
    To wards that held the spirits within.
    Released from bonds by cursed plight,
    Elementals surged into the night."

Sarah gasped. Reg looked at her, unsure whether this was a good gasp or a bad gasp.

Like with many things to do with the magical world, Reg didn't understand everything the homunculus had said. Even with a world of knowledge ready to answer each question she had, she still couldn't always get a straight answer.

But Theodore had mentioned Corvin, confirming Sarah's suspicions that he might be hiding something.

"What is it?" she asked Sarah. "Does that help?"

"*Corvin*. Corvin is the key!"

Reg nodded slowly. "Okay, yes, he mentioned Corvin. Even though I didn't feed him that information," Reg pointed out with a note of triumph in her voice. Theodore had to be getting it from somewhere. A history book about something that had happened centuries before? Personal correspondence? A book of prophecies? Theodore was able to find patterns and make sense of all the disparate information and to bring it together in a way that made sense. A very bright boy.

"Corvin's curse," Sarah said.

"His hunger, you mean, or...?"

"No, the werewolf curse. All of this came about since the werewolf attack. We kept saying that, but I never thought it might actually be causative."

"Of what?" Reg asked.

"That October cursing Corvin started a chain of events that led to Gideon being petrified, as well as the other things you experienced."

Reg shrugged and looked at Theodore, planning to ask him for further clarification. At least he was better than Harrison at answering questions. He seemed to have slipped back into answering in verse for Sarah's benefit. Reg could usually get him to talk in normal language she could understand when they were alone.

"Corvin's woes brought cracks unseen," Sarah repeated. "Corvin being cursed and being unable to use his magic. That is what started everything. The spell that he had previously maintained started to break down. The rest of it…" Sarah looked at Theodore, her eyes penetrating. "It sounds as if Corvin had bound these elementals. Bound them to some artifacts."

Theodore considered, then answered.

"Vessels crafted with ancient lore,
    Locked these spirits evermore."

"But they were not locked up evermore," Sarah pointed out. "Not if they have now been released because of the failure of Corvin's spell."

Theodore clicked a few times, trying to process her comment, then apparently decided that she hadn't asked him a question or that he couldn't answer and stood there just staring at them, waiting for the next question he could answer.

Sarah looked at Reg. Reg nodded.

"So this helped, right? I did a good thing. I helped you to figure out what is going on."

"Experiments with other magical races, especially with breaking the rules that govern those magical races, are never good," Sarah said severely. "You should have known better. I would have thought that after what Jake did, you would avoid such things."

"After what Jake did?" Reg shot back, outraged at the comparison. "He captured and tortured the wolves, drove them insane, and caused Faolan's death! I rescued a lost soul."

"A homunculus does not have a soul."

"This one does," Reg insisted. "Don't you talk about him like he doesn't even exist. Just because he is a creature created by alchemy, that doesn't mean he's any less than any other sentient being. And he *does* have a soul. You think I should just have left him in that forest to wander aimlessly until the end of time? That would have been the ethical thing to do?"

Sarah looked confused. "I don't... you are playing with forces that you know nothing about. I thought that you had learned your lesson about that before. You can't just jump into a situation and start... changing things and acting like you know best when you don't even understand what is going on."

"I understood just fine. Theodore did not die or disappear when Sma died, and that makes him a separate, independent entity with the same rights as any other sentient, self-aware species. You can't say I should just have left him by himself for the rest of his life."

"I don't know what the right thing was," Sarah admitted, her cheeks pink. "You should have come to me. So that we could call together a council of elders to discuss it."

Reg snorted. "And to take ten years to make a decision? Or to decide that he didn't really exist and shouldn't be recognized as a person? No way. He needed help. So I helped him."

"Well, I cannot fault your passion or your instincts. But you don't understand how these things work and the fact that you can make things worse by dabbling in something you don't understand. You need to trust other people. To come to them for advice when you run into a situation that is complex and confusing and you don't know how to handle it."

Reg shrugged, frustrated. "Theodore just gave you a part of the answer you are looking for. Are you going to follow up on it?"

"Yes, of course I am." Sarah shook her head. "You are infuriating sometimes, Reg. I have tried to help you and to guide you, and you still..."

"Can't behave myself?" Reg finished, repeating the refrain she had often heard from foster parents, teachers, and case workers.

"You still won't trust me," Sarah corrected. "I want to help you, Reg. I have your best interests at heart. I don't want to stifle you or to stop you from being yourself. I just want to help you to avoid... painful pitfalls that could be avoided with better choices."

Reg's cheeks heated, embarrassed by her landlady's words. Reg had grown up with every choice and every attempt to be herself resulting in her being punished or shut down, so how could she believe anyone was really willing to help her and let her be herself?

"Okay," she admitted. "I may have some trust issues."

"Yes, you do," Sarah agreed. "And now... we must talk to Corvin."

CHAPTER TWENTY

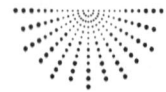

*R*eg wasn't about to let Sarah behind the wheel of the car, so she drove her own car. Sarah glanced at Reg on the way over to Corvin's house.

"Where did you come up with the name Theodore?"

"Oh. He named himself, actually. I couldn't just go around calling him 'hey you' or 'the homunculus.' So, I asked him to come up with a name for himself. I didn't know what to expect. Some demon name or something foreign and unpronounceable. Or a call number. But Theodore is pretty normal. A little old-fashioned. But normal."

Sarah nodded. "Do you ever shorten it to Theo?"

Reg shook her head. "He chose Theodore. If he wants me to call him Theo, he can tell me that. I won't call him something other than what he asked me to. I gave the responsibility to him, so... I need to honor it."

"I'm sure a nickname would be okay."

"If Theodore wants."

Reg was glad that Sarah hadn't seemed inclined to take Theodore with them over to Corvin's house but allowed him to return to the garden where he was comfortable. She hoped that Sarah wouldn't tell Corvin that Reg had a homunculus. Reg didn't want it widely known. Even magical practitioners, who she would think should know better, didn't always treat other species and cultures with respect. They saw species different from themselves as inferior or interlopers, even if they had been there just as long or longer. They thought they were stupid or weird or not as skilled, or said they didn't belong with human society but should be segregated somehow, in their own community or some restricted area.

Reg didn't want to know how they would treat a homunculus, especially one which, as far as she could tell, didn't seem to follow the laws of alchemy by which he had been created.

Reg pulled in front of Corvin's house for the second time in two days. She sighed and tried to relax her muscles. She didn't know how things would turn out, but she would try to be relaxed through it all. She was mostly just an observer. Sarah was the one with the knowledge, the one who would be asking Corvin to explain himself.

Sarah patted Reg on the knee. "Don't worry, dear, it will all be okay."

Reg nodded and climbed out of the car. There were more flyers on Corvin's porch. She picked them up and handed them to him when he answered the door.

"Are you going to come clean up my porch every day?"

"Why don't you? Then I wouldn't have to."

He grunted. His eyes turned to Sarah. "And to what do I owe the pleasure of your company? I didn't think you would be coming over."

"Nor did I," Sarah admitted. "I don't normally show up at the wolf's door."

"Under the circumstances, I don't think you can call *me* the wolf."

"No," Sarah chuckled. "I guess not. The fox, perhaps."

"I like that better," Corvin agreed, giving Sarah a sideways flirty look. But his lips immediately tightened, the smile disappearing. He stepped back to let the two of them into the house.

Sarah declined a drink from Corvin, and it was clear from her look at Reg that she thought it would be best if she did as well. But

Reg wouldn't be pressured into behaving the way Sarah wanted her to. She wasn't there as Sarah's lapdog. When she went to see Corvin by herself, she had a drink. No reason she couldn't have one when Sarah was there, too.

Corvin nodded his approval, apparently deciding this put Reg on his side. But she wasn't on anyone's side. She was her own person. Sarah and Corvin could be enemies—though from what she had seen in the past, they were not really enemies. Sarah just had a healthy respect for what Corvin could do with his powers and understood his nature better than most. They worked together when they had to, and Corvin had done much to strengthen Sarah and preserve her life when the emerald that kept her healthy and young, despite her centuries had been stolen.

"So I ask again, what is this all about?" Corvin demanded. No small talk today.

"I would like to hear what you know about the elementals," Sarah told him. "The elementals that you and Gideon bound."

CHAPTER TWENTY-ONE

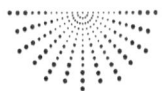

Corvin gaped at Sarah. At first, his cheeks flushed a dusky red. Then he turned pale.

"The elementals," he groaned. He swore. "Why didn't I think of that?"

"Tell me what happened. The whole story," Sarah insisted.

Corvin shook his head and held it between his hands. "I didn't even think of it. I haven't thought much about it for years."

"You have been maintaining whatever spell you used to bind them."

"Well, yes. But I have been doing that for so long that I was barely even aware of it. I didn't need to expend much of my own energy to maintain them. The relics and elementals are powerful themselves, and I was able to... use my gifts..."

"Your curse."

Corvin sighed heavily. "Yes. My curse. The ability to take power from them and feed it back into the binding spells." He rubbed his forehead. "It didn't require much effort."

"You bound them."

"Someone had to," Corvin insisted. "I didn't see you or any other practitioners in the area stepping forward to help at the time."

"Just you and Gideon? Or were there others?"

Corvin looked away, not answering.

"There were others," Sarah discerned. "Who else?"

"It isn't any of your business. What other practitioners decide to do is their own business. You have no authority over others."

"I want to know if members of my coven were involved."

Corvin stared back at her. "You don't have any right to demand that information."

"If a member of the coven has been breaking magical treaties or causing harm, the others in the group have the right to know it."

"Causing harm?" Corvin rolled his eyes. "How were we causing harm? We were addressing a threat to the community. Do you remember what it was like before they were bound? Do you have any memory of that time?"

He didn't say, "Or are you too old to remember?" but Reg heard it insinuated in his tone.

It was Sarah's turn to flush. "Certainly, I remember. There was a lot of concern about it at the time. But no decision was made by the community to bind the elementals."

"What exactly are elementals and what kind of trouble were they causing?" Reg asked, feeling lost.

"Elementals are… spirits of a sort. They control the four elements of our world. Each elemental is bound to a certain element and can influence it. Earth, air, fire, and water. Normally… this doesn't have much effect on our world. They are insignificant. They cause small fluctuations in the weather patterns—a storm here, a drought there, what we would see as normal and natural weather variations or cycles. But sometimes, there are problems. A hurricane, forest fire, earthquake, or long drought…"

Corvin nodded. "Look at the Dust Bowl in the dirty thirties. Hurricane Katrina. The Chicago fire. All can probably be attributed to rogue elementals."

"But those things are normal," Reg protested. "You can't stop bad weather patterns."

"No," Sarah agreed. She gave Corvin a look. "You can't."

"There are times when it is advisable to take action," Corvin insisted. "When people are being killed. When there is great danger to all the homes so recently established in this area. Most people were still in tents; there were few permanent structures. Tents that were easily wiped out by a wind or fire."

"You should have left well enough alone," Sarah said. "Look at what is happening now. Gideon being petrified. Innocent people attacked. There was a forest fire. You know an out-of-control fire could wipe out this entire town, even if we aren't still living in tents."

Corvin spoke to Reg, ignoring Sarah. "What was worse, four elementals, each with an affinity for a different element, were all active. So we weren't just dealing with fire or just with earth. We were dealing with all of them. And they bounced off of each other. They weren't working together, not in any organized fashion, but if they were to start working in concert..."

Reg shuddered, thinking of every weather apocalypse movie she had ever watched. She could only imagine the kind of devastation such an alliance could cause. The town would not just have been facing a forest fire, but maybe also an earthquake, hurricane, and other disasters simultaneously. Or combinations of elements... perhaps a storm raining fire and brimstone.

"That doesn't give you the right to unilaterally decide how to handle the threat," Sarah told Corvin.

"There is no council in charge of all paranormal happenings in the state. There is no coven in charge of rogue elementals. There is no authority over these things, so you can't dictate what anyone else does about it."

"The magical community has historically worked together to come to a solution that—"

"Just because certain groups have agreed to work together does not mean that I am required to work with anyone. And, if you remember, no one wanted me involved in their covens, councils, or communities. You were all quite emphatic about excluding a Hunter from any and all organizations at the time."

Sarah did not argue this point. Reg knew that things had been different back then, that Corvin and his kind had been pariahs, even worse than now. Now, the world was changing and, suddenly, it was discriminatory to exclude someone just because of a curse they were born with.

She thought that things were better before. At least more practitioners would have been protected from him.

But it would have been a miserable and lonely life for Corvin.

"You did not have the right to take these free spirits, these unembodied intelligences, and to bind them. Such a thing is horrific. Unthinkable. You cannot imprison an entity just because you don't like its nature. We never imprisoned *you*."

"I never caused the havoc that the elementals did. They were dangerous to the town. To the entire state. To ignore that and to allow them to go about causing disaster and death wherever they went was irresponsible. Turning a blind eye to what was happening because you didn't want to have to deal with it."

"You cannot bind an elemental. You have to just... give them their time and space. In time, they would have left the area. Gone out to sea, perhaps, or into a volcano. They would have sought out the elements they had an affinity for and gone away, eventually." She shook her head. "We thought that was what had happened."

Corvin snorted. "You believed that all four elementals just suddenly drifted out to sea? Or went in four different directions? All the disasters stopped, and you and the other members of the covens were more than happy to forget anything had happened and go on with your lives."

Sarah opened her mouth.

"Without asking any questions," Corvin pointed out. "You turned a blind eye. You know that is what happened."

"How many of you were involved? I can't believe that I didn't hear anything about it through the coven. People must have been aware of it."

Corvin smirked. "You thought that your own coven was the only one in Black Sands or this part of the country?"

"No. The warlock coven, too, of course. It is as ancient as the witch's coven."

"They were not the only covens operating in the area. You did not have any control over how others chose to practice. You and your leaders had the right to accept only an elite few into your coven and exclude everyone else. But you have no authority over anyone else. You have no right to dictate who else meets or what they choose to do."

"*An' it harm none,*" Sarah intoned. "That is the core principle of our practice. Did you harm none?"

"I protected all life in Black Sands. I and a few select others were the only ones willing to take action to protect you. So you can put this all on me, but you made a choice with your inaction. And you chose to look the other way at the time and pretend that you didn't know what was happening."

"How was anyone outside of your... your shadow coven supposed to know what you were doing? You clearly knew you were doing wrong and did it in secret."

"We knew that some would look on it with disapproval," Corvin agreed. "But we had a higher purpose in mind. We were protecting our homes and families. Are you telling me that you would rather have seen your family killed before you even got that house of yours built?"

"I think you exaggerate the dangers. We could have found another way to deal with them if you hadn't gone off on your own to do something... dishonorable."

Reg could see both sides, and wasn't sure why Sarah was so vehement about what seemed like the only viable solution. Maybe it wasn't what Sarah would have done, and she would have wanted it to be discussed before the coven or some kind of council first. But then what would they do? What were the alternatives?

"So... you and Gideon were both involved in binding these elementals so that they couldn't do any harm," Reg summarized, hoping they could move on. There was no point in rehashing ancient history. Sarah wasn't going to change anything in the past by telling Corvin he had made the wrong choice. "Like when we bound the witch doctor, right?"

Corvin nodded, looking smug. "Exactly."

"No," Sarah insisted, "not like binding the witch doctor. Samyr Destine chose to do evil and had done much harm. The elementals… they had no evil intent. No more than the wind and the waves have evil intent. They could be dangerous, but they were not trying to hurt or kill anyone. Binding them is more like… tying a tiger to a stake so that he cannot move. Or putting a dog in a cage too small to turn around in. There are better ways to deal with wild creatures. We could have found a better way to deal with the elementals."

"Well…" Corvin grimaced. "You'd better start thinking of what that is. Because from your description, two of them have already escaped, and the others will not be far behind. I have no way of maintaining the binding spells in my current condition. The population of Black Sands and of Florida are much higher than they were when I bound them. You will need to find a solution soon."

CHAPTER TWENTY-TWO

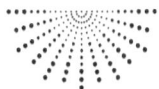

Reg felt like she had swallowed a bowl full of marbles. Her guts were heavy, tight, and cramped. The marbles rattled around, impossible to ignore, and made her increasingly anxious.

She thought of the living stone statues and the fear she felt from the souls trapped inside them. Whether the earth elemental had intended to hurt and terrify them or not, that was the result. She remembered how startled she had been when she had reached out to the fire to turn it back, and the fire elemental had resisted her, had talked back to her, and had stalked her, making it clear that it was not going to go quietly and behave like a normal fire would, but would do everything within its power to fight against her for survival.

Had she banished the elemental by extinguishing the fire? She didn't think so. It wasn't fire itself, but an intelligence with an affinity for fire. Even though she had put out the fire, the elemental lived on, separate and apart from it, looking for the chance to start another forest fire. Or worse, maybe this time, a fire in the town. Maybe in an old, decrepit row of low-income houses, with families jammed into the rooms with a much higher density than had ever been intended. Some of those little rows of houses, either connected or with just inches between them, would go up like tinder.

She closed her eyes and covered them with her palms, thinking.

"What is it, Reg?" Sarah asked softly. She had been using a hard-edged voice when talking to Corvin, but that was gone now. Maybe she had the same feeling of worry and dread that Reg did. Maybe she, too, felt the menace of the elementals and the danger they could do if left to run rampant through the town and surrounding areas.

Or was Reg picking up on Corvin's feelings? Was she being influenced too much by him because of the connection between them? Was she too quick to see his point of view and feel his concern than she was to see the logic and rectitude of Sarah's position?

He was the one who had dealt with the elementals in the past. He was the one who had the best insight into how they operated and what they could do if unleashed on the unsuspecting town.

"If this is what can happen with just two of them being released…" Reg started, lost in her memory of the firefight, the fear of being trapped by the malevolent fire, and the terror of the living statues left behind. "They were already working in concert. The earth elemental didn't stay at the temple where it was released. It joined with the fire elemental in a… in a definite attack on humans."

"You don't know that," Sarah countered.

"I do. I saw the statues in the forest near Davyn's house. Not at the temple."

"But you don't know that the earth elemental has joined with the fire elemental or that they are consciously working together or targeting humans."

"They were both in the same place. You think it was just a coincidence?" Reg looked at Corvin. He was sitting there like his mind was far away. As if it no longer had anything to do with him. "Do you think that the earth elemental freed the fire elemental?"

Corvin focused on Reg, drawn back from his far-away thoughts.

"Do I think they have that much intent? The cunning to do such a thing? I…" He grimaced, and his hand went to his wounded arm. "I can't tell you anything about how they were released, other than the fact that I haven't been able to maintain the binding spells since the werewolf attack."

He grimaced again and doubled over, his face nearly colliding with his knees, making a small cry and a grunt of pain. Reg reached for him, immediately accessing the healing power of her fire, trying to relieve the pain.

For a moment, she felt it herself, a searing pain that raced through her nerves, delivering pain to every cell in her body. She tried to disconnect from Corvin, but he held on to the connection, which only deepened the pain.

But as quickly as it had grabbed her, the pain was gone and only Corvin sat doubled up, groaning.

Sarah looked at him, but her expression was not pitying. Her face was a mask, hiding what she was feeling, blocking Reg from reading her face or using her psychic abilities.

"He tried to access the gem where the fire elemental was held," Reg explained. "To see how the spell was broken and it was able to escape."

"I don't see how it makes any difference," Sarah said candidly. "We already know the inciting factor. The werewolf attack and curse left Corvin unable to maintain the prisons he kept the elementals in. They will all escape, with or without help."

"What are we going to do? Two of them are already free and causing trouble. Two more will be at least twice the trouble, if not more, with the four of them working together. How are we going to stop them?"

"I don't know. I don't even know the rightness of trying to stop them. They are not breaking any laws."

"But they are hurting people. You said that was against your basic principles. Doing harm. They have to be stopped."

"It is against *our* guiding principles as witches," Sarah said. "It is not against theirs. No law applies to the elementals. No treaties.

No understanding between us. What they do is... instinctual. Like an animal. It isn't reasoned or malicious."

Reg thought about the fire elemental and was not so sure. They had certainly had a long time to think about what had been done to them and for their resentment to grow. If they had any conscious thought or awareness of themselves and others, there was reason for concern. Sarah might not think they had any conscious plan of revenge, but Reg wasn't quite so sure.

Corvin was apparently recovering from his attempt to make contact with the ruby and the binding spell that he had fashioned. He leaned back in his chair, head tipped all the way back so his chin jutted up toward the ceiling, breathing through his open mouth. Reg got to her feet and poured him another drink. Not a lot, just enough to cover the bottom of the tumbler. Corvin swallowed a mouthful. He sat up straighter, giving Reg a nod of thanks.

"Can you tell me about how they were bound?" Reg asked. "I don't want to cause you any additional pain; I don't mean for you to have to reconnect with them; just... tell me about how they were bound."

Corvin looked at her, his jaw set stubbornly.

Reg shook her head. "You can't fix this. You can't maintain the binding spells or do anything about the elementals that have already been freed. So if you want someone else to be able to do it... you have to tell someone how they were bound in the first place."

"It was a very long time ago."

"It sounds like you still remember. And you've been maintaining the spell ever since."

Corvin nodded briefly. Reg waited. She understood his not wanting to talk about it in front of Sarah, who was already antagonistic, but Reg would not be able to do anything about it herself. She did not have the skills for any complex spells. They would need at least Sarah and Davyn and maybe others to find a solution.

CHAPTER TWENTY-THREE

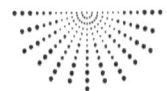

*C*orvin swigged the rest of the drink and looked at her again.

"Each elemental is bound to an object. An artifact or relic that represents its affinity. And each object is protected by a binding spell—*was* protected by a binding spell—and other wards intended to keep the elemental in and potential treasure-seekers out."

Like the ward stones and the electrical field. So if they intended to return the two escaped elementals to their prisons, they would have to get past those wards first, if they hadn't been disrupted by the elementals' escapes. And if Reg needed to access the remaining two elementals, she would have to be able to get past the protections intended to prevent intruders from reaching them as well.

"What is each one bound to?"

"You already know that the earth elemental was bound to the Geode of Gaea."

Reg could picture it in her mind. She nodded. "And how do you get past the ward stones? Or how did the elemental get past them?"

"It must have broken through them in order to escape. You will not need to be able to do it yourself."

"Unless we want to re-bind them again and reactivate the ward stones."

Corvin glanced significantly at Sarah, as if wishing they were alone. "I'm afraid I can't reveal any of that at the moment. I would not want to take the chance of accidentally triggering this foul curse again."

Reg nodded, understanding that it was not his real reason. They would have to discuss it when Sarah was not around, if it became necessary.

"The fire elemental was bound to the Emberstone, a large, heart-shaped ruby. It is—was—guarded by an electrical field generated by lightning."

"Right. I felt that at the fort. I don't know how you did it..."

Corvin shrugged. "A lot of care and study went into each of the protections. We resurrected a lot of ancient magical rites to perfect each... quarantine."

Quarantine. Like the elementals were sick rather than dangerous. Like he was taking care of them.

Sarah had a pinched, sour look on her face. "That's two of them. Where are the other two?" she demanded.

Corvin looked at Reg again, reluctant to go on. If he'd had the full use of his powers, maybe he would have sent her a message telepathically. A picture or piece of information that she could use without telling Sarah about it. But Reg couldn't act without Sarah. She needed the witch to help her to figure out what to do. She couldn't do anything alone.

Reg waited and, eventually, Corvin shrugged. Maybe he didn't even know why he was trying to keep the information from Sarah. What he had done was out in the open now. What further need was there to keep it quiet?

"The Tears of Poseidon," he told her. "Water relic, obviously. A vial of the deepest sapphire blue seawater, forever shifting and swirling with the motion of the earth and moon. Hidden in the keep... a deep underwater cavern."

Reg was going to have to go swimming. Her siren heart thrilled at the idea of a deep dive into the ocean. Logically, she didn't want to risk it. She knew how water affected her. It would trigger her siren instincts and hunger and, if there were a man in the close vicinity... his life would be at risk. Even as she tried to put this out of her mind, the voices of her mother, Norma Jean, and all the siren sisters around the world set up a wail demanding that she anoint with blood the waters she had claimed as her territory. Something Reg intended never to do.

She was probably the only one who could safely dive down to that deep sea cavern to retrieve the Tears of Poseidon. Yet doing so would still pose a danger to herself and others.

"What is it protected with?"

"A combination of hydromancy, natural barriers, and Oceanids."

Reg raised her brows at him and glanced aside at Sarah to see if this had all made sense to her.

"Hydromancy is an ancient art," Sarah said. "How were you able to find enough information to use it?"

Corvin smirked. "I have studied a great many areas in my time. Hydromancy is just one of them."

"Did Gideon teach it to you?"

"Gideon knew less than I did. No. I learned what I needed to guard and protect the Tears."

Reg was still looking at Sarah.

"Water magic," Sarah explained. "Very little is known anymore about this obscure branch of magic once practiced by only the most experienced wizards and sorcerers."

"Okay." Reg would have to get Corvin to give her some pointers about how to get past the magical barriers he had set up. It was clear she wouldn't get that information from anyone else. "And... Oceanids?"

"They are... water spirits. Sea nymphs."

"So, how do I get past those?"

Corvin scratched the back of his neck. "You realize that we intended these protections to be impenetrable. The elementals were supposed to be bound until the end of time. We did not provide a way to get past them."

"But there must be a way. Two of them have already escaped."

"Each is progressively more difficult. As we practiced and grew in knowledge and experience, each was more and more difficult to access."

Great. So, the water and air relics were the hardest to get to. Reg wasn't sure she even wanted to know about the air relic. She supposed it was probably suspended hundreds of feet in the air where the oxygen was too scarce for humans to survive. Guarded by air warriors with lightning bolts.

"So does that mean that you *don't know* how to get past the nymphs?"

Corvin shrugged. "I have developed many more gifts since that time... If I were able to access them... it would be challenging, but I imagine I could find a way."

"You think you could get past sea nymphs? I seem to remember you have a problem with sirens. One taste of siren venom and you go weak at the knees."

Sarah snickered.

Corvin drew himself up straight. "Siren venom is another matter. I would have to develop a potion to reduce its effectiveness... but nymphs have several well-known weaknesses."

"Hmm." Reg wasn't sure he was quite as confident as he pretended to be.

But it should be easier for Reg, as a siren, to negotiate her way past a sea nymph or two than for a fully human male. The ocean was Reg's territory, not Corvin's. And he was natural prey for sea nymphs. Reg figured she could probably get past some sea nymphs. If she found out how to defeat the hydromancy spells. She was hoping that Theodore would be able to help her with that. He had just as much knowledge as Corvin. He was like a computer, and Corvin was just a man.

"Well, I hate to ask, since each one is more difficult than the last... but how about the air elemental?"

"The relic is the Zephyr Pearl. It is installed in the Cyclone Tower... Just as the Tears of Poseidon are protected by the great deep, the Pearl is naturally protected by its height."

"How did you get it there, then?"

"We... had an ally who was able to reach it."

"And where is he now?"

"She is... no longer known. I don't know where she went or if she is still in existence."

That made it significantly more difficult. "Is that all, then? It's just high up?"

"Well, no, of course not," Corvin admitted, scratching his neck.

Reg cocked her head, waiting for him to give her more information.

"Air spirits?" Sarah suggested. "If you used sea nymphs to protect the Tears of Poseidon, I assume you used something similar to protect the Zephyr Pearl."

Corvin nodded. "Sylph guardians," he agreed. "Again, we intended to make it impenetrable. We did not take measures to make sure it was accessible to us later. The plan was not for any of us to retrieve the elementals. It was that they would be forever inaccessible to anyone."

"And how does one get past Sylphs?" Reg asked Sarah. "What weaknesses do they have?"

Sarah sighed. "I'm afraid we will have to do some research. These are... extraordinary measures. It isn't something we can just walk into and defeat with a chant or a handful of salt."

Corvin nodded, looking smug. Despite the fact that they were now in dangerous circumstances because of what he had done, he was proud of the measures they had put in place and how unassailable they were.

"Does that mean that the elementals cannot escape?" Reg demanded. "That we don't need to do anything to check on them or prevent their escapes, because they'll never be able to break free of their prisons?"

"Well, that would be a nice idea," Sarah said, "but I wouldn't want to rely on it. Half of the elementals have already broken out without any help from mortals. If the location of the other relics is revealed somehow, we could have all kinds of ne'er do wells trying to reach them. And you never know who might stumble across the magic needed to free them."

"No one is going to release them accidentally," Corvin scoffed.

"What was Gideon doing in the Temple Orange Grove?" Sarah challenged. "Was he just 'checking on' the Geode of Gaea? And if he was, then how did it escape while he did that? I assume Gideon knew how the elemental had been bound. If he was here to strengthen the bonds because he became aware that you had been weakened, then what happened? Or was it the opposite? Did he decide he wanted the geode for himself? That it was time to release the elemental and he could do so now that you were prevented from using your magic?"

"Gideon would never betray me like that. He knew how important it was to keep the elementals bound. All of them."

"Then what was he doing?"

"He must have been there to check on them and strengthen the defenses," Corvin said. "He became aware that there could be a problem following the werewolf attack. And…"

"He just happened to be there when the earth elemental escaped?" Reg filled in.

"We don't know for sure when it was freed. It might have been free for a while before he approached the temple. It might have been freed the night of the werewolf attack or any time since, and simply had not been stirred into action until Gideon got there."

"If they were able to escape without anyone freeing them… then the same thing could happen with the water and air elementals. We might be too late to do anything. Or arrive just to be attacked like Gideon was."

"I don't remember anyone asking you to retrieve them," Corvin growled. "Sometimes, you need to leave things alone."

"Just like you and your friends did," Sarah suggested.

Corvin rose to his feet.

"I think you have worn out your welcome here. I have been very patient, but I'm tired, and I've had enough. I hope you don't start something you are unable to finish. But for now… whatever you do, do it somewhere else."

CHAPTER TWENTY-FOUR

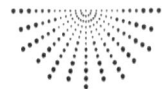

*D*o you think there's more to Corvin's story than he told us?" Reg asked as she drove Sarah back to the house.

"Undoubtedly. There is always more to the story, and Corvin has good reason to hold back. He knows that what he and Gideon did was wrong. And anyone who was helping them." Sarah's lips pressed together as she considered. "I don't know who might have helped him. It was so long ago. Are any of them still around? I hate to think that any of those I have nurtured friendships with over centuries could have been involved in something like that."

"Well, if they were... maybe they lived to regret it later. Maybe they realized that they had made the wrong choice but, at that point, there wasn't anything they could do about it."

"It's possible," Sarah agreed, sounding relieved at Reg's suggestion. "We have all grown since then. It was a very different world we lived in when I first came to Florida. It was... very wild. We didn't have the laws and structure that we have today. There was much more freedom just to do things as you wanted. Although, of course, we were not free to practice magic openly. The trials were over, but there was still a great deal of misunderstanding about the craft. A witch could still be hanged, though they would say it was for some other crime."

Sarah sighed and gazed out the window before going on.

"We were all young and reckless, eager to explore this new frontier and to make our place in the world. Mistakes were made; I can forgive Corvin for that, I suppose. I made many of my own as well. But I didn't hang on to them and defend them."

"He's defensive," Reg said. "He's tired and in pain because of the curse and inability to use his gifts. He's like a big, grumpy toddler. Maybe if he was feeling better, he would act differently about it. But what was he supposed to do? Release the elementals after he decided it wasn't the right choice? What would have happened if he had tried to do that?"

"I imagine he would be where Gideon is now. The elementals are clearly not happy with the way they were treated. I am not sure they have conscious thought processes as we do, or personalities or self-awareness. But I think it is clear that they are angry about their incarceration."

Reg nodded. She had only encountered one of them so far, but she could attest that the fire elemental had not been ready to let go of its resentment of being bound and to simply enjoy its newfound freedom.

Far from it.

"Are we going to free them?" she asked Sarah. "Do we have the skills to do that? And can we free them without ending up…" Reg trailed off.

"Like Gideon?" Sarah finished.

"Yeah. And we still have that challenge, too. Figuring out if there is a way to reverse the petrifaction."

"And if it is the right thing to do," Sarah added. "If he helped to bind the elementals for all of this time, maybe it is appropriate that they bind him in turn."

"But what about the others in the forest? And whoever else the earth elemental runs into in the next little while? It's more than just Gideon."

"Yes, of course, you are right," Sarah admitted, frowning. "We must find out how to reverse the petrifaction, regardless of what happens to Gideon."

Reg pulled in to the curb in front of the house.

"We will have to do what we can," Sarah said before opening her door. "We need to restore what we can. Set things right as much as possible. Corvin is right about one thing… we let this happen without doing anything about it. What did we think when the trouble being caused by the elementals ceased? That they had all washed out to sea? Decided to go somewhere else? Or to stop causing chaos? We should have done something back then to see whether we could live in peace with the elementals or to find a way to drive them out. Instead, we stood by while someone else took action."

"What Corvin did wasn't your fault."

"In a way, it was. We should all have known what was going on. We should have been holding council and coming up with a plan of action. Instead, we were too caught up in our own exciting lives to take any responsibility." She paused. "Or I was; I cannot speak for anyone else. I take responsibility for my part in what happened. In my ignorance."

Ahead of Reg was a truck she recognized. One with dragon scratch marks on the roof. As Sarah got out of the car, Davyn stepped out of the truck. He walked toward them. Reg glanced up at the sky, but didn't see or feel Ember anywhere close by. He must have stayed at the house.

"Is everything okay?" she asked Davyn. "Ember?"

He smiled. "Ember is fine. What are you worried about?"

Reg rubbed the back of her neck. "Everything. All this stuff with the elementals, but also about him getting too big and going away… becoming more independent. Worrying about him getting hurt."

Davyn looked at Sarah. "All this stuff with the elementals?" he repeated.

Sarah nodded. "We have just been talking to Corvin about what happened to Gideon and the artifacts Reg discovered at the temple and the fort."

"Oh." Davyn's face grew pale. He swallowed. "What exactly did he do?"

Sarah motioned to the house. "Let's go inside. It is best not to talk about this out in the street."

She led the way into the house, and Sarah gave Davyn a brief rundown of what they had learned.

"Corvin and Gideon and an unknown number of practitioners formed a shadow coven and… bound these four elementals to four artifacts. Corvin has been maintaining the binding spells and protections over the years. But that ceased when he was injured and cursed by the werewolves."

"And the earth and fire elementals have been freed."

"Or broken free. So it would appear."

Davyn rubbed his face. "Well… this is a situation."

"It is indeed," Sarah agreed. She opened a sideboard in the parlor that Reg had not seen her access before. Reg saw it was a liquor cabinet. Sarah had refused to drink with Corvin, but felt that she needed the fortification now.

Once they had all been supplied with drinks, Davyn looked at Reg and Sarah. "We will need to act quickly. Two of the elementals are free. The others may follow quickly. We need to at least check on how secure the arrangements are."

"We need to retrieve the relics and free them," Sarah insisted.

"Perhaps, yes. But we don't know what the consequences of freeing them would be. Corvin and Gideon decided many years ago that the only way to protect Black Sands from the influence of the elementals was to bind them. What solution do we have? Unleashing four angry spirits into the environment does not seem like the wisest course of action."

Sarah looked at Reg. "Maybe Reg can communicate with them. Convey to them that we are trying to help them, to restore their freedom to them and atone for what was done in the past."

The only one Reg had encountered so far was the fire elemental, and it had not seemed very open to any kind of explanation.

"I don't know. I can try, but I don't know if I'll have much luck."

"Knowing what they are will help," Davyn assured her. "When you encountered the fire elemental, you did not know what it was.

We will need to do some research." He rubbed his forehead. "Of course, the person with the most knowledge about ancient relics and spirits is Corvin. I take it he is not willing to share?"

"He told us a little about them. How they are bound and protected. But he said they were meant to last forever and to be unassailable."

Sarah nodded her agreement.

"Well, clearly that is not the case," Davyn said. "But I do not know who to go to that will have the best knowledge of these ancient rites."

Reg looked at Sarah. "To Theodore, of course."

Davyn raised his brows. "Theodore. Who is Theodore?"

CHAPTER TWENTY-FIVE

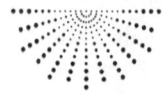

*D*avyn's reaction to Theodore was pretty similar to Sarah's "What have you done?"

"I don't understand why everyone is so worked up about it," Reg told him. "I didn't go out and perform some kind of forbidden magic. And you keep telling me," she pointed this remark at Sarah, "That there is no such thing as dark magic. As long as it doesn't harm anyone. And what does it hurt anyone for me to have a homunculus? It isn't even like I created it. I'm just using what Sma left behind when she died."

"The homunculus should not even exist after she died," Davyn pointed out.

"I understand that. But you can't deny that he does. Well, you haven't seen him, but Sarah has, and he's real, right?"

Sarah nodded reluctantly.

"So if he exists, why can't I use him? It would be better for him to just keep wandering the forest with no home and no master, no purpose, and for all that knowledge to disappear? I thought you need someone with that ancient knowledge."

Davyn's confusion over this suggestion was humorous. Reg could see that he wanted to tell her that she should not, under any circumstance, have had anything to do with the homunculus. And yet, he had just said that he needed the very knowledge that Theodore possessed. And he couldn't say that she had done anything wrong by rescuing Theodore. How could it have been wrong? Why should she avoid having anything to do with him just because he was created using alchemy that she didn't understand?

"Reg... there is danger in delving into these ancient arts."

"I haven't done anything. Other than giving a homunculus some reading material..."

"You are shameless."

"Why should I be ashamed? I am not the one who created him. I haven't done anything wrong."

Davyn shook his head.

"Theodore told Sarah that it was because of Corvin's spell breaking that the first elementals got out," Reg informed Davyn. "We didn't know that, but he did."

"I'm going to have to think about this."

"What is there to think about? You need the knowledge he has. How long can we put this off?"

"I at least need to think about it tonight. I'm sorry, Reg, but I can't just jump into this. I am an example to others in this community; where I get my knowledge or what means I use to acquire it is important. These are dire circumstances. I have heard of what happened in the days before they 'disappeared.' And we know the kind of power they have to cause severe storms, forest fires, and other disasters. But I need a day. I need time to think it through."

"Okay." Reg shrugged. "I have appointments tonight. We'll talk tomorrow and see... whether you are going to help or not."

He looked surprised. "Of course I'll help, Reg. I wouldn't abandon my community when they need me. The question is only the method we use to approach it. I will consult other resources tonight and consider the issues involved."

"Well, I will be talking to Theodore."

Reg said it flatly, wanting him to understand that she wasn't asking his permission or approval. The homunculus was a huge help, and his knowledge was much easier for her to access than books, the internet, or some other practitioner in the community. She wasn't going to ignore the one really good source that she had.

* * *

Reg was more concerned about who else would be helping out with their quest. She had Sarah and Davyn for sure. She knew they would both be helping, even if she was using a source of information they didn't approve of.

She was sure they would come to accept Theodore and be happy to use him when it came down to the crunch. She bet they would even come to like him.

But she also didn't know whether they would recruit others to help. Letticia? Damon? Other witches or warlocks who had been away for centuries that she didn't know? She didn't want too many people involved or for word to spread throughout the community about what they were doing. If they could keep it to just a nice small group, she felt they had a better chance of success than if they involved a lot of people.

She didn't know much about elementals, but it seemed they might get agitated with more people around. Sometimes, it was better to be able to fly under the radar and not stir things up.

Especially when those things could wreak havoc on the entire state.

CHAPTER TWENTY-SIX

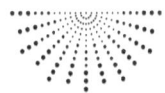

*R*eg finished her readings and a seance and thought she would be able to fall asleep fairly quickly. It had been a long day, and she had barely slept the night before. Fighting wildfires and elementals was not easy work.

But she kept reviewing everything Corvin had said about the remaining elementals and wondering how she and the others would achieve their goal. Or even what their goal was. To free the elementals? To make sure that the two that remained could not get out and attempt to bind the earth and fire elementals or drive them away? To gather them together and try to come to an understanding that wouldn't endanger anyone in Black Sands?

The longer she lay in bed, the more she tossed and turned. Starlight, who normally either slept on the bed or watched out the window while she slept, eventually snorted and huffed and strode out of the room in irritation. She'd tried to explain why she was so restless, but he seemed to have no interest in the doings of elementals, and she already knew his opinion of Corvin.

Eventually, Reg got out of bed. She was too irritated with herself to stay there any longer. She went out to the garden and summoned Theodore. Despite her disagreement with Sarah and Davyn about whether she should have taken on Theodore, she had never summoned him anywhere but the garden. She was wary of inviting anything into her cottage, especially creatures she didn't understand. She had learned a lot about homunculuses—homunculi—since first meeting Theodore, but she still couldn't say that she really understood what he was or how he continued to exist.

"From soil and stone, by magic spin,
Theodore reform, our work begin."

It was more difficult to see him forming in the darkness, but she didn't want to turn on any outside lights and attract Sarah's attention in the big house. There was something magical about watching Theodore form in the moonlight. He seemed more tranquil than during their daytime encounters.

Theodore peered at Reg.

"Bound by craft and ancient lore,
In service, I arise once more—"

"No, no," Reg waved away his opening verse. "I told you that you don't need to say all that. It's just you and me here, and I don't go in for all the rhyming stuff. Just talk to me like a normal person."

He clicked and cocked his head.

"What do you wish?"

"I just have some questions." Reg paced, trying to work out the restless tension. "How much do you know about elementals? You know, the ones that Corvin bound."

"Earth, air, water, and fire. A completed whole. They work together to cause havoc and disaster."

"Yeah. That's what I heard." Reg paused at the garden bench, but was too restless to sit down. She kept walking. "We are going to try to... visit the two that are still bound. Water and air. Corvin told me a little about how they are bound and protected. But I'm worried..."

"What is your goal?"

"I don't know," Reg admitted. "I guess that will depend on how things work out. Maybe we will be making sure that they stay bound, and maybe we will try to free them and convince them to go somewhere else with their natural disasters."

"You wish to free them?"

"Maybe. I mean, not really, but from what Sarah has said, they shouldn't have been bound in the first place, so I kind of think it's the right thing to do. Only, I don't want to... you know... unleash chaos and all that."

"Your heart is true."

"Uh, okay. I guess that's nice, but how will that help me?"

"You have what you need if you set your mind to it."

Reg remembered Harrison telling her something similar when they had fought the Witch Doctor and his draugrs. And Harrison had been right. By pooling everyone's talents and abilities, they had been able to defeat the witch doctor when they never should have been able to. He had been so much more powerful than they were. But he'd had weaknesses. In the movies Reg had seen, the bad guys always had weaknesses and, by exploiting those, the heroes were always able to come out on top.

Reg talked with Theodore long past her usual bedtime until lights started turning on in the big house, letting her know that Sarah was up. If Reg were going to get any sleep before they started on their mission, she knew she'd better get to bed and at least close her eyes for a few minutes.

CHAPTER TWENTY-SEVEN

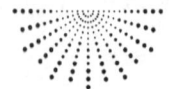

*A*s Reg had expected, Sarah knocked on her door all too soon. Sarah knew that Reg didn't normally get up until almost noon, but it was apparently a thing that all magical quests had to start early in the morning. How was anyone supposed to accomplish anything unless they started first thing in the morning?

Storytellers had a lot to answer for. Reg was sure she couldn't be the only quester ever to be a night owl. How was a company supposed to stay up late into the night drinking beer with trolls or gathered around the fire telling the feats of their forefathers if they got up early every morning?

Sarah had a key and, as usual, let herself into the guest cottage at will. She started the coffee brewing, the surest way to get Reg out of bed, and rattled noisily around the kitchen pretending to prepare breakfast, hoping to make enough noise to wake Reg up. Reg just turned over and went back to sleep. It should have come as no surprise that a few minutes later, Sarah knocked on her bedroom door, abandoning the pretense of being polite and progressing to *assertive.*

"Oh, Reg, I'm sorry, did I wake you up? You probably had a rough night, but I was just wondering… Davyn is here, and we were hoping to start before too long. We don't want to burn daylight, as they say. When were you planning to get up?"

Reg groaned and pulled the sheet over her head. "Couple more hours."

"Hours?" Sarah demanded, aghast. "We can't wait for two more hours."

"Did we have an appointment?"

"What do you mean? No, we hadn't set up a specific time for when we were going to start but, you know, Davyn had to take time off work, and I've made time in my schedule. It's rude to make everyone else sit around and wait while you sleep…"

Reg tried to ignore Sarah and go back to sleep. If she engaged with Sarah, she would not be able to fall back asleep.

But already, she was composing arguments about why she shouldn't have to get up yet. It was too late. She wouldn't be able to get back to sleep. She pulled the sheet down to glare at Sarah.

"You know what my sleep schedule is like. Isn't it kind of rude to plan to start a quest when I am normally sleeping?"

But Sarah didn't flinch at the suggestion. "Most people are out of bed by now."

"So?"

"Well, you're awake now, so…"

Reg groaned. "Next time we plan a trip, we are starting in the afternoon. Not the morning."

Sarah shrugged. "We'll have to see." She turned her head as the coffee machine trilled a happy tune. "That is your coffee."

Making coffee was not going to get Sarah off the hook for scheduling a quest for when Reg was normally still in bed and then forcing Reg's compliance.

But it was a start.

Starlight was already in the kitchen and yowled a couple of times as Reg shuffled past him to go to the bathroom.

"Where is Davyn?" Reg asked suddenly, looking down at her sleeping outfit. "Did you say he's here?"

"I left him at the big house. I didn't know what kind of condition you would be in."

"Oh. Good."

Though it probably didn't matter. It wasn't like he hadn't seen her in shorts and a T-shirt, her usual sleepwear. That *was* how she had shown up to fight the forest fire.

With Sarah hovering impatiently, Reg muddled through her morning routine of getting washed, dressed, and caffeinated. The cat was fed. Reg did *not* get the chance to check her videos and social media with Sarah standing there watching her like a hawk.

"All right," Reg said eventually. "Is it just the three of us? You and me and Davyn?" She looked at Starlight. "How about you? Do you want to come hunting with us?"

Starlight stared at her without blinking. It was a definite "no." Reg chuckled. But Starlight was probably right. A deep-sea cavern and some kind of tower in the sky were no place for a cat. Starlight would have to assume a human form, and he only seemed to do that when it was an emergency and there was no other way to help Reg.

"Yes, it's just us," Sarah confirmed.

Even when all they had been doing was going to the mountain to destroy a fairy blade, they had taken more people than that. And certainly when they had fought the witch doctor and the draugrs. But there was something to be said for staying lean and agile, and Reg's instinct was that they needed to keep their company small.

"I guess this is it, then. Do I need to bring anything?" Reg grabbed her big shoulder bag and started to jam things into it. She should probably have thought the day before about what she would need for the quest. She threw in a few granola bars and an energy drink. Maybe a hat? She wouldn't need one for diving, but maybe when they went up the tower after the Pearl she would need a visor to keep the sun out of her eyes. But the winds would probably just blow it right off. She looked at Sarah for her advice.

"Just bring yourself, Reg. None of us knows what we are going to need other than that. I'm not sure what good any books or magical artifacts will do. You just need yourself and your skills."

Reg sighed. It didn't seem like very much. It seemed to her that any magical quest might hinge on having just the right tools along.

A special dagger, ring, or talisman. How many books had she read where they had needed some special object at the climax of the quest, even if it were just something like the words of an enchantment or prophecy or a piece of chewing gum.

"Come on," Sarah encouraged, maybe sensing the inertia Reg felt, the inability to get moving. To actually start the quest.

Or maybe she was just impatient.

Reg motioned to the door, "After you."

Sarah exited the cottage, and Reg followed her, hefting her somewhat heavier bag up on her shoulder.

Davyn was waiting at the house. He was standing still when they walked in the door, but Reg got the feeling she had interrupted his pacing. He smiled and nodded to Reg and didn't criticize her for sleeping in and keeping them waiting.

"Well, are we ready to begin?" he asked.

Reg gave a nod. She wasn't sure what they were up against, but she had prepared the best she could. She felt like she at least had an idea of what she was talking about after quizzing Theodore for half the night.

"How clear was Corvin about where they hid the Tears of Poseidon?" Davyn asked. "There is… a lot of sea out there. I'm hoping you will be able to sense it like you sensed the other artifacts, but if it is far away…"

"I got a bit of a picture when Corvin was talking about it. And I talked to Theodore about it. I think I know about where it is."

"How do you want to handle this? Do we drive and rent a boat? Is it in local waters or halfway around the world?"

"Everything is close by. I don't know why they kept everything in one area. When Francesca bound the witch doctor to the kattakyns, we sent them all around the world so that they weren't all so close together. Anyone trying to get them together would have to travel all over the world to track them down. And when the enchantment wore off, it would take the different parts of his sah a longer time to migrate toward each other."

"Travel was… rather restricted a few centuries ago," Sarah reminded her. "You couldn't just hop a plane to fly anywhere in the world. You had to arrange for passage on a ship, and it took months to get around the world."

"And I don't imagine taking priceless artifacts on a ship like that was very safe," Davyn suggested. "Pirates and pickpockets and all…"

Reg hadn't considered how much society and travel had changed since then.

"Besides, Corvin and Gideon were just young fellows back then," Sarah pointed out. "It might not have occurred to them to separate the elementals. They didn't think they would ever be freed and able to get back together. And being close by would allow them to check on the artifacts to ensure they were still secure."

All of that made sense. Reg probably should have thought of it herself. She returned to Davyn's question.

"Let's take a car to the harbor," she suggested. "And then I'll see whether I can feel the vial. I don't know whether I'll need a boat or any other equipment yet. But… there is one problem…"

They both looked at Reg expectantly.

"When I get close to the water, I… am not exactly myself."

Davyn had seen this up close and in person at least once before. A look of understanding came over his face. Sarah was mystified.

"Not yourself?" she repeated tentatively.

"Because of the siren thing," Reg said, embarrassed to bring it up. "When I get close to the water, and get the sea spray in my face or step into the ocean… I might not be able to control myself. If Davyn is close by, or another man… well…" She shrugged, her face hot. "I need to know that you'll make sure no one gets too close. I don't want there to be… an incident."

"Of course," Sarah agreed. "Oh, forgive me for not understanding. I didn't even think about that. I was just thinking how much of a benefit your siren abilities would be."

Reg appreciated that Sarah had considered Reg an asset rather than a liability. A flush of appreciation joined the embarrassment already heating her cheeks.

"I will stay well back," Davyn promised. "And we will help to keep anyone else away from you."

Reg nodded. "Yeah, that would be good."

Davyn also had a gift for invisibility, but Reg suspected that would not be any help at all. She would still be able to smell him and would know that he was there. Despite his gift, she could still see a shadow where he was. An ability that was probably tied to being able to see spirits and other things that remained hidden from normal people.

CHAPTER TWENTY-EIGHT

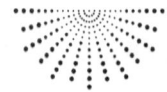

*R*eg felt like they should have packed better for the trip, even though they were only going to the harbor. It felt significant, like something that deserved a big send-off. As it was, there was no luggage to load into or on top of the car. They simply climbed in and fastened their seatbelts.

Davyn drove. He probably felt like he wasn't doing enough on this mission if his only function was staying out of Reg's way.

Reg wasn't sure what his role in the quest would be, but she was sure they would need his knowledge and skills at some point. He was a lot more experienced than she was.

It was fairly quiet at the harbor. Reg looked up and down the line of boats. A few were occupied with fishermen coming or going but, mostly, the boats were silent. It was probably late for those who got up early to fish and too early for those going out on pleasure trips. Reg had not appreciated being roused from sleep so early, but the timing was not bad.

"Okay." Reg took a deep breath in and let it back out. The tang of salt air filled her senses. The sun sparkled on the surface of the water, too bright, making her want to dive deep down to where it was darker and there was more to explore. She had always wanted to go diving in clear water filled with brightly colored fish and coral. "Let's go down to the end, away from the boats."

"To the beach?" Sarah suggested.

"No, there will be more people there. Where there are no boats and it is too deep to wade. I want to be able to slip into the water without attracting attention."

She wouldn't want someone calling for an emergency rescue because Reg dove into the water and didn't come back up again. With her siren powers, she should be able to stay under the water for as long as she needed to. Certainly longer than any normal human.

"Down there, then," Davyn said, pointing. "I know a good place."

They drove a couple of miles farther, and Davyn pulled into a little corner of beach with large rocks, where the water was the dark azure of the deep. It was quiet, isolated from the rest of the coastline by dense trees and large rocks. Maybe a good make-out point, but not much good for much else, other than what Reg was about to attempt.

"Looks good," she told Davyn. "This is perfect. You'd better stay in the car."

He sighed and didn't argue. Of course he wanted to get out and participate but, as soon as Reg touched the water or got spray on her face, he would be in danger.

Reg opened her door and climbed out of the car. Sarah got out as well. They walked toward the rocks at the water's edge. Gulls wheeled and mewed far overhead.

"Tell me your plan," she told Reg.

"Dive down here... swim to the point where I can access the underwater keep. Find the Tears of Poseidon."

"That's pretty basic. How are you going to get past the various wards?"

"I did some research on hydromancy." Reg didn't bother mentioning Theodore. Sarah could imagine Reg having spent the night poring over magical tomes if that made her more comfortable. "I should be able to get past most of the wards just by being part siren. The Oceanids… mostly, they don't have anything to do with sirens. They stay out of each other's way. This is my territory, so they can't claim that I am somewhere I shouldn't be. Wards that are aimed against humans won't be effective against me. Probably."

"But the Oceanids have been tasked with protecting the Tears. You can't just walk in and take the vial."

"Yeah. I have some ideas. I'll just have to experiment, see what works."

Sarah shook her head in disapproval. "This is foolish. You do not have a solid plan. You don't understand what you are facing."

"You can't go down there, but I can. Any human would have to wear a dive suit and would be susceptible to all kinds of problems —equipment failure, hallucinations, disorientation—but I'm not going to have any of those. It is safe for me. Yeah, I'll need to figure out how to get past the Oceanids, but I'm pretty good at talking my way past guards." She mustered a smile for Sarah. "Lifetime of talking my way around the rules."

"Well, you *are* very good at it," Sarah admitted. "But I don't think you are prepared for what you will face."

"Do you have any advice?"

"If you need help… call on someone. I don't know what you are going to find down there, but if Corvin and Gideon set it up, then there must be a way for humans to survive for at least a short time. A chamber filled with breathable air. Some kind of way station. A way for them to check on the integrity of the prison. You can call on one of us if you need help."

Reg nodded. There was a lump in her throat. She was sure Sarah didn't particularly want to be trapped in an underwater cave with no way out except Reg's abilities. What if Reg were injured or killed? Then Sarah would be trapped down there with no way out.

"Thanks."

"Has it been long enough since you ate?" Sarah asked, looking at her watch. "You're not supposed to swim for an hour after eating. You don't want to get cramps."

Reg laughed. "I don't think I'm going to get cramps."

"You could. Do you really want to risk it?"

"Yes. I didn't eat that much, and I've never had cramps when swimming in my life. It will be okay."

Sarah patted her on the arm. "Well... you be careful. Remember that we are here to help you. I don't have your psychic skills, but I will listen for you."

"All right." Reg swallowed. "See you in a bit."

She had dressed with swimming in mind. She undid the wrap-around skirt and dropped it on top of one of the rocks so it wouldn't be filled with sand. She had left her big shoulder bag in the car, so she didn't need to worry about that being left on the beach. If she were a long time and Davyn and Sarah had to go for some reason, either because some beach patrol security company told them they had to leave or because they needed something to eat or a bathroom break, her things would not be left on the beach for thieves to paw through. She put her towel on top of the skirt and weighed them down with a rock so they wouldn't blow away.

The wind blew salty sea spray up into her face. Reg's senses all immediately sharpened. She closed her eyes and reached out for the Tears of Poseidon. This was her territory. These were her waters. She was entitled to know everything that went on under the surface.

It took a few minutes, and she couldn't see it clearly, but she knew what direction to go. Reg looked at Davyn in the car, where he watched her carefully. She could not smell him with the doors and windows closed up tightly. She felt a pang of disappointment that Corvin was not there. She had claimed him as hers. Reg felt a longing to take him down into the water with her. She reached out her senses to try to determine where he was and what he was doing at that moment.

It came as no surprise that he was still at home, shut up like a hermit. Studying his books and trying to avoid triggering any of his multitude of magical gifts. He raised his head for a moment as she reached out, then his hands clenched into fists and his face into a grimace of pain. She shouldn't have reached out to him and risked triggering his own telepathic response. But she needed to know where he was and that he wasn't waiting for her in the underwater caverns, waiting to see if she would show up to tamper with the Tears of Poseidon and the water elemental.

Reg turned to wave at Sarah, then jumped into the water.

CHAPTER TWENTY-NINE

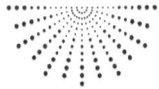

*S*he was home.

Reg loved the pressure of the water on her skin and the stillness she felt when holding her breath. The tumult of voices in her head quieted, and she heard only the chorus of siren sisters happy to welcome her into the water. It was different from the silence she had felt when Corvin had taken away her powers—that echoing, empty chamber in her head; instead, she was filled with a sense of quiet and peace with the siren sisterhood singing quietly in the background. Not the discordant wails she often heard as they urged her to take actions she was unwilling to pursue. This was more like what she had imagined the sailors in ancient Greece had heard when they were lured into the water by the magical voices of the sirens.

She pulled herself through the water with her arms and kicked with her feet, torpedoing through the incredibly clear water. She aimed toward the place where she knew the Tears were being guarded. The water was very deep, and she continued to dive as she moved forward, seeking the ocean floor.

Then she entered a magical fairyland. This was what she had imagined years ago when her foster parents had gotten her a little swimming pool, and she would sit or lie on the bottom, dreaming of brightly colored schools of fish and the twisted and variegated beds of coral.

She was far from the surface of the water, yet she could still see the light from the sun up above her.

Schools of fish swam around her unafraid, as if she were one of them. Their scales shimmered like underwater jewels. Gentle currents caressed her skin, and Reg felt a sense of belonging she'd never found anywhere but in the water.

She glided through the crystalline waters, reaching out again to find the vial that contained the Tears of Poseidon and the water elemental bound to it. She needed to keep her focus on her mission. She wasn't there just to enjoy the embrace of the ocean and the beauty of the underwater garden.

It took her a while to reach an opening into the underwater caverns where she knew the relic rested. Reg knew she was crossing a threshold as she entered the tunnel. It was more than just a physical entrance into the cave system. She had crossed a magical barrier, the first layer of protection around the vial.

Reg looked around, wary, watching for an attack. Would it be the Oceanids right off the bat? Or would there be something else first, something smaller to test her or to deter those who were only exploring and not really after the Tears?

The passageway was narrow. Not a problem for Reg, but for a big man or someone with dive gear, it would have been a squeeze. Most people would not go exploring a network of underwater caves like that without a guide or someone who had been there before. Even if they were small enough, most people would have found the space claustrophobic and turned back.

Maybe that was the first test. Just having the sense not to explore dangerous places. The tunnel grew dark as she swam on. Reg trailed her fingers along the bottom, letting her other senses guide her. She found she could build a picture of the tunnel in her mind just by listening to the sound as she moved through it. Siren radar? That was cool and unexpected.

Bioluminescent plants were sprinkled here and there, providing a soft glow. Her eyes quickly adjusted to the darkness so that even the tiny bit of light provided by the plants was enough to guide her.

The tunnel was long and winding. Reg stuck to the main one even though there were a number of passages that led off of the trunk line. She kept her focus on the pull from the Tears of Poseidon. She noticed that the luminescence of the plants tended to be stronger in the side tunnels. Perhaps designed to lead unsuspecting explorers away from the keep, to get lost forever in the winding passageways. Reg filed it away for future reference. Don't follow the light.

The farther she got, the more tempted Reg was to explore the other passageways. Was it possible that the tunnel she was in was just a big loop and she would keep going in circles forever and ever? She felt like she should get out of it. It would certainly be more interesting to explore the other passageways.

She focused on the Tears. No, she was going the right way. It was the hydromancy that was trying to distract her into following trails that would only lead her away from the prize.

But the other passages became increasingly tempting. Reg wanted to get out of the darkness and find the Tears of Poseidon. How long had she been swimming aimlessly through the tunnel already?

Theodore had suggested that Reg's powers as a firecaster might be just what she needed to counter the hydromancy and water spirits. She focused on her inner fire, thinking about it and wondering whether she would really be able to use her fire while underwater. It was certainly not something she had practiced with Davyn. She knew she wasn't supposed to try anything new without him there to help and make sure things didn't get out of hand.

But could her fire really get out of control or do any damage underwater? The idea was ridiculous.

Still kicking her feet to propel herself forward, Reg held her hands in front of her as if holding an invisible basketball. She moved her hands slowly and encouraged the flame. She didn't believe she could do it underwater and was prepared to give up after only a cursory attempt.

But they needed to get the last two elementals before it was too late. They needed to prevent further disasters in Black Sands. Did Reg really want the town to be flooded? Or for half the state to plunge into the ocean? And what about the air elemental? She kind of liked being able to breathe. When she was not underwater, anyway.

Reg persisted and saw her fire start to glow between her hands, a tiny light in the middle of the water.

"Yes," Reg murmured. "That's right. See this little fire? Do you see what I can do, hydromancy? I bet you never thought I could do that." She grew the flame a little bigger, trying to remember the words that Theodore had taught her. She repeated them in her mind a few times before saying them aloud. Of course, that actually was little more than just mouthing the words since she wasn't breathing while under the water.

Flamma viae veritatis

There were shrieks from the siren sisters in her head. Of course, none of them had fire power, so they would never have attempted to use the incantation.

Flame of the true path

The flame lit the way before her, brightening the space around her so that she could see more clearly and the luminescence was dimmed. Reg laughed to herself.

"How about that, Corvin? Never thought you would have a firecaster down here, did you? Sort of puts a crimp in your plans to make the Tears of Poseidon unassailable, doesn't it?"

She swam faster. Not because she needed to breathe; she just wanted to get the vial and get out of there. After the Tears, there was still one more relic to retrieve. And how would she battle the forces of the air and wind? Her affinity toward water was much stronger. She had no idea what she would do to overcome the guardians in the air. Maybe Davyn and Sarah could take care of that one, and Reg could be the one to sit in the car and wait for them.

CHAPTER THIRTY

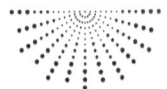

*R*eg burst forth from the tunnel and found herself in a large, open chamber.

Finally! The keep.

She kept her fire burning as she turned around, taking it all in.

Once more, she was surrounded by colorful fish and coral, even more impressive than before. The brilliance and variety of the plants and animals were amazing.

Reg fought to keep her focus amid the mesmerizing beauty. She knew what she was there for, and it wasn't a sightseeing tour. She regretted not bringing an underwater camera with her.

She followed the tug at her heart, pulling her toward the Tears of Poseidon. They were there. She didn't have to find another passageway to continue her search.

The Tears led her down to the bottom of the chamber. Amid the colorful twists and blooms of coral, of plants and anchored animals, she spotted the sapphire glass.

There it was. The vial holding the Tears of Poseidon.

It emitted a faint glow. Brighter than the bioluminescent plants, but not as bright as Reg's fire. She swam toward it, eager to complete the next part of her quest.

For an instant, all her concerns about the hydromancy and the

Oceanids were gone. She was alone. She had only to grab the vial and she could return to Sarah and Davyn on the beach.

As she reached the vial, the coral and seaweed around it transformed. Turning around and stretching out, they changed into the shapes of three beautiful women, their faces cold and striking, their hair flowing seaweed, their bodies composed of coral and sand.

The Oceanids.

They surrounded the vial and picked it up in their hands, heads close together, protecting each other, keeping watch in all directions at the same time.

They were so lovely, Reg hated having to oppose them. If she could have, she would have just left the vial with them. It felt wrong to take their treasure, even though Reg was trying to protect the lives of her friends and the other people in and around Black Sands.

I have come to claim the Tears of Poseidon, she told them. *The time has come for them to be removed.*

Siren, one of the Oceanids protested. *This is not your place.*

This is my territory, Reg told her. *I have every right to be here. These are my waters just as much as they are yours. And everything in them can be claimed.*

No. The Tears are not your affair. Stay out of it.

Friends have already been hurt by the elementals released on the land. I must take control of this one.

It is not yours to take.

Corvin sent me.

They looked at her, frowns of disapproval on their faces, but they were not sure what to think of this. They obviously knew Corvin's name. He was the one who had left the Tears there and had given them directions to keep the vial safe. If Reg now represented him...

How do we know you tell the truth? one Oceanid demanded.

He has been cursed. He cannot come and retrieve it himself.

You lie.

How else would I know where it was? Or how to get here?

They watched her warily. Reg got closer to them, looking for her chance.

She started to hum in the back of her throat. Quietly at first, and then growing in volume. The siren sisters joined their voices with her, discordant at first, but Reg was the only one who could hear them. She used their strength, played off of their notes, and began weaving her magic through the underwater cavern. The Oceanids raised their heads to listen to the song, distracted for a moment from the sapphire vial. They tilted their heads, looking at each other and looking around the beautiful cavern that teemed with underwater life.

Reg edged closer. She didn't take her eyes off the prize, the Tears of Poseidon, whirling around in the little vial. Her song began to echo around the cavern, creating waves, rocking everyone back and forth. The hands holding on to the vial dropped away one at a time until only one of the Oceanids was left holding on to it, barely touching it.

Reg swam forward and grasped the vial. *Her* vial. This was what she needed to fulfill her quest and see to it that Black Sands did not fall prey to the four elementals again. As her hand closed around the vial, the three Oceanids reacted, trying to stop her both physically and with more hydromancy. Reg had constructed a psychic shield as soon as she had the vial in her hand, so she was not hurt by the spells, but they pelted her shield again and again, driving her back from the Oceanids.

No! The Oceanids wailed a protest and tried to stop her. Reg's heart raced as she swam quickly away from them. It had been easier than she had expected. All she had to do now was to get back up to the surface and meet Davyn and Sarah.

That was when she hit the wall.

Reg's escape came to a crashing end. She fell backward and had the sensation of falling, though she didn't know whether she was really descending, or just knocked silly. She looked around, trying to see what she had hit.

But there was nothing in front of her. No solid wall like she had felt. Just open water.

More water magic. Somehow, they had blocked her escape route, turning the water into a solid barrier, even though it still appeared exactly the same. Reg called on her fire, trying to blast her way through it. Heat bubbles formed and sizzled, but she could not get through the barrier.

Reg turned back toward the Oceanids so they could not take her off guard. She didn't want to turn her back to them. They tried to find a way to approach her, to get around her shield and get the vial back from her. Reg held on to it tightly. They were not going to get it back, not after everything she had gone through. Not with so many lives at stake in Black Sands.

There had to be another way out of the chamber. It didn't make sense that there would only be one way in and out. There needed to be an escape, a back door, maybe several of them. Reg reached out and touched the coral-covered rock wall, looking for any break. It could be hidden. There could be an illusion that was preventing her from seeing it. She pushed herself along the wall, searching.

Her mind raced. Somewhere down here, there must be a cave with breathable air. That was what Sarah had suggested. A bubble where Corvin and Gideon could rest when they came to check on the Tears. The way that Reg had come in had been too narrow to admit diving gear and too long for Corvin or Gideon to traverse it holding their breaths, even if they had managed to extend their abilities. They had to have come in a different way.

Reg wailed her song, listening for the echoes to come back to her, visualizing what they told her about how the wall of the chamber was constructed and what was on the other side.

The Oceanids tried everything they could to persuade her to return the vial, crying, begging, and threatening. Reg shut out their cries, focusing on the picture she was building of the network of tunnels and caves around her and how she could use them to escape.

There was another large chamber and, from the empty echo, Reg thought it was filled with air rather than water. She pounded on the wall of the chamber she was in, trying to find a way to access it. There had to be a way to get to it, or it would have been filled with water. A room full of air would not naturally occur so deep under the water.

There was a hollow knock as Reg hit the wall. It sounded different. She had to be close to the solution. She had to find the door or illusion that connected the two.

At last she visualized the entrance hole with her echolocation map at the same time as her hand met with no resistance. She could see the wall with her eyes, but she could not feel it and the echoes told her it was a tunnel. Reg held the vial tightly in one hand as she cautiously swam through the passageway, the other hand on the wall. The tunnel was big enough to admit her. She heard the Oceanids in pursuit behind her. She tried to keep the psychic shield in place while still doing everything else she was trying to do, but it was weakening. Her energy and focus were waning. Despite her siren heritage, maybe the depth was getting to her. If she didn't get out of the reach of the Oceanids, she was going to be in trouble.

Reg swam swiftly down the passageway, kicking her feet hard. The Oceanids pursued her, squawking to one another, determined to catch up with her and then dispose of her.

Then she burst through the surface of the water. Reg instinctively took a huge gasp of air, even though she had not been holding her breath underwater, able to breathe in the water just as naturally as if she had been on dry ground. She looked around her. It was the chamber she had visualized with her echolocation.

Reg scrambled up a shallow slope onto a rocky platform that rose above the water. She retreated to the other side of the cave, getting as far from the water as she could.

As she expected, the Oceanids were not far behind her and broke the water's surface soon after she did.

But unlike Reg, they could not breathe the air in the chamber. They were water creatures.

They made gagging noises and retreated, settling back into the water and communicating in their high, piping voices. Reg breathed heavily, exhausted by the chase, and leaned against the rock wall. She was safe from the Oceanids for the time being. But she would need to figure out a way to get out of the underwater caverns without having to pass the Oceanids. The dry cave was large and she would need to explore it once she'd had a chance to rest and relax for a few minutes.

She looked at the vial, turning it over in her hands. She couldn't tell whether the sapphire blue came from the glass of the vial or the ocean water inside. Maybe from both.

It was heavier in her hands than it ought to have been. She hadn't realized that when she had been underwater; it had felt nearly weightless.

Inside, the water swirled in whirlpools and settled into a rhythm like waves breaking against the shore. Even when she held the vial perfectly still, the waves inside still moved. Was that the effect of the relic itself or the elemental imprisoned within?

The Oceanids threatened to crawl out of the water to attack Reg and take the vial from her but, as none of them broke the surface again, Reg didn't think that was likely. They started to chant, their voices rising and falling in rhythm. Reg closed her eyes and listened to them for a minute. It was a compelling rhythm, like the thump of war drums deep under the water.

Reg brushed the surface of the rock floor with one hand to make a tiny pile of sand. She threw a pinch of it in front of her and summoned Theodore.

"From sand and stone, by magic spin,
　　Theodore reform, our work begin."

She wasn't sure if it would work with the small amount of sand she had, or if Theodore needed the soil of the garden or forest to properly form.

The sand did its thing, forming a miniature dust devil, then gathering more sand from the rock's surface and eventually forming the familiar shape: a somewhat dirty and disheveled child with flat black eyes.

He looked around the chamber, clearly surprised to find himself there. He nodded to the vial in Reg's hand. "You have succeeded in finding the Tears of Poseidon."

Reg nodded. "Found and stole… but I'm not sure what to do now. I'm kind of stuck here."

"Go back the way you came?" Theodore suggested.

"The Oceanids are not very happy with me. I don't think that's a good idea."

"Then you must find another way out." Theodore looked around.

"Sarah said to call on one of the others if I ended up getting stuck. And she said there would be a place like this. She was pretty smart to figure that out without knowing how Corvin set this all up. But even if I call one of them here, I'm not sure what they can do. How can they help? I don't want to trap them too."

Theodore cocked his head and clicked, thinking about it.

"You can call others? Bring them here?"

"Yes. But what is anyone else going to do to help me?"

"But you cannot transport yourself, only others?"

"Uh…" Reg furrowed her brow. She had needed to come to the chamber where the Tears of Poseidon were kept the usual way, since no one but Corvin knew anything about the setup. There were problems with transporting herself or anyone else to a place she had never been before and knew nothing about. She had known there would be many dangers in the underground caverns that she couldn't know of without seeing it for herself.

But transporting back out? She could send herself to anywhere familiar. Back home. Or to the corner of the beach where she had left Sarah and Davyn.

All she needed to do was envision the place she wanted to transport to.

CHAPTER THIRTY-ONE

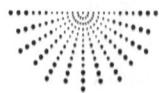

$\mathcal{R}$eg laughed at herself. "Now, why didn't I think of that?" she asked Theodore.

But his attention was not on her. He was looking at the water, where the Oceanids were still chanting their compelling war chant. Reg noticed that the water was rocking, sloshing back and forth like it had not been doing before. She stood up, looking at it without getting any closer. She had assumed that the Oceanids were no longer a threat, but maybe she had counted them out too soon. They couldn't come after her when she was out of the water where they couldn't survive. So she was safe.

But now doubt crept in. If it had been nothing and they weren't a threat, then Theodore wouldn't be looking at the water with such concern.

The water lapped up onto the stone floor like the tide coming in. But, of course, there was no tide down there. The dry cave was not actually above the water line, but was magically created and maintained.

She swallowed and stood on her tiptoes, scanning the surface of the water and trying to see down into the depths, but the water was dark, and she couldn't see what the Oceanids were doing to make the surface shift like that.

"This is not good," Theodore warned.

"What's going on?"

"They have called the guardian."

Reg swallowed. "I thought *they* were the guardians."

Theodore continued to stare at the heaving water, his black eyes wide and unblinking.

"They have awakened ancient magic dormant in the ocean depths."

"Is this... another trap that Corvin set?"

Theodore shook his head. "The guardian existed long before Corvin Hunter came to the earth."

"Did he know about it? Trigger some kind of spell to wake it up if someone tried to take the Tears of Poseidon?"

Theodore shook his head slowly. "It is impossible to know what was in the warlock's mind," he reminded her. He had never even met Corvin. Whatever knowledge he had of the warlock was gleaned from Sma or her library. "The guardian was called by the Oceanids. Whether Corvin foresaw this... I know not."

Reg eyed the water. "What *is* the guardian?"

"Guardian of the deep. Terror of the trench. Depths' Doom."

"But... what is it?"

The water lapped at Reg's feet. Suddenly, something broke through the water's surface. A green-gray, seaweed-draped tentacle. It reached toward the rocky shelf on which Reg stood. A rotten, fishy smell filled the chamber.

Reg's heart sped in panic.

She needed to get out of there.

What was she doing still standing there watching the approach of something that could snatch her off of the rocks and drag her down below the surface of the water?

She might be able to live and breathe underwater, unlike most humans, but she was not immortal. She couldn't live there forever, and she had a feeling that the creature from the depths had plenty of other ways to deal with her than just drowning her.

The tentacle that rose out of the water was as thick as a man's thigh and undoubtedly as strong.

Trying to keep calm, Reg pictured herself on the beach with Sarah. She imagined the sun on the sand, her friend waiting for her, her skirt lying where she had weighted it down with a rock.

But nothing happened. When she opened her eyes, she wasn't on the beach again. She was still in the magical chamber, the water touching her toes and the creature filling the pool, rising slowly out of it to grab her and pull her back in.

Maybe it would squeeze her like a python. Maybe it would deliver her to the Oceanids to do with as they would. Maybe it had a mouth lined with tiny teeth the tentacles would pull her into. Or a beak like a squid.

She really didn't want to find out.

"Now would be a good time," Theodore prompted. "If you can transport yourself…"

"I know. I'm trying. But it isn't working."

He looked at her. "Perhaps try harder."

Reg again pictured the beach. She smelled the tang of the salt water. The way the sun had shone on her face in the early morning. The silence, interrupted only by the mew of seagulls.

Still, she was not transported there.

"I don't understand it. Does it have magic that is preventing me from transporting?" Reg looked around the chamber for another escape route. There had to be a dry tunnel she could get out through. She couldn't see anything, but that didn't mean it wasn't there. She ran her fingers along the wall, hoping to find it as she had found the tunnel between the two chambers, feeling for the opening behind the illusion. She looked for a rune that might mark the exit.

"Perhaps you prevent yourself," Theodore suggested.

He was looking anxiously toward the water and the multiple tentacles now reaching out from it.

Reg knew her panic was probably preventing her from being able to transport herself. She needed to be calm and clear-headed, and it would come naturally to her, just as it had the previous times she'd needed to transport herself.

One of the tentacles had nearly reached her but seemed to be stopped by an invisible barrier.

It wasn't until then that she realized she was still using the psychic shield she had formed to protect her from the attack of the Oceanids. She could not transport while using the shield. She had experienced that in Egypt when she'd tried to simultaneously use defensive measures and active transport.

It was impossible.

She could only use one at a time.

CHAPTER THIRTY-TWO

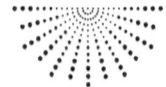

*I*t took a great force of will to drop the shield while the tentacles reached for her. Everything in her resisted dropping the only protection she had. But she needed to get out of the cave, to escape the danger entirely rather than just hold it off for however long she had the strength to do so. When her shield finally failed, she would have no more energy to transport.

As soon as she was able to drop the barrier, she found herself standing on the beach. The sun shone on her face just as she had imagined, and the salt tang in the breeze flooded her senses. She was back.

Sarah pressed a hand over her chest. "Oh, Reg! You startled me." She took a deep breath. "I thought you would come back from the water." She indicated the spot where Reg had dived in.

Reg collapsed to the sand, her legs shaking. One of the tentacles had touched her skin just as she had finally managed to get the transportation to work, and she pressed her hand over the stinging skin. It had been a very close call.

"Reg! Are you okay?" Sarah hurried over to her and took her by the arm.

Reg breathed deeply. Her heart was still pounding hard, like she was in danger. But she was safe now. Beyond the reach of the Oceanids and whatever that creature of the deep was.

"Yes, I'm fine. It was just… close." Reg breathed out, trying to slow her breathing. "I'm fine."

She rubbed her leg where the tentacle had touched. It burned. Reg saw a puffy welt. The tentacle must have had some kind of poison on it. A good thing it hadn't done anything more than brush the surface of the skin as she had managed to whisk herself magically away from it.

She could picture the tentacle now, pounding the surface of the rock in frustration. She would hate to be woken up after centuries of inactivity to chase after prey that just managed to slip through her fingers. Or her tentacles.

"What's that?" Sarah demanded. "Did you scrape it on a piece of coral? Some of those are tipped with poison. We will need to clean it and treat it."

"It wasn't coral. It was just…" Reg trailed off. There really wasn't any way to minimize it and pretend that it had been nothing of concern. "Well, it was some guardian of the deep with tentacles and it reached me just before I got out of there. I don't know; I don't think it was bad. It barely touched me."

"Oh, my goodness." Sarah shook her head. "Who knows what kind of substance it might have on its tentacles? I will need to do a cleansing ritual… and maybe a poultice… it wouldn't hurt for you to ask your… you know…"

"Theodore?"

Sarah looked away, shaking her head. "Yes, Theodore. Perhaps he will have some knowledge of it."

"He did… I'll ask him if there is some accepted treatment. In a few minutes, when I've managed to settle my heart down."

Reg looked around and realized she hadn't brought Theodore back with her. But that was okay. He would just disappear once she was gone, and she could reconstitute him when she needed him. The guardian of the deep couldn't do anything to harm the alchemical creation.

"What happened?" Sarah asked. "You were successful, but I was worried about you diving into this without a solid plan."

"It went… it mostly went just fine. It was a lot easier for me to do as… you know… part siren, than it would have been for any human to do. I'm still not sure how Corvin and Gideon set it up, since I don't see how a person could get in there without dive gear, but the entrance was too narrow for anyone wearing dive gear and too long to get in without it."

"He probably has some sort of back door. Another way to get in that is less obvious."

"They must have had a way to check on the relic to ensure it was still safe. They couldn't have just left it there for centuries without checking on it."

"No," Sarah nodded, "I'm inclined to agree."

Reg rubbed her leg. "I managed to get the vial from the Oceanids, but they weren't happy, I'll tell you that. And then they awoke this… whatever it was, this guardian from the deep, and it nearly got me before I managed to transport out of there."

"You were very lucky."

It wasn't just luck. Reg had used her skills, both her physical nature and her gifts and logic, and the research she had done with Theodore to get her through it.

Reg would give her a more complete description of what had happened later. When they were sitting in the kitchen with a cup of tea and a plate of cookies.

Reg ran her fingers through her red box braids, which were still dripping down her back. She was safe. Everything was fine.

She heard the car door open and looked up to see Davyn standing there, one leg out of the car and one leg still inside.

"Is it safe to come over?" he called out.

Reg evaluated herself. She was exhausted and still recovering from the incident in the cave. She wasn't in the water and, although she was still dripping wet, she was not experiencing the sharpening of senses that occurred when her siren nature was triggered. More-over, she didn't consider pulling Davyn into the ocean as she looked at him. That was a good sign.

"Yes, I think it's okay," she agreed. "Just… come slowly so I can warn you if you're in any danger."

Davyn nodded. He left the car door open and approached slowly, his hands raised slightly as if she were holding a gun on him. The wind shifted, and Reg waited, listening to her body and seeing whether the wind would bring her the scent of Davyn's blood.

But everything seemed to be normal. Reg could sit there and talk to Davyn without worrying about what she might do to him.

"What happened?" Davyn asked, bending over slightly to address Reg. "Are you okay?"

"Yeah. Everything is fine. It was just… a little bit more arduous than I figured. Corvin said what to expect, but he neglected to mention that the Oceanids might be able to wake up something sleeping in the depths of the ocean."

"Maybe he didn't know," Sarah said. "I think he would have told you if he knew."

"Yeah, maybe," Reg agreed. "I knew he wasn't telling me every-thing, but I thought he told me the dangers. It could have been the end of the line for me."

Davyn took a knee beside Reg. "I think you're right. Corvin thinks a lot of you and I don't think he would have sent you into anything where he thought you might be killed because of some-thing that he failed to tell you."

Reg hoped not. But then, Corvin hadn't sent her to get the water elemental. He had not suggested that it would be a good idea. He knew that she would try it anyway and, as Davyn had said, she didn't think he would allow her to go into it completely uninformed about such a significant risk.

"Reg was injured," Sarah pointed out, indicating the small, raised welt on Reg's leg. "I think we'd better treat this as soon as possible. We don't want to take any chances."

Reg rolled her eyes. "It isn't anything. It hardly hurts at all. It just barely touched me." She studied it closely. "Maybe just some aloe or antibiotic cream and a bandage. It really isn't bad."

Davyn looked at the injury, moving his face closer to get a better look at it. He glanced back and forth at Sarah and Reg before pulling a pair of glasses out of his pocket. He put them on and again leaned closer.

"Seriously?" Reg said. "You're embarrassed about needing glasses?"

"I don't need them for everything," Davyn dismissed. "Just close-up work. I want to get a better look at that welt. What exactly caused it?"

"I don't know exactly what it was. Some kind of leviathan of the deep. A sea monster that had been dormant for years, but the Oceanids woke it up. I didn't get a very good look at it because it was under the water. But it was big. Very big. And it had tentacles and was covered with seaweed. It reached out of the water and grabbed—and tried to grab me. It just barely touched me before I managed to transport."

"Well, that's leaving it until the last minute. Why didn't you transport as soon as you had the Tears?"

"I was sort of busy getting away from the Oceanids. I forgot that I could, and then forgot that I couldn't do it while I was using a psychic shield, or forgot that I was using the psychic shield, and I couldn't transport until I let it go. So..." Reg shrugged. "I took a few extra minutes."

Davyn nodded. "It must have all happened very quickly," he allowed. "Sometimes it's hard to know what to do when things are moving so fast. We forget all the things we had been trained to do."

"I didn't forget everything. But I wasn't expecting that... thing."

"Is this it?" Davyn asked, looking at the sapphire vial. "This is the water elemental?"

Reg held it up so he could better see the swirling seawater inside. "Bound in the Tears of Poseidon."

Davyn stared in fascination. "I never thought to see such a thing myself. We talk about these things as if we know all about them, but what we really know about elementals and similar beings wouldn't fill a teaspoon. Or..." he nodded to the vial. "A small vial of seawater."

They were all silent, pondering this fact for a few seconds.

"What do you think?" Sarah fussed, nodding toward the welt and addressing herself to Davyn. "This is very worrisome. So many things in the ocean have poisons and stingers and such. It doesn't look bad now, but who knows what could happen if we let it go without treating it?"

"Aloe is a good idea," Davyn said, "like Reg suggested. It has protective powers and will accelerate healing. You might also try a poultice to draw out any toxins. But it is hard to know exactly how to treat it without knowing more about the creature that caused it."

"We should talk to Corvin," Sarah said reluctantly. "He obviously knows much about the lore of the Oceanids and may have come across this creature in his studies."

"I really don't think it is anything to be worried about," Reg assured them. "It doesn't hurt that much. It's just like poison ivy or something. Kind of stings and itches a little."

Davyn nodded. "We definitely need to find out anything we can about this creature and the injuries it can cause."

Reg felt like she was talking to a wall. The more she told them it was nothing, the more concerned they seemed to be.

But it wouldn't hurt to talk to Corvin. He would let them know that it wasn't anything. She could see whether he was feeling any better, over his irritability of the day before. If there were something more that she could do for him, she would.

And it meant she would have a break before they had to go on to the next relic. The air relic. She didn't know what to do about the Zephyr Pearl, suspended in the Cyclone Tower. What was a Cyclone Tower? Was it a tower used to create cyclones? To hide from them? Observe them? Or was it just called that because of the high winds surrounding it? She'd never heard of it before and didn't know if that was because it was a sacred place or just really obscure.

Maybe it was one of those things that she should know about, but hadn't because of the way she had been neglected and moved around during her childhood. She sometimes found that with children's stories like the Pied Piper of Hamelin or Three Billy Goats Gruff, or sometimes with other things that she just hadn't had any experience with, like the fact that platypuses were real animals and not some creature from mythology.

"Okay," she said with a sigh. "Let's go see Corvin."

CHAPTER THIRTY-THREE

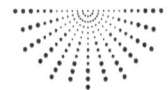

*R*eg pulled on her wraparound skirt, tied it in place, and wrapped the towel around her shoulders so that water from her braids wouldn't keep running down her back. With the skirt on, the welt on her leg was out of sight, and she could pretend that it didn't exist—other than for the stinging and itching.

"We should stop for something to eat," Sarah suggested, looking at her watch. "I'm sure Reg has probably burned through all of her calories from breakfast."

Reg was feeling a little nauseated and shaky, but she supposed that could have been due to low blood sugar. She didn't feel like eating but, sometimes, she found she needed to eat in order to feel better, even though she didn't feel like it at the time. Sarah stopped at a drive-thru for burgers and distributed them to everyone. Reg nibbled at hers but didn't find it appetizing. She had only eaten a bite or two by the time they got to Corvin's house.

Sarah led the way, a woman on a mission. She rang the doorbell with purpose, and looked irritated when Corvin didn't answer immediately.

Reg would normally have reached out to him psychically but, since the werewolf curse, that wasn't an option anymore. She didn't want to cause him pain. She knocked hard on the door when repeated presses of the bell did not bring him to the door.

"Maybe he is out," she suggested.

Davyn looked around. He walked over to the garage and peered in the window. "His cars are still in the garage."

"He might be driving something else," Sarah said, "Or be out for a walk. Maybe he decided after yesterday that he needed to do more than just sit around at home all day. So he went out for an early afternoon constitutional."

That did not sound the least bit like the Corvin Reg knew. She reached out her senses tentatively. She still didn't want to do anything that might trigger Corvin to use his powers, but she was getting concerned. Maybe he just didn't want to let them in, but it could be something worse. Maybe there had been another werewolf attack. Or maybe the injury and curse he had been afflicted with in the werewolf attack had worsened. They thought it was healing and all he was left with was the curse that would give him pain if he tried to use his powers. But they could be wrong. They had been wrong about other things.

She could feel Corvin's presence nearby. So he was still at home. Was he thinking about leaving? Going somewhere without talking to them? Maybe he had decided that he had worn out his welcome in Black Sands and it was time for him to move on. Reg had wondered more than once why he had not moved on to better hunting grounds. There had to be better places for him to live than Black Sands, where he was known by the general populace and there were very few with magical powers whom he could draw into his net.

She reached out to touch Corvin's consciousness lightly. He was aware that they were there. But he did not make any move to answer the door.

"We need your help," Reg told him firmly, no longer trying to avoid triggering his psychic powers. "I am injured."

And then, for an instant, she could feel his pain knifing through her, so sudden and so strong that she fell against the door, and both Davyn and Sarah had to grab her to keep her on her feet.

"Whoa. Take it easy, Reg," Davyn told her soothingly.

"We need to take her inside," Sarah told him briskly. "Let's get that door open."

Davyn supported Reg on one side, though she tried to take her weight on her own feet again. She was still a little wobbly. "Let's get it open?" he repeated. "How do you propose to do that?"

Sarah put her hand on the doorknob and said a few words aloud that Reg did not understand. Then, there was a click as she turned the handle. They shuffled in together, supporting Reg awkwardly.

"He's in here," Reg murmured. "I'm okay. Let go. We need to find him."

They all looked around. Reg had half expected to find Corvin at the door. He knew they were there, even if he didn't want to let them in. Most people would at least go to the door to look out the peephole and listen for any snatches of conversation as they stood on the front step discussing developments. But he wasn't. He wasn't within sight of the door.

Davyn and Sarah let go of Reg experimentally, both looking concerned.

"It wasn't my pain," Reg told them. "It was his. When I reached out to him. But we need to find him because I think something is wrong."

They agreed, and all walked together rather than going in different directions. They were in a powerful warlock's home uninvited; it wouldn't be outside the realm of possibility for there to be a number of magical booby traps or wards set to protect him from the ill-intentioned. He had been attacked in his home once before. If he hadn't put any defenses in place before, he surely had now.

"We come in peace," Sarah said aloud, looking around. "We have come seeking help and medical treatment."

There was no response. But likewise, no booby traps. No curses flung at them from unexpected directions. No creatures roused from the deep.

Reg walked into the kitchen and was immediately overcome by a sense of deja vu. This was where Corvin had been the last time she had come into the house uninvited. He had been knocked out, and the gas had been turned on in an attempt to fill the house with gas and cause an explosion. But this time, he wasn't lying there on the floor. Reg sniffed the air, but there was no scent of natural gas. But there was something else—a whiff of sulfur? Something was wrong. Something was out of place.

Sarah looked around, shaking her head. She obviously felt the same thing. Something was going on that they didn't understand.

"What do you think it is?" Reg asked softly.

Sarah put her finger to her lips to silence Reg and again shook her head. After making sure that Corvin wasn't in the living room or kitchen, Reg led the searchers to Corvin's study.

It was filled with dark, heavy furniture. A very traditional, masculine library or study. Bookcases full of books from the floor to the ceiling on each wall of the room. A decently sized double window on one side of the room had heavy velvet curtains pulled across it to block out all sunlight and prevent anyone seeing in from the outside.

At first, it appeared that the study was empty and that Corvin had commissioned a life-sized statue of himself. But as soon as Reg processed the thought, she knew it was not true.

Corvin himself had been turned to stone.

"No," Sarah whispered, staring at him.

Davyn was the first to approach the statue. He touched it gently, as if he were afraid he might still be able to feel the warmth of his skin or the pulse in his throat. But of course, he couldn't. Corvin was stone, just like Gideon and the others who had been petrified.

And, like with the others, Reg could still feel him there. Still feel his consciousness struggling to comprehend what had happened to him, to somehow communicate with the outside world.

Only the curse was still active, and if Reg tried to contact him, it just triggered the pain from the werewolf curse. Wasn't there anything they could do about that? Reg resolved to talk to

Theodore later about the curse and see whether the homunculus had any suggestions of what to do to help them.

"How did they get here?" Reg asked. "How did they know where to find him?"

Sarah shook her head. "The elementals do not have brains; they do not have logic. They just act and react. If the elementals were here… it was only because they are free, and perhaps recognized Corvin's energy. I would imagine that after being imprisoned for several centuries, they have a pretty good recollection of who put them there and reacted when they happened to come across him."

"Couldn't he keep them out? Why didn't he set wards to make sure that they couldn't enter his house?"

"Wards only work against those with will," Davyn explained slowly. "Something like an elemental, which is only… shade or specter… has no will of its own and just flows around like water until it finds its level."

"And it found its way here. Purely by happenstance," Reg said, aware of the sarcastic edge in her tone. She couldn't control it.

Davyn nodded. "It isn't such a big world," he told Reg. "I think… they were pretty much fated to find each other, and to find the others who had imprisoned them."

"And who are the others? How many other people are going to be petrified? Isn't there any way to stop them other than to bind them like Corvin did?"

"There are other ways," Sarah insisted. "That was what I tried to tell Corvin. We could have helped him to find another way."

But Corvin had been determined to do things his way. He and Gideon and whoever else had banded together with them had decided that binding them was the only way to be really sure of stopping the elementals from causing any more destruction. Everyone else, they said, was just kidding themselves if they thought there was another way.

Maybe they had been right.

"What do we do now?" Reg demanded. "How do we get him unpetrified?"

"We will continue to work on that," Davyn said, sounding

uncomfortable. "But the first thing we must do is retrieve the last remaining elemental. To ensure it cannot get free and cause even more destruction. Or that... somehow we shape things so that... it isn't a threat."

"If it doesn't have a will, how do you negotiate with it?"

"You'll see," Sarah told her. "We'll figure it out one way or another. The first thing we need to do is not to get the air elemental. It is to deal with your injury."

CHAPTER THIRTY-FOUR

*I*t really isn't bothering me," Reg told Sarah. "It just itches and stings a little. I don't think it is anything to worry about."

She could feel Corvin's concern as well as Sarah's and Davyn's. She didn't know what he could see or hear in his petrified state but, if nothing else, he was picking up on her thoughts and Sarah's and Davyn's feelings of concern. He still had his powers even in this petrified state. Or some of them, anyway. Just as Reg had used the psychic shield against the Oceanids, she could block herself from feeling Corvin's pain, as long as she didn't let it take her off guard.

"It's okay," she told him aloud. "I'm fine. Everybody is fine. We have the water elemental, and we just need to get the air elemental now. Then, we'll be able to reverse the petrifaction. You don't have to worry."

Davyn and Sarah both looked at her with disapproval. They each had doubts about whether they could figure out how to reverse the spell and didn't think that she should make promises to Corvin that she couldn't keep. But Reg was determined to do it. She would find out how to reverse it and save Corvin, Gideon, the people in the woods, and anyone else who had been petrified by the earth elemental that they didn't know about yet.

"We will figure it out," Reg repeated firmly.

She hoped.

"You know what? Theodore could help," Reg said, looking around the study. As well as Corvin's vast library of books on the shelves, she saw filing cabinets that were probably filled with his own research and notes, maybe copies of lectures that he taught, maybe even Corvin's records of what had happened hundreds of years ago when he and Gideon had bound the elementals.

It had been complex and he had been proud of what they had done, so he must have written it down. He wouldn't want to forget any detail of what he had done. Reg knew how easy it was to forget a new recipe or something she had figured out if she didn't make some kind of record of it. The trouble was that she hated writing anything down and rarely did.

She was the queen of forgetting things and having to relearn the same lessons over and over again. Maybe with the advancements in technology, she would one day be able to record everything she knew and retrieve it again when she needed it. The technology was almost there with voice memos and AI technology. One day, she would be able to just tell her phone everything she wanted to remember, and then ask it later, and it would not only regurgitate what she had recorded, but analyze and apply it.

Or maybe she already had what she needed. She had Theodore, after all. She could talk to him and ask him questions whenever she wanted to. She couldn't exactly do that discreetly, though. People might notice if she summoned Theodore into a restaurant to ask him questions. It was easier to pull out her phone and ask it questions quietly without attracting people's attention. Because everyone else was talking to their phones.

There was a large potted plant near where Reg stood. It nicely complemented the stone statue beside it. Reg grabbed a handful of soil and tossed it in front of her.

"From soil and stone, by magic spin,
    Theodore reform, our work begin."

The dirt formed a dancing dust devil that eventually resolved into the familiar childlike face with flat, black eyes.

Sarah shook her head. "Isn't there a way you could summon him without having to throw dirt around?"

While it was a petty criticism, Reg had already been asking herself the same thing. What if she hadn't been able to summon him in the cave because she couldn't scrape together enough sand from the crevices of the rock floor? What if there hadn't been a ficus in Corvin's study? What if she was somewhere there just wasn't any dirt lying around?

"I don't know," she admitted. "I'll have to ask him. Maybe the incantation would be enough now that I've been using him for a while. I don't know if I need the soil or if it was just helpful initially."

Theodore looked around at all of them. He hadn't been in Corvin's house before and looked about in interest.

"Is this your house?" he asked Reg.

"No. Corvin's." Reg motioned to the stone statue.

"Oh." The homunculus took in the warlock's appearance and nodded wisely.

"Theodore, you see all the books and records here?"

He nodded. Of course he could see everything there.

"You read all Sma's books and scrolls and added them to your knowledge. Can you read all of Corvin's books, too?"

Theodore nodded again. "All you see becomes part of me."

Reg rolled her eyes. She had told him multiple times that he didn't need to always speak in verse and rhyme, but he still slipped into it regularly. Reg guessed that was just the way that homunculi were supposed to speak. Or how Sma had designed him. Reg hadn't exactly been a part of his initial programming.

"I want you to do that, then. We have to get the Zephyr Pearl. Maybe you could give me a little bit of advice on that. And then… there are other questions we will have. We will need to reverse the petrifaction spell on Corvin and the others."

Theodore blinked and clicked and tilted his head. "Why?"

"We need to return them to the way they were. Before they were cursed."

"But he is dangerous."

Reg looked at Sarah and Davyn. She couldn't exactly argue the point. They all knew Corvin was dangerous, especially to Reg and those like her.

"I know, but... some things in life are dangerous. You can't eliminate all of them. And we can't just let everybody who is petrified stay in that state. It isn't right to take away people's freedom of movement or choice."

Theodore clicked a few times, thinking about this.

"The more immediate question," Sarah spoke up, "is what to do about Reg's injury."

Theodore looked at Reg, his head moving slightly as he looked her over. Reg lifted her skirt to show him the welt on the back of her leg.

"It really isn't anything. It's just that the creature from the deep touched me just before I managed to transport. He had a stinger on his tentacle or some kind of substance like poison ivy. I don't think it is anything to worry about, but Sarah and Davyn are concerned."

Theodore stared at the welt on Reg's leg, not moving.

"Do you know what to put on it?" Reg pressed. "Aloe or some kind of poultice?"

"Aloe or some kind of poultice," Theodore repeated. "Aloe speeds healing and is a protective herb. It also relieves pain and itching from poison ivy and other irritants. There is no need to be concerned about poison ivy; it is not life-threatening unless you are allergic to it."

Reg nodded her agreement. "Exactly," she agreed, nodding at Sarah. "You see? Just like I said. What other herbs can be used for healing? I'm sure Corvin has good stores of herbs, so we can whip something up and then get on with retrieving the air elemental."

Theodore clicked and twitched, calculating his answer. He raised one hand to command their attention.

Comfrey's strength to soul restore,
Calendula blooms soothe and more,

Echinacea's guardian will shield
wounds and toxins to it yield.

"Comfrey, calendula, and echinacea," Sarah murmured. "I am sure Corvin will have those in his stores. Give me a few minutes in his kitchen, and I will prepare a poultice to be applied. Or should I make a tea?" she wondered aloud.

"No, no," Reg protested immediately. She did not need to deal with one of Sarah's foul-tasting teas on top of everything else. If she were going to be in her best form for the trip to the Cyclone Tower, she did not want to be nauseated or in a bad mood from drinking a wretched medicinal tea. "I think the poultice will be the best. It is applied directly to the skin to be the most effective. Right, Theodore? A poultice is best."

"A poultice is best," Theodore agreed. "It is applied directly to the skin and will draw out the poison."

"See?" Reg nodded. "That would be the best."

"Okay," Sarah agreed. She left the study, heading for the kitchen.

"Dodged a bullet there," Davyn murmured.

Reg laughed.

CHAPTER THIRTY-FIVE

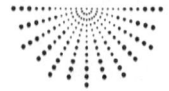

*R*eg wandered around Corvin's study as they waited for Sarah to prepare the poultice. Reg could hear her singing to herself and banging around in the kitchen, preparing the remedy for Reg's leg. It was actually burning more than she let on, so part of the reason for walking around the study was that she didn't think she could sit still and put up with it. It was a little better if she could move around and distract herself.

As a firecaster, Reg hadn't had to deal with a lot of burns, but she had been burned a couple of times when caught unprepared.

There were a lot of books in Corvin's library. Reg didn't know how long it would take Theodore to integrate them all. When she had given him the instruction to read Sma's library, she had left him alone for several days, and didn't know how long it had taken him to do it. Theodore walked to the shelf nearest him and pulled out a heavy book. He rested it on the desk and flipped swiftly through the pages. Like a computer, he seemed to take in a page at a glance and didn't need to stop and read each and every word. Or he scanned the information in and processed it later. She didn't know how it worked. She didn't need to.

There were a lot of thick, heavy tomes on the shelves. Not all of them had writing on the spine. Some of them were just leather-bound books without any indication of how old they were or what they contained. She imagined the amount of wisdom that existed in the room and what it would mean to have access to it all through Theodore. She often felt inadequate, raised by non-practitioners who were unaware of her gifts and the true magic that surrounded them. She'd gone all those years without knowing that a parallel world existed.

There were a lot of holes in her knowledge of the non-magical world, too, due to her learning disabilities, early neglect, and being moved from family to family and school to school. She always felt like she was behind everybody else. Theodore was her savior. He would fill in those gaps and tell her everything she needed to know.

Davyn was also watching Theodore, but his gaze was not one of approval.

After half an hour, Sarah returned to the study. She had a bowl of green mash, white bandages, and medical tape.

"Have a seat, Reg, and let's get this done."

Reg sat in one of Corvin's large armchairs, pulled her skirt up, and stuck her leg out. Sarah positioned a footrest so that Reg could extend her leg without having to hold it up. Reg had to turn her leg slightly to give Sarah access to the injury on the back of her calf. Sarah leaned close to peer at it.

"It is starting to blister. We are none too early getting this poultice on it. I hope it will ease the pain immediately."

Reg nodded. Sarah started to spread the mash of herbs onto the skin, her touch light. The poultice was cool and soothing, and Reg relaxed after the initial touch, no longer worried that it would cause the injury to sting even more.

Sarah recited the incantation that Theodore had provided.

Comfrey's strength to soul restore,
Calendula blooms soothe and more,
Echinacea's guardian will shield
wounds and toxins to it yield.

Theodore looked up once from the books he was scanning, looking as though he might have something to say about the ritual. But then he looked back down at his book and kept reading.

Reg waited to see if something else would happen. Maybe the welt would fade away to nothing. Or it would throb or tingle or do something else to tell her it was working.

Nothing special happened. The mixture was cool and soothing. Reg shrugged at Sarah. "That feels good. I'm sure it will be fine now."

Sarah nodded and started to wrap the bandage around Reg's leg. It seemed like a bit much. Maybe it needed a couple of Band-Aids, but not the whole swath of cloth Sarah seemed to be planning to use.

"Don't make me into a mummy," Reg laughed. "Just wind it around there once or twice and tape it down."

"We want to make sure the poultice doesn't slip. You will be active and we don't want it to cause problems."

"Well, I'd rather have it stinging a little bit than be worrying about the poultice slipping. If we're going to get the air relic, we need to be able to focus."

Sarah shook her head at Reg's foolishness but did as she'd asked and just taped down the bandage after a couple of layers. It felt slippery and a bit loose, and Reg suspected she'd end up ripping it off as soon as they started the invasion of the tower.

But maybe Sarah wouldn't notice.

Sarah put her hands on her hips, surveying the bandaged limb. "Well, that will have to do. I suppose we should be getting on our way to the Cyclone Tower."

Reg's stomach tightened. She had no idea what they would be facing there. More guardians, in the air this time. She had been able to escape the Oceanids because they could not leave the water. She would not be able to escape the Sylph guardians the same way. She hoped that Sarah had learned everything there was to know about the weaknesses of the sylphs.

Sarah had not said anything about them within Reg's hearing. Hopefully, she and Davyn had discussed it. Maybe while Reg had been navigating the underwater cavern or while they'd been waiting for her to wake up that morning. It seemed like a long time ago now.

CHAPTER THIRTY-SIX

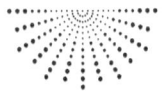

"here exactly is the tower?" Reg asked as they piled back into the car.

Everything was close to Black Sands, so she knew it would not be far, but she had never heard anything about the sacred site of the Cyclone Tower in the time she had been there.

"It is inland a little stretch," Sarah offered. "They would not want it too close to the coast where it might be vulnerable to storms."

Reg would have thought that a building with a name like Cyclone Tower would be built to withstand the strong winds Corvin had mentioned and whatever stormy weather the coast could throw at it. Why name it the Cyclone Tower if it was nowhere near the path of the storms that blew in off the ocean?

"Is it a ruin?" she asked. "Has it been there a long time?"

"Well, since the time that Corvin and Gideon imprisoned the last of the elementals," Sarah said with a shrug. "From what I can glean, it took them some time to catch and bind each of the elementals and to put into place the protections and guardians for each."

"It was a precursor to the modern technology," Davyn contributed. "Built as a prototype long before Finch's design."

Reg shook her head. "What?"

Sarah laughed. "You don't know anything about the Cyclone Tower?"

"No... I thought maybe it was like... I don't know... a watch-tower to look out for approaching storms before we had all the satellite technology and everything. Or maybe like Rapunzel's tower, to protect someone or something from the rest of the world."

"Well, those are good guesses," Sarah said, "but no."

Reg waited for an explanation about what she should know about the Cyclone Tower, but Sarah did not provide any details.

"You should probably just wait until you see it," Davyn advised. "I wouldn't want it to be a disappointment."

"But it is magical," Reg suggested. "Corvin and Gideon wouldn't have chosen it as the site for the Zephyr Pearl to be safe-guarded otherwise, would they?"

Sarah and Davyn exchanged a look and didn't answer directly.

"It won't take us long to get there," Sarah told her. "For now... why don't you close your eyes for a few minutes and rest? You've already tired yourself out retrieving the Tears of Poseidon, and Davyn and I are fresh. You might as well grab whatever shut-eye you can."

Reg sighed. She sat back and delved into her shoulder bag for a snack. She watched out the window while she nibbled on an energy bar. She hoped it lived up to its name, because she wasn't sure what good she would be against the Cyclone Tower and air spirits.

* * *

Davyn and Sarah talked in quiet undertones intended to avoid disturbing Reg while she rested. They didn't seem to have anything to say about the dangers they would be facing, but talked about some of the other things going on in their community. Event plan-ning and milestones. It was hard to believe they would want to discuss such unimportant issues.

"Reg?"

Reg opened her eyes and looked around, realizing that she had, in fact, drifted off while she'd been resting her eyes. Part of the power bar she had been eating was melted into the upholstery beside her. Reg tried to pick up what was left of it and rub the chocolate out of the fuzzy fabric of the seat without much success.

"What?"

"We're approaching it now. You'll be able to see it in the distance as we get up this hill."

Reg sat forward in her seat, her eyes fixed on the hill. She watched the horizon for any sign of the Cyclone Tower with some explanation of what exactly it was and why Corvin had chosen it.

As they reached the top of the hill, she saw a large metallic tower. It looked like something out of a steampunk nightmare, a dull brass structure with a confusing jumble of pipes or ducts all leading upward.

She couldn't see much detail at first but, as they got closer, she could see a lookout tower or light enclosure like on a lighthouse up at the top. A bubble that obviously enclosed the critical functions of the tower, whatever they were.

"That's it? What exactly is it? What does it do?"

"It uses cyclonic actions to sort particulates," Sarah told her.

"What?"

"It creates a cyclone inside. Like… one of those fancy vacuum cleaners. It uses the cyclone to sort and filter different sizes of… dust and sand. The new ones are used for purifying natural gas. But this one isn't that advanced. This was pretty cutting edge for its time, way ahead of its time."

"What does that have to do with the Pearl? I thought… that it was built to safeguard the air relic."

"The tower uses the zephyric resonance of the Pearl to power the winds used to create this cyclonic effect that has… industrial applications." Sarah shrugged. "I don't understand why they are sorting these particles or what they are used for when they hit the market. People have uses for everything, I suppose."

"I guess so," Reg agreed as they approached the tower. They reached an outer perimeter fence with red warning signs on it.

No trespassing

Danger

Zephyric resonance in use, safety protocols must be followed

All employees must wear protective gear

Reg felt her eyes widening. She had been worried about sylphs and storms. She hadn't expected to be faced with new technologies and energy that she'd never heard of before.

"Is this safe? I didn't bring any… protective gear."

"Of course," Sarah assured her, "Would I have brought you here if you were going to be exposed to radiation or something? Zephyric resonance is perfectly safe."

"Then why all the signs?"

"To scare off trespassers."

"Oh. Well, they are doing a good job."

"This facility has been in operation for hundreds of years and I am unaware of any accidents affecting either employees or trespassers. It's just a bluff. Cheaper than guard dogs."

"Guard dogs…" Reg looked around, expecting to see or hear dogs on chains. She had previously had run-ins with a few guard dogs and she did not want to encounter any more. Especially after the guardian of the deep. That was enough for one day.

"There aren't any guard dogs," Sarah repeated. "It is perfectly safe. We are prepared to go in, retrieve the Pearl, and leave again without anyone the wiser."

"How are you going to take the Pearl if that is what powers the tower? Don't you think they'll notice that?"

"Don't you worry, Reg. It is powered down for maintenance every Thursday afternoon. So we're right on time."

Reg wasn't so sure. Sarah seemed awfully sure of herself for someone who hadn't known anything about how to get the Pearl just a day earlier.

Maybe that was the same way Sarah had felt about Reg diving into the ocean to retrieve the Tears of Poseidon. That she couldn't possibly know everything she needed to or have a plan that would lead to success.

And look how that had turned out.

Reg had been successful, but she had certainly not gotten out without a hitch. She had nearly been caught by the creature from the deep. And even though she had escaped with the vial, the beast had managed to scrape the skin of her leg, which, truth be told, was throbbing again now, reminding her that they were about to enter uncharted territory without a good plan for the second time in a day. Or at least, without any kind of plan Reg had been told about. What was she supposed to do, sit in the car and wait for them to return?

"So… you have this all planned out," she said.

"Of course," Sarah assured her. "No need to worry. You've done your part; now it is up to me to do mine."

Reg looked at Davyn. Was he just along for the ride this time as well?

"I'm… providing support," he offered. "Sarah seems to have it under control."

Reg looked at the tower and shook her head. "How are you going to do this? You're just going to walk in there and take the Pearl? Is there even an elevator?" She tried to imagine Sarah being able to climb more than a couple of flights of stairs. She wouldn't be able to breathe after three. Reg loved the older witch, but she wasn't in the best shape.

Not that Reg would do much better herself, but Sarah was several centuries older than she was.

Davyn stopped the car in an employee parking lot and pulled into one of the "reserved" spots. There didn't seem to be many other people around, to judge by the emptiness of the parking lot.

Because the tower was being shut down for maintenance, of course.

"I don't need an elevator," Sarah told Reg, and opened the door.

Reg looked at Davyn to see if he were as doubtful about this course of action as she was. Sarah put on a pair of sleek wraparound sunglasses that were probably more expensive than anything Reg owned. She walked around to the back of the car. Davyn reached down and hit the trunk release button.

Reg couldn't see what Sarah was getting out of the trunk.

"Please tell me she isn't flying on a broomstick," Reg told Davyn.

He looked back at her, his expression blank. "A broomstick? Witches don't ride broomsticks, Reg."

Reg giggled to herself. "There have been so many things I have discovered over the last couple of years. Things that I thought couldn't possibly be true, and then they were..."

Davyn nodded his understanding. Sarah set something down, then stepped onto it and floated over to Reg's window. Reg stuck her head out the window and looked down. Sarah was standing on top of what appeared to be a large Roomba self-propelled vacuum. It hovered over the ground, a cloud of dust disrupted beneath it. Multicolored lights blinked on the front, and a dot grid of LEDs formed a status screen on the top. Sarah had appliquéd some non-slip stickers on it to give her some grip. She held a remote control in one hand.

"Broomsticks are so last-century, Reg," Sarah told her. "I am of the school of thought that we need to keep up with technological advancements. Some witches will hide in the woods and avoid using a phone or TV or any other modern conveniences, but I like my indoor plumbing, Amazon Prime delivery, and everything you can get online. Do you know I got these on Etsy?" Sarah indicated the non-slip stickers with the toe of one shoe. They were in the shape of bird silhouettes.

Reg shook her head in amazement.

"You just relax here," Sarah told Reg. "I'll be back in a few minutes." She looked at Davyn. "You ready?"

Davyn held up a walkie-talkie. Sarah had a matching one in her other hand. "You can never get a cell signal out here," she told Reg.

Davyn got out of the car.

"Do you have a Roomba too?" Reg demanded.

Or did only witches fly and not warlocks? Maybe warlocks preferred hoverboards or Segways. Or maybe he preferred to fly in the comfort of a car, like Reg had once seen in an old Disney movie. Reg touched the handle on the side door of the car, wondering if it were capable of flight. Was there a little special something under the hood, just in case?

"No Roomba for me," Davyn admitted. "Honestly, I'm a little afraid of heights. I'm hoping that I can provide ground support only. A little reconnaissance, another eye on what's going on, maybe a well-directed spell or two as she attempts to get in and out."

He had flown with dragon Reg without any complaints about the height. If he was afraid of heights, Reg was extra proud of him.

Sarah clicked the remote and started to rise.

"Do you really think she can just fly up there and take the Pearl?" Reg asked Davyn.

"I don't think it will be any easier than what you did. Maybe significantly harder or more dangerous. But that's why I'm here for support. And you're here too, so there are three of us."

"And how many of them?" Reg looked up toward the top of the tower.

Davyn looked around the parking lot. "Not too many. Since today is the day that they take it offline for maintenance, we are hoping there will only be a skeleton crew and little resistance."

Reg watched Sarah start to rise up the side of the Cyclone Tower. She manipulated the remote control without looking at it. She apparently flew on the thing often enough to be familiar with the controls. At least it wasn't something she had bought just for the occasion and was hoping would be helpful.

A few times, the craft suddenly shifted direction, blown around by the winds surrounding the tower.

But somehow, Reg doubted that Sarah would be able to just fly to the top of the tower and steal the Pearl. As Davyn had suggested, it would be at least as hard to get as the Tears of Poseidon. Corvin said each one was harder to get than the last, so the Pearl should be the hardest of all. At least there were two of them there to help, though Reg didn't feel like she would be much good, since she hadn't even been briefed on what Sarah was planning to do.

She and Davyn watched as Sarah rose to the top of the tower without setting off any alarms or being challenged. Sarah then worked her way around the top until she came to some sort of access panel or window. They couldn't see what she was doing, but she hovered there, performing whatever spell would dissolve the glass, or maybe cutting a witch-sized hole with a diamond glass cutter.

Suddenly, sirens started to blare. Reg tensed immediately. She glanced at Davyn. He was looking up, but didn't offer Sarah any advice or ask her what was going on. Maybe this had been expected.

There was a mechanical noise that originated within the tower. It sounded like huge gears turning to lower a drawbridge, very slowly and methodically, perhaps one person operating a crank.

Then, there was an earsplitting cry, and a stream of guards began to fly out of a large window or gate on the far side of the tower.

Reg stood there, her mouth hanging open as the guardian spirits took to the sky.

She had expected them to be ethereal, composed of insubstantial matter, just enough to take form. But they had armored breastplates to shield them from attack, and were very large and solid-looking. She hadn't known whether to expect actual wings, or if they would just float around and aim spells at Sarah. She hadn't expected them to be actual warriors with spears and magic. Some of them had arrows.

Reg's stomach twisted with anxiety. She had imagined that the Sylphs would be in beautiful human shapes, female probably, angels with long wings like she had seen in books.

But instead, they were a shape that had haunted her nightmares for many years.

Ever since she had seen a showing of the old *Wizard of Oz* movie and had seen the wicked witch unleash flying monkeys on the unsuspecting Dorothy.

CHAPTER THIRTY-SEVEN

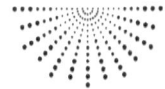

*D*avyn swore.

"Did you know about this?" Reg demanded. They might have at least warned her. She thought that winged monkeys warranted at least a heads-up.

Davyn nodded. He was holding the walkie-talkie up to his face, but he didn't say anything to Sarah, and she hadn't transmitted anything to him yet.

"We knew the tower was protected," Davyn said.

"By flying monkeys?"

"Well... by some kind of Sylph guardians. I hadn't quite expected this."

Reg was glad she wasn't the only one. Davyn seemed a little concerned with the threat, but he didn't immediately jump into action, pulling a rocket launcher out of the trunk. Maybe the situation was not as bad as she feared.

"Do we have anything to combat them?" Reg asked. They seemed to be armed with spears and close-combat weaponry. She couldn't shake the images from her mind of the winged monkeys in The Wizard of Oz snatching up Dorothy and her companions and flying away with them. Her heart was thumping hard and fast. So far, the Sylphs did not appear to have noticed their presence, only

Sarah's breach of the tower, but it was only a matter of time before they realized she wasn't alone.

"You and I are firecasters," Davyn told her calmly. "Fire is a natural weapon against animals and ethereal creatures."

"They don't look so ethereal to me," Reg snapped. "They're pretty solid. I thought the Sylphs would just be... like spirits. At the worst, like clouds. Not like this."

"By ethereal, I mean they rely upon the air for their power and locomotion. Like the Oceanids can only operate in the water and would die if removed from it, the same applies to ethereal creatures, those that can only survive in the air."

"They are susceptible to fire."

"To the other three elements. Earth, water, and fire. They wouldn't be able to survive in any of those three environments."

Reg nodded, calming a little. She knew how to use her fire. It wouldn't even be the first time this week. She had fought the fire elemental and the Oceanids. It couldn't be much harder to fight the monkeys with fire than it had been to fight fire with fire or light her flame underwater. The monkeys would not want to get close to the flames. She and Davyn could surround Sarah with flames, and she would be fully protected.

"Okay, yes," she agreed, nodding. "That makes sense."

"Fire burns up the oxygen in the air. The sylphs need the oxygen to breathe and fly."

"Great." Reg was calming now that she knew the plan. She could handle this. Even though she had retrieved the water relic earlier in the day, she still had enough energy for a little fire power.

The monkeys were flying close to Sarah, harassing her, but none of them had speared her or were close enough to use knives or other small weaponry. Hand-to-hand combat would not be easy up in the air. The monkeys had probably trained that way, but not Sarah.

As the monkeys dove and moved in close to Sarah, she performed several complicated maneuvers to escape them without any apparent effort.

"Looking good, Sarah," Davyn said on his walkie. "We're awaiting any instructions."

"The vacuum has built-in evasive tactics," Sarah told them, sounding calm and unconcerned about the attack by the flying monkeys. "You just input the destination or goal, and the vacuum uses advanced algorithms to plot the best course."

Reg had heard rave reviews from robot vacuum users about how well they worked, independently navigating around hazards and keeping floors swept clean. But she'd also heard some tales of disaster when things went wrong, and the machine unwittingly spread filth around the house, got tangled up in a sleeping owner's hair, or tripped people up. They weren't foolproof by any means.

Sarah had probably fortified the machine's algorithms with some spells of her own to ensure that it wouldn't accidentally dump her off or get distracted by a bird or dust ball, but Reg didn't completely trust the technology. There was using cutting-edge technology, and then there was being too close to the edge.

As if the vacuum knew what Reg was thinking, Sarah's craft experienced a sudden drop in altitude. Sarah didn't have the button pressed on her walkie-talkie, but Reg still heard the little scream she gave as the machine plummeted toward the ground and then recovered.

"Sarah, you okay?" Davyn asked.

"Just got caught in a gust of wind," Sarah explained. "It's pretty windy up here."

"We knew it would be."

"Yes, and I thought I had compensated enough for that, but I didn't have a long time to prepare. I didn't have time to test it in a wind tunnel."

Reg gazed up at Sarah. She again traveled up toward the top of the tower. Of course, no method of flight was perfect, and wind gusts could take any small craft down. Maybe Sarah should have considered another method of scaling the tower to access the Zephyr Pearl. A grappling hook, maybe.

"Is she going to be okay?"

Davyn nodded. "Sarah is an experienced flyer. I'm sure she'll be fine. She can override the vacuum's algorithms and control it herself, just like with the old technology."

At Reg's look, he shrugged.

"Broomsticks."

Reg had thought Davyn would think her silly to believe that witches could fly on broomsticks as they did in the old stories, but he didn't mean that they never had; he just meant that it was out of vogue, and they had other ways to fly now.

Maybe Sarah shouldn't have been so quick to adopt the new technology.

The monkeys seemed to be adapting to the movements of the flying machine. They were getting closer to Sarah, pointing their spears and shouting and making threats. Sara seemed unconcerned. She ignored them and focused on returning to the top of the tower and the panel she had removed. Reg tried to construct a psychic shield around Sarah to keep her safe, but she was too far away and Reg's energy was already depleted. She should have eaten more when she'd had the opportunity.

"There is water and food in the cooler," Davyn said, not looking away from Sarah but motioning toward the car and the soft-sided zip-up cooler on the backseat.

Reg reached into the car and pulled it out. She cracked a water bottle and took a swig, handing one to Davyn as well. She had a feeling their firecasting services were, in fact, going to be needed, and probably soon. It was crucial to avoid burning through their body's water supply without rehydrating. Most of the food in the cooler was healthy stuff. Reg grabbed a banana as she pawed through the rest, hoping to find something more appealing.

She found a couple of wrapped chocolate muffins and pulled them out. Maybe not a black forest cake like Harrison would have provided, but they would do for a quick snack and energy booster.

Sarah tinkered with something on the side of the tower. Monkeys dived at her and shrieked loud warning cries. Sarah just worked, ignoring them as if they were shrieking magpies warning of a cat's approach when the fledglings were too close to danger.

One of them jostled Sarah. It hadn't used its spear, as far as Reg could tell from her position on the ground, but it had bumped into her, and Sarah tipped slightly, having to take a step to the side to stabilize herself. The status screen on the craft flashed warnings and an alarm beeped. Sarah fired a spell that sent the monkey wheeling away with another shriek and turned back to her work.

"Davyn, I think it is time for a distraction," she told him over the walkie-talkie.

"Distraction coming up," Davyn agreed.

He grinned at Reg and, without any warm-up, opened his hands and aimed a pillar of fire into the sky. He didn't aim it toward the monkeys, but they immediately set up a hue and cry as if he had targeted them.

A number of them broke away from the group and turned their attention to Davyn, dive-bombing him and shrieking incomprehensible threats.

It was good that Reg and Davyn had become accustomed to Ember's customary opening tactic of dive-bombing them, stopping only inches from them. It made the monkeys' tactic seem rather amateurish. They didn't get nearly as close as Ember would have.

Davyn surrounded himself with a wall of fire that sent the monkeys back to a safer distance.

Reg opted for a more targeted approach. She remembered how she had lit Corvin's cloak on fire in anger before she had known she was a firecaster, and how she had rescued Zora's cubs from Channelle not long ago by burning away the straps of the leashes Channelle held them on.

She focused on the leather straps and hinges holding the monkeys' plates of armor in place. Several of them squawked and flew farther away from her, trying to hold the armor in place, but were eventually forced to abandon the ruined vestments.

They howled angry imprecations against Reg and Davyn. Reg looked up at Sarah to see how she was doing. It was hard to tell whether she was making any progress in defeating the security in place at the tower. She reached out to Sarah mentally, hoping to get a better sense of what she needed and how close she was to getting into the tower to get the Pearl.

More time.

"She needs more time," Reg advised Davyn.

He nodded. "That gives us a bit more time to play with fire," he suggested with a smile.

"Yeah." Reg focused on a couple more monkeys and stripping off their armor. They were less likely to attack if they felt vulnerable. Davyn did some showy fireplay, shooting balls of fire toward the monkeys that exploded in front of them. Not injuring them, but intended to make them startle and take their focus off the attack on the intruder. He shot eye-catching pillars of fire into the sky in various colors.

Reg glanced at him. "You're going to attract attention to the attack."

He considered this, then apparently decided she was right and toned it down a bit. They didn't need people to realize that something was happening at the Cyclone Tower and drive over to see it. Especially not the owners or human security forces. If they hadn't already been alerted by the security alarm, Reg would prefer they stay away.

Another alarm started ringing, louder than the first, and then it was abruptly cut off. Everything went silent. The monkeys were startled but did not withdraw when they realized the alarm had stopped. They were clearly not programmed or instructed to stop just because the alarm had been cleared.

Sarah rose to the top of the tower, where the power source or workings were apparently enclosed and stepped inside. She had managed to open whatever door or window she had been working on, and now she was one step closer to getting the Pearl.

The monkeys turned away from Reg and Davyn and focused on Sarah. Several of them flew into the tower after her.

"Uh-oh. I think we'd better do something," Reg advised.

Davyn tried a few fiery displays to see if he could distract them again, but it wasn't working.

Reg bent and grabbed a handful of dust. She tossed it in front of her.

"From soil and stone, by magic spin,
    Theodore reform, our work begin."

CHAPTER THIRTY-EIGHT

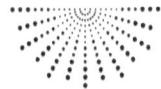

*T*he dust whirled around on the ground for a moment and then was swept away by an upward gust. Reg covered her eyes and blinked rapidly, trying to wash away the stinging grit.

She looked up at the top of the tower. Sarah was out of sight. There was no way to tell if she was okay or was engaged in hand-to-hand combat with vicious monkey fighters who were now all wound up by the fireworks display by Davyn and Reg.

"Do you think she's okay?" Reg asked. She stared at the dust swirling on the ground and didn't know whether it was still Theodore trying to form or the wind that normally blew around the Cyclone Tower. She tried the summoning again,

"From soil and stone, by magic spin,
   Theodore reform, our work begin."

It wasn't working. The dust swirled faster for a few seconds, and then it was gone again.

"Is something blocking the magic?" Reg worried aloud. "Is it blocking my powers?"

She ignited a ball of light between her hands as a test to see whether she could still perform other tasks, and the friendly ball of light flickered for a moment and then it blew out.

"Dang it." This time, Reg was sure that it was the wind. Perhaps there were unseen wind spirits as well as the winged monkeys, and they had now identified Reg as a threat that needed to be dealt with. Or perhaps it was the winds themselves that made the decision. Even the power of the air elemental trapped inside the Zephyr Pearl inside the tower. At least it wasn't like the guardian of the deep; a pterodactyl or some huge air beast swooping down to stop her where the flying monkeys had failed. The monkeys were bad enough. She didn't need a flying King Kong on top of everything else.

"She could be in trouble up there," Reg told Davyn worriedly.

He clicked the button on his walkie-talkie. "Sarah? Are you okay? Come in."

They both waited anxiously for an answer. There was no response from Sarah. Maybe she couldn't hear them inside the tower and that was all it was. But more likely, she was too busy fighting flying monkeys to answer the call. Or she was already disabled or dead. Reg couldn't let that happen. Sarah was her friend, and Reg needed to do whatever she could to protect her.

Her fire had failed. Summoning Theodore for more ideas, or his magic had failed. Davyn had some skills that Reg didn't, but she couldn't see him climbing the tower or finding a way to levitate up there at a moment's notice, Not when he was afraid of heights and had planned to stay on the ground for the entire operation.

But how was Reg going to get up there to help Sarah? She didn't have a hoverboard or robot vacuum cleaner. There were plenty of flying monkeys available, but she didn't think they would be interested in carrying her up to the top of the tower to see if she could help Sarah. She had a talent for communicating with animals; she had always been able to talk to cats, and recent events had shown that she was able to talk to werewolves. But the monkeys did not respond when she tried to reach out to them. She probably didn't want to know what they were thinking anyway. They weren't going to help her, even if she explained nicely how

Sarah was her friend and Reg needed to help her if she was injured or overwhelmed.

"Isn't there anything we can do?" she asked Davyn.

He looked at her and shook his head. "I don't have any way to get up there. Unless I can get in at the ground floor, and… hopefully, there is an elevator. But with the age of this building, there is probably not. Stairs are going to take a while."

Reg blew out her breath in frustration. "Come on… there has to be something we can do."

"There is only so much a firecaster can do. And most of it relates to lighting things on fire. I can't see how my invisibility would help either, so I'm afraid… it's down to prayers and incantations."

He closed his eyes, took a deep breath, and then let it out slowly. Reg looked up at the tower again. Her leg muscles tightened. She wanted to burst up there. She wanted to just gather her legs under her, stretch out her wings, and fly into the air to help her friend.

And so she did. Without even forming the intent in her mind, Reg transformed into her dragon form and took flight, shooting up like an arrow straight to the opening Sarah had entered through.

It wasn't nearly big enough for an adult dragon to fit through. But Reg wasn't going to let that stop her. Fitting her head and neck and forefeet in through the opening, she dragged herself forward, first sucking in her ribs and making herself as small as possible, then drawing air into her lungs, expanding her ribs and steeling the muscles in her sides to expand the opening, popping out two more windows, one on either side, to make enough space to crawl in.

There were howls and shrieks from the monkeys who had followed Sarah into the tower and were now trapped, blocked from getting out again by a raging dragon. Reg responded with a roar of her own, so loud that it shook everything in the little room at the top of the tower.

Sarah turned around, taking off her sunglasses to stare at Reg in surprise and horror.

Reg tried to telegraph calming thoughts to her so she knew she wasn't about to be ripped apart by a dragon. She hadn't ever seen Reg in her dragon form before, so how was she to know?

It's just me. It's Reg. She sent Sarah a picture of herself. Using telepathy as a dragon was not quite the same as it was when she was in her human form. She had to rely on the way a dragon brain worked.

Sarah mouthed "Reg?" in amazement, and Reg gave a little nod of confirmation.

The monkeys ran at her with their spears. Their backs were to Sarah, and she cast her spells quickly, doing her best to disarm and slow the Sylphs down. Reg gave a directed blast of fire but could not use the full force of her fire within the enclosed space without roasting Sarah in the process. The monkeys jumped back, most of them not seriously hit, but the weapons fell from their hands, wood on fire and iron searing hot. The acrid smell of singed monkey fur filled the tower. Reg roared again. They were frantic to get out and ran at the windows on the other side of the tower to try to break out. A blast of fire popped out several windows, and most of the monkeys fled.

"Thank you, Reg," Sarah said coolly, putting her sunglasses back on. "I doubt anyone thought of making the place dragonproof when it was being built or when Corvin and his little friends decided to use it to imprison the air elemental."

Reg snorted fire at a couple of winged monkeys who had stayed behind to fight but were still trying to figure out how to approach her and take her off guard. They jumped back a few paces, hovering above the stone floor and chattering at each other. Reg tried to use her telepathy to understand what they were saying, but it was hopeless. Understanding human thoughts was hard enough. The monkey brains of the Sylphs were beyond her reach.

Bird brains, she snorted.

Sarah was hunched over an ancient steampunk computer that clanked and whirred with visible gears. Reg couldn't imagine how it was still working hundreds of years after being installed or even only a hundred years ago. Her phone was obsolete within three years of purchase.

Reg envisioned the Pearl in her mind, prompting Sarah. Why was she on the computer when she should be retrieving the Pearl?

Sarah turned and looked at her. "What do you think I'm doing? As long as I can work on the machine uninterrupted, I will be able to get it."

Reg blew more fire out her nostrils and sat back on her haunches, watching the remaining monkeys. She would have to fend off any renewed attacks until Sarah was finished with the computer. Then they could get the Pearl together, and Reg could go home, eat, and take a nap. It had been a long day and, even as a dragon, she felt fatigued.

The monkeys outside clustered around the windows, peering in at her, chattering to each other. Trying to devise a strategy that would expose her flank so she was vulnerable to attack. Unfortunately for them, her flank was well-armored. Her most susceptible areas required a frontal assault, one that would put her foe directly before her claws, teeth, and fire.

She entertained herself by blowing fire out the various windows, enjoying the shrieks of the monkeys, watching them fly away, and then sneaking back when they thought they were out of her range of view. Like a dragon game of whack-a-mole. Unfortunately for the monkeys, a dragon had a very wide peripheral field of vision, and it was almost impossible to sneak up on her. She looked back over her shoulder at Sarah to see if she were making any progress. Sarah was muttering as she worked the various dials and levers on the ancient computer.

Reg got up and paced restlessly to the window to stick her head out and look down at Davyn, who was still standing by the car but was in a relaxed posture now. He was leaning against it while he looked up toward the tower. He waved at Reg and folded his arms.

CHAPTER THIRTY-NINE

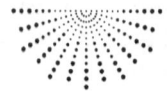

*T*here was a mechanical noise similar to the one that had sounded before the monkeys had been released, and Reg was instantly alert. She looked around and cocked her head, trying to see what was happening. The noise was coming from within the tower, so she couldn't see anything.

Doors opened to Sarah's right, and a tall man with a clipboard stepped into the control room. He looked around at the intruder, the broken windows, the monkeys and the detritus they had left lying around, and the dragon sitting there waiting patiently. "What the heck is going on here?" he demanded, outraged. He looked down at his clipboard as if he expected to see the answer there. Maybe a block on his schedule that said "Attempted Invasion."

Sarah turned her head to look at him. "Oh, hello," she said in a friendly voice. Her old grandmotherly attitude made it seem like she was just there for tea and had brought along some cookies for him. "Are you the mechanic?"

"I'm not the mechanic," he growled, indicating his clipboard. "I am the manager!"

"Oh, yes, of course. Is the mechanic available?"

"For what? What are you doing here? How did you get in here, and what do you think you're doing?"

"There is a problem with the Zephyr Pearl," Sarah told him. "I'm sure it can all be straightened out quickly enough. But I think we need the mechanic."

"You can't be in here. You don't work here, and…" he looked down at his clipboard, "…you don't have an appointment!"

"Yes, I'm sorry about that. Our timeframe was rather limited. What with everyone being petrified. We needed to get over here to deal with it quickly. So… the mechanic…?"

"He is working on maintenance issues." The supervisor looked around the room again, his nostrils flaring at the chaos left behind by the monkeys. He spotted the most loyal guards who had stayed behind to try to work out the problem of how to get the dragon out of the room and then deal with the human intruder once the threat had been removed. "What are you doing inside? Shoo! Shoo! Get out!"

The monkeys resisted at first, their postures aggressive, taking a few steps to charge him. But the manager wasn't about to be bullied by his own staff.

"Go on! Go on, get out!"

The last few monkeys were chased out of the control room, their wings flapping loudly as they made their retreat.

"*Who* are you?" the man demanded of Sarah. "And is this your dragon?"

"Yes, sorry about that. It was the monkeys…"

He shook his head, sighing loudly. "Have you ever tried to supervise flying monkeys? It is like herding cats. And I would know."

He frowned, studying what Sarah was doing on the machinery. She moved over slightly to block his view of what she was up to.

"Well, if you could call the mechanic up here, I could be out of here much sooner."

He shifted, trying again to see over her shoulder. "What exactly are you doing?"

"I told you, it is a problem with the Zephyr Pearl. Now, if I could just get that, I can take care of it, and we will have it back in place in no time. The longer you take, the longer the machinery will be down for maintenance."

"But we have a schedule," the man protested. "It is very important to stick to the schedule. The maintenance protocol takes two hours, and we must be back online again immediately after completion."

"Exactly. I need to get the Pearl. We need to take it out for cleaning. Otherwise, your performance is going to continue to suffer."

He flipped through several pages of his clipboard, frowning worriedly. "Why wasn't I told that it needed to be sent out for cleaning? This delay could have been avoided if everyone would just follow the communication protocols that are in place for exactly this reason."

"Tell me about it," Sarah agreed.

Reg focused on the manager, trying to feed him as many pictures as she could of low-efficiency graphs, downward trend lines, and chaotic schedules. He grew noticeably more agitated. He clicked the button of the walkie-talkie mounted to his shoulder.

"I need Spanner up here right away. Why can't anyone keep me informed on these developments?"

There was a staticky reply on the walkie-talkie that Reg could not understand. Maybe it was in a different language. She had a feeling that the man was something other than human. His rigid reactions to what was happening and Sarah's calm replies to being discovered were baffling. She had expected a big scene, more guards, and having to hold off any other employees while she gave Sarah more time to get the Pearl.

The man paced back and forth, grumbling and flipping through the pages of his clipboard. He gave sharp orders over the walkie-talkie several times, addressing different sectors and activating different protocols. He even called the research department to get back to him on protocols regarding dragons in the control room, but they were slow to respond with any helpful answer.

The doors opened again and, this time, a tiny old man came out. He was as short as Forst, Sarah's garden gnome, with a very wrinkled, wizened face. He had huge, foxlike ears, and his skin had a greenish-brown cast. He looked around the control room and did not take it as calmly as the man with the clipboard.

"What is going on here? Where are the Sylphs? How could you let a dragon into the control room? You're the one who is always so stuck on following policies and procedures, are you telling me this is according to policy? And you?" he yelled at Sarah, "Who are you? What are you doing in my control room?"

"Your control room?" the man with the clipboard demanded, "According to the policy manual, as your supervisor, it is my—"

"I don't care what the policy manual says, Skippy. If you want this control room to keep operating, it is *my* control room. Now get the dragon out of here, and you," he indicated Sarah, "I want to know how you got in here!"

Skippy, if that was the supervisor's real name, did not make any attempt to push Reg out the window or to call on the flying monkeys to carry her away. She was happy she was too big for a flying monkey to pick up. Or even several flying monkeys.

He held his hand up to demand silence from Spanner, the mechanic. "This woman needs the Pearl. It needs to be cleaned if we are to get the efficiency that we need. It's no wonder our numbers have been decreasing the last few months."

"This woman? Who is this woman? I haven't asked anyone to clean the Pearl."

"Well, you aren't part of management, are you? You do what I tell you to. She needs the Pearl. Let's get this done. The sooner she can get it, the sooner we can get it back."

"She's going to take it away?" the little man sputtered.

"How else is she going to clean it?"

"You can't just give the Pearl to anyone who comes here asking for it!"

"Does it look like that's what I'm doing?" Skippy displayed his clipboard, which had several crossed out entries and new notes about Sarah's role in the maintenance of the Pearl. "If it's on my clipboard—"

"You just wrote that on your clipboard! That's not official. This woman hasn't been vetted!"

"It's on the clipboard," Skippy insisted.

"Let me see that."

Spanner stepped forward and reached out his hand for the clipboard. Skippy held it in front of his face but wouldn't let him grab it out of his hand. "It's my clipboard; you are the mechanic. You don't get a clipboard."

Spanner grabbed at it several times, but Skippy was much taller and kept pulling it back from him. Then Spanner went postal and launched himself at Skippy, biting and tearing at him until he managed to wrestle the clipboard out of his hand and leap away with it. The clipboard snagged on Skippy's blue uniform, and buttons popped as Spanner tore the clipboard away. Skippy's shirt was ripped, exposing his undershirt.

Spanner froze, looking at what he had done. Skippy was flapping his hand, which Spanner had bitten to get the clipboard away, and didn't notice his open shirt for a moment. They all stared at the silk-screened words on the t-shirt beneath his uniform for a long moment.

World's Best Troll

Skippy pulled his shirt closed, muttering something to cover up his embarrassment. He made a couple of calls on his walkie-talkie, giving random orders.

"You need to give my clipboard back," he told Spanner. "I *told* them you were going to be trouble the day you first interviewed. 'We're an equal opportunity employer,' they said. 'We have to give everybody an opportunity based on their performance, not prejudices.' I told them that hiring a gremlin as a mechanic was not a good idea! The last mechanic never bit me! And his efficiency ratings were much higher than yours! Hiring a gremlin as a mechanic. They think they're so progressive. Diversity hires might look good in the annual report. But not when your efficiency tanks!"

CHAPTER FORTY

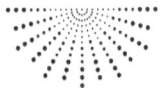

*W*ith the large, iridescent pearl clamped under her arm like a motorcycle helmet, Sarah stepped aboard her Roomba hovercraft, flew out the window, and gently descended to the ground. Reg had a more difficult time reversing her position and getting back out of the hole she had widened in the side of the control room, but she managed to squeeze her way through it again. Skippy stood near the large hole, frowning at the damage and making copious notes on his recovered clipboard.

Reg braced herself for another attack from the flying monkeys, but instead of dive-bombing Sarah, they simply hovered, flapping their wings slowly, watching Reg as she exited the Cyclone Tower and followed Sarah to the ground. They chattered comments to each other, but they were not the threatening or panicked cries Reg had heard from them before, but calm, possibly sarcastic tones that she was glad she didn't understand. She didn't need to know what they were saying about the dragon who had bested them or stulti-fied supervisor Skippy and his mistreatment of them. Reg thought that a couple of them had sustained fire damage but, on closer examination, saw that they were smoking fat cigars as they watched the witch and the dragon leave the tower with the Pearl.

At the bottom of the tower, Sarah stepped off of her vacuum

and put it back into the trunk of the car. Davyn stared at the soccer ball-sized pearl clamped under her arm.

"You got it? What happened up there?"

Sarah shrugged. "We asked them nicely, and they gave it to us."

Davyn looked at Reg in disbelief. She couldn't communicate with him very well in her current form, but she did manage a stiff shrug. Davyn looked back at Sarah.

"You asked them, and they gave it to you."

"Yes," Sarah agreed.

"Asked who? I can't imagine they let you simply walk away with it."

"Well, I did promise to clean it and return it to them. Which I will do after we finish with it. A witch should always follow through on her promises."

"Of course," Davyn agreed. His eyes were narrow.

"They were very accommodating once we got past the initial communication issues."

"I see."

They both climbed into the car. Davyn looked at Reg. "Do you want to transform and come with us?"

Reg always found transforming back to human a little awkward and embarrassing. She enjoyed her dragon form and was never too eager to leave it behind. Especially if she thought there were any danger of a further attack or other circumstance that might require her special powers as a dragon.

She no longer feared that she might be unable to transform into a dragon. It seemed that when it was a necessity, the transformation was easy enough.

She could follow the car in flight and ensure that no winged monkeys attacked it and that there were no hazards on the road ahead. But the monkeys seemed to be off the clock and showed no interest in any of them.

Reg took a deep dragon breath and pictured herself in her human form, sitting in the car and digging into the cooler for another snack. Looking down at herself, she saw that she had transformed back to her familiar human form. She opened the back passenger door.

"That was… interesting," she commented.

Sarah made a noise of agreement as she put on her seatbelt and settled in for the ride. "Do you think you could find me something edible in there?" she indicated the cooler. "Maybe some fruit or cookies?"

Reg held up a banana, and Sarah shook her head. Reg dug further and decided that even though Sarah had suggested fruit, that really wasn't what she wanted. Reg found a package of Oreo cookies and ripped it open. Sarah took a couple of cookies for herself and handed two more to Davyn. Reg put on her seatbelt and relaxed into the comfortable seat, eating one of the cookies herself before asking anything else.

She washed it down with water. It was too bad that Davyn had only packed water and energy drinks. It was the one circumstance where Reg would have preferred milk.

"What was Skippy? A troll?"

"Yes," Sarah agreed. "They do remarkably well in supervisory positions. At least, those where the supervisor is expected to follow strict policies and procedures and not to do a lot of creative thinking or deal with unforeseen circumstances."

"You encountered a troll?" Davyn repeated.

"Yes."

"But he didn't smell bad," Reg pointed out.

"No, they are usually reasonably clean creatures."

"But the one in the Everglades, Tybalt, he…" Reg wrinkled her nose, remembering the rank, rotting smell that had hung around their tour guide.

"In the Everglades? That wasn't a troll," Davyn told Reg. "That was a swamp goblin, from what Julian said."

"Oh, right." Reg tried to remember the details. "They're not the same thing?"

"Trolls and goblins?" Sarah asked. "Oh, no. They're as different as night and day. I don't think I would want to run into either one in a swamp, but trolls are usually quite reasonable. Territorial, mind; you don't want to cross a bridge guarded by a troll without the proper toll and travel papers. But they aren't as likely to kill and eat you as a swamp goblin." She grimaced and shook her head. "Foul creatures. You can't reason with a goblin."

"No." Reg sniffled and wiped her nose, the memory bringing back the foul smell and the terror she had felt when Tybalt had captured her and there did not seem to be any way to escape. She shuddered and shoved another Oreo in her mouth. "I wouldn't have wanted to run into one of those in the tower," she said around the cookie.

"Oh, but you wouldn't," Sarah assured her. "Swamp goblins do not like heights."

Reg snorted, barely managing to avoid inhaling cookie crumbs. "Oh, of course."

Sarah nodded and reached her hand back toward Reg, who gave her a few more cookies.

"And the other guy? Spanner? He wasn't a troll or a goblin."

"No, a gremlin. Nothing like the creatures in the movie," she declared, rolling her eyes. "Sometimes it is hard to believe how far Hollywood gets from the truth."

"A gremlin. And they're not like trolls or goblins."

"Not much," Sarah agreed. "I mean, they are all humanoid and have been portrayed in fiction as being evil or bloodthirsty creatures. But in real life, you can't paint them all with the same brush. Prejudice is alive and well in interspecies communications, and we must be careful not to adopt other people's stereotypes."

"Like hiring gremlins as mechanics."

"They are not usually considered suitable for such things," Sarah admitted. "They are associated with the sabotage of mechanical equipment. Putting a wrench in the hand of a gremlin and giving him the go-ahead on fixing your equipment would normally be considered... folly at best."

"He seemed like he was capable."

Sarah shrugged. "He didn't have any trouble sorting the computer out and retrieving the Pearl when he was ordered to. It was… quite a complex machine. They say that only good can come from increased diversity in the workplace."

But there was doubt in her voice. She might have misgivings and prejudices of her own about the suitability of gremlins in the workplace.

"They aren't normally good with machinery?"

"Good at breaking it. The RAF experienced a significant number of problems with gremlins in World War One. They were quite a problem for the Allies, especially causing problems with the aircraft."

"Gremlins were working against the Allies in World War One?"

"Oh, yes. There was quite a bit written on the problem. If you are interested in reading about them—"

"No," Reg hurried to stop any suggestion that she read through Sarah's thick tomes on gremlins or any other magical creatures. If she did any research on the matter—and she really didn't care anything about gremlins as long as they were not fouling up her car —then it would be using Theodore and YouTube. "That's okay. I was just wondering because I hadn't ever heard of a gremlin in that kind of position before. He seemed perfectly capable."

Hyperactive, maybe, but Reg couldn't fault him for that. Some jobs took a lot of energy and might as well be filled by those who had it. Spanner had jumped back and forth between a number of tasks in quick succession, but he had been able to sort out the computer and fetch Sarah the Pearl.

"So what is our next step?" Davyn asked. "We now have the two remaining elementals. What do we intend to do with them? I had hoped that Corvin would hold the answer, since he was involved in binding them in the first place. But now that he has been petrified, he will not have any answers for us."

"If there was anything in his books, Theodore should be able to tell us by now," Reg reminded him, "He should be finished reading them."

Davyn looked at Sarah. He apparently also had reservations about the use of the homunculus.

"He's very useful," Reg insisted. "I don't care what you think of homunculi; he does a great job sorting everything out and answering questions. He told you that it was Corvin who bound the elementals, right?" Reg directed this latter at Sarah.

"Yes, he did," Sarah admitted. "I can see the utility of such a creature, but… this kind of magic is not… it would be rejected by most practitioners. It is a… forbidden area of magic."

"You're the one who keeps saying that the only thing that determines whether magic is good or bad is whether it harms anyone. How does Theodore harm anyone?"

"One area of concern is where he gets his energy. An alchemical being or an automaton usually gets its energy from the practitioner who created it, which is one of the reasons that it is no longer active after she dies. But with Theodore…"

"He didn't die when Sma did. But that's because her spirit is still here, and he continues to operate until her spirit is completely gone," Reg said with more confidence than she actually had. She was, after all, only speculating on how Theodore had survived the demise of his creator.

"That does not sound right," Sarah disagreed, shaking her head. She looked at Davyn. "What do you think? Have you ever heard of such a thing?"

He shook his head slowly. "I think there is something else going on here… Another possibility is that Sma was not his creator, but someone else was. And that means that he is still in service of that person, whoever it is. Or when she created him she somehow tied him to another person or energy source other than herself. Such a thing should be impossible, but she was a wily old witch and may have discovered some ancient magic that would allow her to do so."

"Why is it always ancient magic?" Reg mused. "Why couldn't it be something new and innovative?"

"Well, okay. Maybe Sma came up with something new and innovative," Davyn obliged. "But what? Where does Theodore get his energy? Who is he serving?"

"Me."

"Are you sure? How did you change his alliance?"

"*He* changed it."

Davyn pressed his lips together and stared at the road ahead of him. "A homunculus does not have will of its own."

Reg sighed and slumped back into the seat. "I don't understand how you can see something with your own eyes and not believe it. You're as bad as the non-practitioners who won't believe what they see with their own eyes. There is no magic because they refuse to see it. There is no telepathy or psychic power because they can't measure it. Theodore has *will*."

"All the more reason not to trust him," Sarah declared.

Reg rolled her eyes and stuffed two cookies in her mouth at once, which made it too full for her to talk. Sarah, who had been turned around to talk to her, faced front again, irritated.

"Back to Corvin's house?" Davyn suggested. "Or should we go back to the temple? That was where everything started. Perhaps we must begin and end in the same place."

Sarah rubbed her head.

"We will still have to go to the temple," she said. "To deal with Gideon, if nothing else. But to begin with, let us return to Corvin's, where we have some privacy."

Davyn nodded his agreement.

Sarah sat with the Pearl in her lap, stroking it and turning it around to look at every side. Was she looking for flaws? There weren't any that Reg could see. Could Sarah see how to unbind the elemental that was imprisoned by it? Did she want to?

Reg had no idea how they were going to fix what Gideon and Corvin had started hundreds of years earlier. Had they made a mistake? Or had they done the only thing they could, and they would have to put the same measures back in place to protect the people of Black Sands?

CHAPTER FORTY-ONE

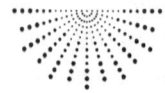

*S*arah had taken Corvin's spare key when they had left the house earlier so, this time, she did not need to perform any magic on the lock to break in, but instead just let herself in.

They returned to the study. Reg wasn't sure whether she would find Theodore there. He *did* have a will of his own and could not be expected to stay in one place after finishing his assignment. She didn't control where he went when she did not need him.

And Reg had tried to summon him at the tower, so she didn't know if his essence would be there, still trying to re-form in the erratic winds surrounding the building.

But they found him in the study, sitting in the chair at Corvin's desk and studying the petrified Corvin.

"Theodore." Reg nodded a greeting to him. "Did you finish consuming all the books and records in the study?"

"Yes," Theodore confirmed. "I am finished."

"Did you read everything?"

"Yes."

Reg looked at Davyn and Sarah for their reactions, and then back at Theodore again. "How do we reverse the spell and turn Corvin back into himself?"

He clicked and his head tilted as he thought about it, searching through the stores of knowledge.

"Element one invoked this curse and three be required to break it. Dragon fire and siren song combine thou to carry on."

It wasn't a rhyme, but she could tell he was struggling to put his usual verse response into plain language she could understand.

Reg took a deep breath in and let it out slowly. "Dragon fire and siren song," she repeated, looking at her companions. "Fire and water. That's only two. But we need three. The Zephyr Pearl?"

Sarah shook her head. "We cannot take the chance of loosing the air elemental before we know what we are going to do with it. While it is currently bound to the Pearl, we cannot assume it will stay that way without strengthening the spell. And I do not want to be complicit in what Corvin has done. I will not strengthen the spell. We must move forward as quickly as possible."

"But we need the third element." Reg looked at Theodore. "How can I use the third element? What about air?"

"Dragon fire and siren song combine," Theodore repeated.

"That's only two elements."

"Element one invoked this curse and three be required to break it."

"I know. Fire, water, and air. That's three. But you only gave me two, dragon fire and siren song."

"Dragon fire and siren song combine."

"Theodore!" Reg had dealt with nonsensical answers from him before. He seemed to get stuck in his own solution sometimes and couldn't see reason. "How many things is that?"

"Dragon fire and siren song are two things."

"Yeah. And how many do we need?"

"Two things," Theodore echoed.

"No, we need three things. We need fire, water, and air elements."

"Dragon fire and siren song combine—"

"No!"

Sarah chuckled, shaking her head. "These problems are not unusual with Large Language Models," she informed Reg.

"I just need to make him understand…"

"There is not much you can do when they get stuck."

"Let's think this through," Davyn intervened. "He did not recommend using your firecasting power, but dragon fire."

Reg hesitated, unsure where Davyn was going with it. "Yeah…"

"And what powers do you have as a dragon? Especially that you do not have in human form?"

"Well, size and strength, and…" Reg laughed. "Flight."

"Flight. Mastery of the air."

"And do you remember the pictograms you saw of sirens?" Sarah contributed. "You were surprised because they were not shown as mermaids or part fish."

"They were birds," Reg remembered. "Birds with women's heads."

"The earliest pictures of sirens always showed them as birds."

"I didn't choose to take bird form, but I could have," Reg remembered the first time she had changed, trying to find her form. Fish or bird, serpent or dragon… "I chose dragon instead."

"Birds and dragons both have flight."

"So dragon fire and siren song combined is all three elements? Fire and water and air?"

"Element one invoked this curse and three be required to break it. Dragon fire and siren song combine thou to carry on."

Reg let Theodore give the full answer again. She nodded her acceptance and tried to understand what was expected of her. "So what do I do? I sing and blow dragon fire? And that reverses the petrifaction?"

She, Sarah, and Davyn all looked at each other, uncertain.

Reg looked at Corvin. In the state he was in, it shouldn't matter if she blew dragon fire on him. Fire wouldn't hurt a stone statue, would it? Of course, if he were a living human, she wouldn't do that, but he was just stone, so it should be perfectly safe.

Reg scratched the back of her head, trying to decide.

And she hated singing in front of other people. Davyn had heard her sing before, when she had transformed into a dragon the very first time, and it hadn't been a pleasant experience. Reg had never sounded very good when she sang.

In fact, she had sounded terrible. Music teachers at school had despaired and asked her to lip sync rather than singing out loud. As they instructed everybody else to sing out, they asked Reg to be quieter, so everyone else would drown her out.

It wasn't very encouraging.

Reg didn't think Sarah had ever heard her sing. She'd certainly never heard Reg's siren song. According to the old tales, the siren's song was enough to drive any man mad. But that didn't necessarily mean because it was so unbelievably beautiful.

Though it did have a wild beauty if Reg and the siren sisters all sang together. What started out as raucous, discordant voices somehow blended to be so beautiful that it hurt.

Of course, a siren would think that. Reg had never actually asked Davyn what he had thought about her song that day. He had never brought it up. He had also never suggested that she sing again or that he thought she had a musical bone in her body.

"I assume that you cannot do both at the same time," Davyn said logically.

"No, I don't think so."

"Do you think it matters what order they are in? He did say to combine them."

"He probably just meant combined in one spell," Sarah suggested. "Not simultaneously."

Reg looked back at Theodore. "Well, Theodore? Which is it? Do I have to do them both at the same time? Because that is kind of impossible."

He clicked and cocked his head but didn't come up with any clarifying answer.

"The worst that could happen is that it doesn't work," Davyn said.

"No, the worst would be that he is unpetrified halfway through, and then I end up incinerating him alive with dragon fire."

"Well, that *would* be unfortunate," Sarah admitted, though she didn't sound like she would regret it too much. She had been pretty mad at Corvin since she learned about the four elementals being bound. She would probably get over it. Sooner or later.

"Well..." Reg took a deep lungful of air but still didn't feel like she was breathing properly. "Shall I try?"

CHAPTER FORTY-TWO

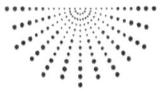

$\mathcal{N}$o one seemed to have any further advice for Reg. She was worried about how it would work. Could she really just do a mini talent show and revive Corvin from his stony silence?

It seemed like a bit much to expect.

"Okay," Reg said eventually, bracing herself. "I'm going to do it, then. Uh… if anyone doesn't want to stay for this part, I'll understand."

They looked at her blankly. Davyn was the only one who had an inkling of what Reg was talking about.

"You just go ahead," he encouraged. "Anyone who doesn't like it can block their ears."

Sarah raised her brows. No doubt she thought Davyn was being rude when really he was being supportive.

Resisting the urge to say, "Okay, I'm going to do it" again, ask permission, or ask another question to put off the actual deed, Reg steeled herself.

She started a hum in the back of her throat. She could hear the voices of her siren sisters rising up in her ears but didn't know if the others could hear them as well or if she was the only one. Their voices encouraged her to grow louder and sing out. Sirens were not ones to sing in a modest voice; they belted it out, no matter how loud and discordant it sounded to anyone standing near her. Reg gathered strength as her song waxed louder and grew, encouraged by the other sirens.

She was aware that Davyn was, in fact, covering his ears, as was everyone else in the room other than Corvin. He probably regretted that he'd let himself be petrified even more than ever.

As she broke into a full-throated cry, Reg transformed into her dragon form for the second time that day. No longer singing, she let out a roar. She breathed in two dragon lungs full of oxygen and blew out fire, aimed directly at the statue, trying to baptize the whole thing with fire.

After blowing out all that fire, Reg roared once more, and then she returned to her human form, wanting to communicate fully with the others as soon as she could. As the smoke cleared from the room, it seemed that Corvin's form was a little less gray than it had been.

"Come on," Reg murmured. "Did it work? Should I sing again?"

"No, please," Sarah intoned so quietly that Reg almost didn't hear her. Even Theodore looked at her like he thought that was the worst idea in the world. He was the one who had come up with the formula. The least they could do was support her to the end.

But he shook his head silently, disapproving.

Reg felt slightly disappointed in her friends, the people who should have supported her. She looked away from them, back at Corvin.

He was the one she should be thinking about. It was his life that hung in the balance, not hers. No one cared whether she was a siren or not, whether she could carry a tune in a paper bag. She wasn't singing to show off her talent.

It was all about Corvin being reanimated.

Corvin moved slowly, creakily, his face still gray and his body obviously stiff and sore. Reg's heart leaped. No matter how hard it was or how she needed to humiliate herself to do it, Corvin was moving. She had succeeded.

She watched him, mouth open, trying to decide if she needed

to try again. To provide a little more siren song or a little more dragon fire to speed the process.

"Regina," Corvin's voice was hoarse from disuse. He swore grumpily. "What was that?"

Reg looked at him and shrugged. "Well… it was the formula that Theodore gave. To reanimate you. And it worked. Mastery of water, air, and fire…"

"Is that what you call it?" He groaned, stretching his limbs and rubbing his neck and back. "I think I'd rather stay petrified."

Reg would have been offended, but she knew it wasn't true. He was grateful for what she had done, and he was glad to be alive and able to move around again. Corvin loved to get her goat.

"I guess I shouldn't have tried then," she told him smartly. "I should have just left you as a statue. It created a nice ambiance. You should think of commissioning one."

Corvin cracked his knuckles, then his neck. Reg grimaced. She hated the sound. It made her cringe every time.

"Well, welcome back," Sarah told Corvin. "Now, there is work to be done."

Corvin shook his head. "There is something to be done, all right," he said grumpily, taking a few steps toward his desk, where Theodore was still seated as if he owned the place. "Where do you get off bringing a homunculus into my home? Setting it free in my library. Indeed, even coming into my house yourself uninvited!"

"Oh, quit being a curmudgeon," Sarah told him. "It doesn't suit you well. You know why we broke into your house. You needed our help. You couldn't exactly call for help or give us permission when you were petrified. We had to take the initiative and let ourselves in. As far as the homunculus goes…" She looked at Theodore with clear disapproval. "I am inclined to agree, and I have already made my opinion on the matter known."

"If I hadn't asked him to review your library, you would still be stone," Reg pointed out. "It was Theodore who told us what to do to get you back."

"Theodore?"

Reg nodded. Why did everyone think that was such a strange

name for a homunculus? Theodore had picked it out himself, so it couldn't exactly be inappropriate.

"The creature needs to be returned to its master. And how are you going to return to me my library? You had no right to go poking through my personal library and research files. This information is very valuable. It was not yours to take."

"I didn't take anything away; it is all still there. That's how Theodore knew how to save you. By reading the books. He probably knows them better than you do now. He can recall everything."

Corvin growled. "Do you think that makes me feel better? That's what I am telling you. That knowledge was not yours to give or to access. You should not have touched it or given it to this creature you cannot control."

"He is mine. He doesn't belong to anyone else."

"Yours? You did not create him. You do not have the alchemical knowledge or experience to do such a thing. This requires very advanced magic and many years of practice and study."

"Well, I didn't create him, but he is attached to me now."

"It doesn't work that way."

Reg threw up her hands in frustration. She clenched her teeth to avoid going on another rant about how people wouldn't believe what was in front of their own eyes when it came to Theodore.

"He is my homunculus," she insisted. "He doesn't belong to anyone else."

He didn't even belong to her, as far as she was concerned. She didn't own him like a slave or a piece of computer equipment. He had his own free will. The law might not consider him a person unto himself, but it hadn't considered women people either, and she definitely was one. But Theodore was attached to her and to no one else. She was the only one who could give him instructions. He would have been lost without someone to talk to and act for, even if he did have free will. Even though he looked like a child, she knew he was not one. But she still felt protective and affectionate toward him, as if he were a child she was looking after for a while.

"The issue is my knowledge," Corvin insisted. He moved

toward his chair and sat down, Theodore scooting out of the way at the last minute so as not to get sat on. He looked at Reg, aggrieved at being removed from what he felt was his rightful place. "What are you going to do to return my knowledge, all of my long years of collection, research, and experimentation to me? How are you going to pluck that out of its head and give it back?"

"I can't."

"If it is your homunculus, then it is your responsibility to deactivate it so that this information cannot be used."

"No way! I'm not going to do that to him!"

"I spent years accumulating this knowledge, don't you understand that?"

"It's not *yours*," Reg insisted. "You can't own knowledge. Anyone could have that knowledge."

"No, anyone could not. Only I could, after my many years—centuries—of work and accumulation."

Reg looked at Sarah and Davyn, but neither seemed to know how to deal with this claim.

"If I didn't give him all that information, we would not have been able to free you."

"It wasn't yours to give."

"Well, it is too late now. What do you expect me to do?"

Corvin folded his arms. "I already told you what I expect you to do."

"I am not going to deactivate him."

"Homunculus," Corvin addressed Theodore in a commanding, pompous voice.

Theodore looked at him but did not show him any reverence.

"Consumed you *everything* in my library?" Corvin demanded.

Theodore clicked. "Yes."

"Everything?"

"Yes."

"Every book, file, and journal in this room?"

"Yes."

Corvin leaned forward, leaning on his elbows on the desk. "What about the locked books?"

"Locked books?" Reg echoed. "How do you lock a book?" But even as she said it, she thought of the little journals some of the girls had owned when she was younger. Little diaries with tiny locks and keys to keep their thoughts private.

Of course, it didn't work; anyone with a screwdriver could pop one of those locks. But Reg had still envied them, both their locking diaries and their secrets.

Corvin's journals or secret books were probably locked with locks that were a little more secure than that. And possibly also with spells and traps.

Theodore cocked his head. "Not the locked books," he admitted.

"You lied to me?"

"I was mistaken. I did not read the locked books."

"Are you sure?"

"Yes."

"So you did not read the entire library?"

"I did."

Corvin rolled his eyes at Reg. "Your homunculus has a problem with the truth."

"It's just... he doesn't always understand. He doesn't think the same way we do."

CHAPTER FORTY-THREE

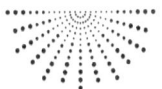

*C*orvin," Davyn said evenly, in a formal manner, "I think that we need to focus on the matter at hand. Although you are not happy with how Reg handled the situation and you have suffered a loss, we need to focus on how to remedy the situation with the elementals. We have retrieved the water and air relics, but I, for one, am not sure how to proceed."

Corvin looked at Davyn, scowling. He clearly still wanted to argue with Reg about his stolen knowledge, but there were more urgent matters at hand. He was the one who had been petrified and, if she had not managed to reverse that spell, he would still be standing like a statue across the room. Others were still in danger, and they were still vulnerable to attack by the earth and fire elementals.

"Fine," Corvin said, laying his hands palms down on his desk as if stabilizing himself for something arduous. "You are correct, of course. This matter can be put aside while we deal with the more pressing concerns."

"Thank you," Davyn acknowledged. "I am sure that you and Reg can come to some solution or understanding later about the use of your library. For now... can you tell us what happened when you were petrified? We have not been able to talk to others who were petrified, so our knowledge about what happened is sadly lacking. You are the only one who can provide us with this information."

Reg thought Davyn was laying it on a little thick, but he had known Corvin for longer than she had and had a better idea of how to handle him. Reg had learned that flattery went a long way toward getting what she wanted from men like Corvin and those in authority. It was hard to flatter someone like Corvin too much. If he objected, it usually meant she needed to go bigger, not back down.

Corvin nodded slowly. He was the only one who had that knowledge and could communicate with them at the moment. He also had further background knowledge of what had happened with the elementals before they had been bound and how he and the others in his shadow coven had bound them. If there was one person holding all the knowledge right now, it was not Theodore, but Corvin. Who knew if he had put pen to paper to record any of what he and Gideon had done in secret. If he had, Reg assumed it was in one of the locked books.

For a powerful warlock like Corvin, knowledge was leverage. The fact that he valued it so greatly was evidenced by how upset he was that Theodore had consumed his library. Who else would have been upset about anyone reading his books in order to save him from a fate like petrifaction?

"Can you tell us what happened before you were petrified?" Davyn prodded. "How it happened? Were you aware of anything… unusual happening before you were attacked?"

Reg admired Davyn for the way he handled Corvin. Clearly, he knew Corvin well and had deep knowledge about how to handle him. Terming the petrifaction an attack made it clear that nobody blamed Corvin for what had happened to him. It made it sound unprovoked and unfair rather than retaliation for something Corvin had done wrong.

"I was here, in my study," Corvin made a small motion to indicate his surroundings. "I had been studying, trying to come to some understanding of how to recapture and bind the elementals that had escaped and how to reverse the petrifaction process on Gideon. Gideon was one of the few people who could have helped me with this matter. It seems cruel that he should be the one afflicted when he was the one with the greatest knowledge of the matter."

Or perhaps that was precisely why Gideon had been the first one petrified. Maybe the earth elemental knew that Gideon was the biggest threat to its freedom.

Davyn nodded gravely. He sat in one of Corvin's guest chairs and pulled it forward, leaning toward Corvin to show he was engaged in the conversation. He didn't ask any questions, letting Corvin take the lead.

"I had been able to do some research and to read my notes from the periods before, during, and after binding the elementals. We had learned a lot during the process, and I needed to refresh my memory."

Corvin turned to grab a glass and splash a little liquid into it. He swallowed it down and wiped his mouth with the back of his hand.

"Gideon was the one among us who had the best under-standing of what was going on with the elementals. They had not been so disruptive to human life before. Humans and the elementals had been able to live together in harmony for many years, but something had disrupted them recently. With that disruption, they seemed to have targeted humans instead of living in harmony with them as they had previously."

Davyn nodded.

"I remember," Sarah said. "It was a very challenging time. Many wondered why things had gotten so bad. There were speculations that it was the beginning of the end of the world, of Armageddon."

"It was a frightening time," Corvin agreed—not admitting that he had been frightened, but acknowledging what had been going on at the time. "There were many who warned about the end of the world. Many of the signs that had been predicted seemed to have been fulfilled."

"Did *you* think the world was going to end?" Reg asked.

He cocked his head slightly and shrugged with one shoulder, not answering the question.

"It was very serious. Many people were being killed or injured by these storms and other natural disasters."

Reg nodded. It must have been very disconcerting to live through such a time, wondering if the earth's clock was running down.

"I suddenly became aware of something in the room," Corvin said slowly. "There was no actual intruder. Nothing that had to come in through a door or window. But some… presence."

"Were you able to do anything to protect yourself?" Davyn asked.

"I could not. With the curse laid upon me, any attempt to use my powers is excruciating. I could not do so much as raise a shield around me or *see* what was in front of me."

Reg's skin prickled with goosebumps. She looked around her, realizing that the elemental or presence he had detected could still be there. It had not necessarily gone on somewhere else. Corvin was the last one they knew of who had been petrified. Though there might be many other people in their houses or the forest who had suffered similar fates and simply not been discovered yet. Or their afflictions had been kept out of the media while the police or magical investigators looked into what had happened.

"Were you aware of the moment in which you were petrified?" Sarah asked. "Did you… have any unusual sensations? A smell or a feeling?"

Corvin's head went up slightly at this question. He considered. "There was… just a hint of a whiff of forest," he admitted, "of pine, perhaps."

"When we first came into the house, I thought I could smell sulfur," Reg offered.

Sarah raised her brows and nodded. She didn't offer what any of this might mean. Reg had no idea whether it was significant, or if it were just a distraction.

"I had gotten up to put away a few volumes," Corvin nodded to the shelves where he had been standing as a statue. "And then… I couldn't move my feet. Couldn't raise my arms. I thought I might be having a stroke or a seizure. But nothing happened. I didn't fall to the floor or have any pain; I just was there and couldn't move. I couldn't see or hear, I just... existed in suspended animation. Until you arrived."

"How did you know we were here?" Davyn asked.

"Reg... she reached out to me and touched me... I could sense her."

Reg remembered the pain she had caused him by the psychic connection and was ashamed. But it had been all that she could do. She hadn't done it to hurt him, but had wanted to help him and to reassure him that they would do everything they could to help.

And Gideon and the others were still out there, still suspended and unable to see, hear, or move. They would not have the pain that Corvin did when she reached out to him, but they were still afraid, wondering what was going to happen to them. She had been able to sense that when she had seen them.

"Does any of this help us?" Reg asked. "Does it tell us what to do next? I can reanimate the others the same way I did Corvin, let them start living their lives again..."

Davyn held up his hands in a calming gesture. "Reanimation is not our only concern. We can keep reanimating everyone that the elementals petrify... and they can keep petrifying them, and do more damage. More forest fires, earthquakes, sinkholes, and whatever else they can do. And not only the earth and fire elementals. Before long, the water and air elementals will also be on the loose, and we will have storms like you have never before seen. Hurricanes that wipe out half the coast. Death and destruction you cannot even imagine. A few petrified people are the least of our worries."

CHAPTER FORTY-FOUR

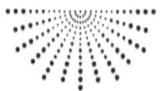

*R*eg was silent. She didn't want to think about destruction on the level Davyn suggested. She liked to think of the elementals as small, mischievous sprites who had escaped their unfair imprisonment and wanted to get back at Corvin and Gideon for what they had done. That was manageable. She could imagine being able to come to a resolution on that level.

But the level of destruction that Davyn suggested was daunting. How were they supposed to stop something like that from happening? The elementals were not just tiny, ephemeral entities that Corvin and Gideon had unfairly imprisoned. They probably would not have done such a thing in the case of such an insignificant problem. The problem they had seen had been vast and overwhelming, and they had done the only thing they could think of.

And now they had to come up with a solution that was different, that was better, and that would work in the long term. And that did not treat the elementals unfairly again. They had to find a way to treat them with care and respect and with fairness and balance. Or they would end up right back where they had started.

She looked around the study uneasily. "Why are we sitting around here? The elemental could come back at any time and petrify us all. Then what are we going to do? We should… go out and reanimate Gideon, at least. He can help."

Corvin chewed on his lip and didn't answer. The others didn't jump in and say that was a great idea, either.

"Why not?" Reg asked the silent room. "Isn't he the only other person who knows what happened when you bound the elementals the first time?"

Corvin nodded. "But I have already told you all about that. He would not be able to provide any additional information I do not have."

"He might remember more or different things. You had to go back and reread your notes; that means you didn't remember everything."

Davyn and Sarah looked at her, and Reg realized what everyone else in the room already knew. That Corvin hadn't told them everything and didn't intend to tell them everything. Perhaps he didn't even want Gideon to be reanimated because of what he could tell.

She rubbed her forehead. "We can't just sit around here talking about what happened. That doesn't get us anywhere."

"Reg is a woman of action," Corvin said, smiling. "I'll bet you could never stay in your seat in school."

Reg thought about how teachers had constantly told her to sit back down and do her work. She had been restless, needing to get up and move around to think things through. Sitting in her seat was practically a guarantee that she wouldn't be able to do the work. And while she was at least standing in Corvin's study rather than sitting down, she still felt the need to get out and do something.

"Yeah," she agreed. "I was, and we need to go. We need to move."

Corvin sighed and leaned back in his chair. He seemed reluctant to go anywhere. "You said you got the water and air relics?" He shook his head. "I thought we did a better job of protecting them. If they were that easy to get ahold of…"

"The spells you had woven to protect them had waned," Sarah

reminded him. "When the werewolves attacked and cursed you, you were no longer able to maintain them. There were other protections in place that you did not have to constantly maintain, but… we were able to overcome them."

Reg smiled, proud of what she and the others had done. And thinking back to the confrontation in the control room of the Cyclone Tower. There were definitely circumstances that Corvin had not expected in play. He had not foreseen that the supervisor at the tower would be a troll who could be talked into giving up the Zephyr Pearl, simply handing it over after they had managed to breach the security of the tower. No number of flying monkeys could stop their boss from simply handing the relic over.

The leg injury from the sea creature gave a sudden throb of pain. Reg bent down and rubbed it gently, hoping that it would settle down again. Touching it hurt. Not a good idea. It would have been better if she had just left it alone.

"Are you okay, Reg?" Sarah asked in concern.

"Yeah, it's fine. It's nothing."

Sarah looked at Corvin. "She was injured retrieving the Tears of Poseidon."

"Oh?" Corvin looked at her. "Do you want me to…" He trailed off, realizing he couldn't use his powers to heal her. "I have herbs in my stores. We can dress it with—"

"I have already done so," Sarah said. "Forgive me for acting as if it were my own house, but we needed to act quickly, and I did not have time to go home for my own supplies."

"Of course, of course. I would have insisted," Corvin assured her. Apparently, stealing his herbs was not nearly as offensive as reading his books. "Are you okay, Reg? Do you need the dressing changed?"

The injury sent bolts of pain up Reg's leg, but she shook her head. She didn't need Corvin touching her or giving her attention. She didn't know what the odds were that he would be able to tend to her without accidentally using his magic, but she didn't think they were very good. Even touching or standing near each other could be a problem.

"No, it's fine," she insisted.

If she had to transform into a dragon again to reanimate the other statues, then she would be fine. When she was a dragon, the pain seemed to go away. Maybe she should remain a dragon for a few days until it was healed. She could just imagine how Sarah would respond to that. Reg smiled and shook her head slightly.

Corvin met her eyes; he was serious and wanted to make sure that she wasn't just brushing him off, but she did anyway. "Really. It's just like poison ivy. Stings and itches a bit when I'm thinking about it, but I can manage. We need to worry more about what is happening with the elementals. We need to get everyone back to normal and to… figure out what to do about the elementals."

"We need to bind the earth and fire elementals again," Corvin said, leaning forward on the desk. "There is no other way to handle them. It was the only way to take care of it back when they were first bound, and it is the only way to handle it now."

Sarah shook her head. "There has to be a better way," she insisted. "It is wrong to bind entities for their natural behavior. They are incapable of doing wrong and are only doing what comes naturally to them. Yes, it affects the humans around them and potentially many others in the area, but it isn't because they are malevolent and want to do us harm."

Reg remembered the fire elemental and was not sure. But she kept her mouth shut. They didn't need to know that. Not until a decision was made.

"We did not rescue the water and air elementals to ensure they could not escape," Sarah told Corvin. "We want to ensure their safety and help them… reintegrate into their natural lives."

"That would be a mistake. You know what havoc they will wreak."

"Not if it is handled properly," Sarah insisted.

Corvin rolled his eyes. "You think you can just reason with these entities? You cannot. They don't have the ability to reason. They only have the ability to target and destroy. That is what they do naturally. You want them to do that? To take out half the population of Florida while they're at it? Destroy your home, your town, and everything you hold dear?"

Sarah favored Corvin with a glare. "You may think you have more experience and knowledge on this matter than anyone else, but you remember that I have lived longer than you. I was a grown, practicing witch when you were just a young pup. Don't talk to me as if I were a child."

Corvin grunted and leaned back in his seat again, petulant.

"Can we go?" Reg asked. "We need to reanimate Gideon next, right? And that is what we know how to do already, so let's do it."

"Reg is right," Davyn said. "We can take the next step, so we should. Maybe we don't know what else to do yet, but we may as well take the step that we know, and to find out what Gideon knows that could help us. He may hold the key. Perhaps that is why he was here to begin with."

"You go, then," Corvin growled. "I have work to be done here. You will fail in your efforts to save the world by releasing the remaining elementals, and then you will be back here looking for answers. Given enough time, *maybe* I can find something helpful. Since I cannot perform any magic, it will all be up to you. I will not be able to do what I did last time."

Reg stared at him in disbelief. "You're not going to come?"

Corvin shook his head, his expression sour. "No. There is no point in me coming. I would only be in the way."

"But you may be able to advise us…"

"Not if you plan to release the elementals." Corvin looked at Sarah and then back at Reg. "Such a venture is bound to result in disaster. When enough people have been killed, maybe you will be ready to come back and listen to what I have to say."

Reg looked at Sarah, hoping that there was some way they could be reconciled and Corvin would come with them. But Sarah stubbornly stood her ground. "Let's go then, Reg. There is no point in delaying." She raised her chin. "If Corvin isn't even grateful enough to thank you for what you did…"

"Of course I am grateful," Corvin said quickly. "I owe you a debt. But for the fact that you have... commandeered my library. You and I will have to sort that out later. For now... you have work to do."

"Okay." Reg shrugged. "I'll see you... tomorrow maybe. Once everyone has been reanimated and things have settled down."

CHAPTER FORTY-FIVE

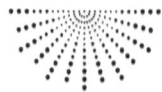

They were subdued in the car on the way to the Temple Orange Grove. Reg wished that she had something to say. If not something supportive and encouraging about the quest that they had set out on, then maybe a good joke that no one had heard.

Did you hear the one about the earth elemental who...

Reg couldn't think of anything funny to say.

She stared out the window, thinking about reviving Gideon. She would bring him back to life just as she had Corvin. They would find out what he was willing to tell them that Corvin had not. They would find out why he had been there in the first place. He must have gone to the temple with a plan. And then... everything would fall into place, and it would all work out as it should.

She had another bottle of water and a handful of Oreo cookies. She knew that she should have something better for her. Sarah *had* packed fruit. But Reg didn't feel like fruit. The thought made her nauseated. The Oreos were good and they would have to do for the time being. Not full of vitamins and other nutrients, maybe, but at least the energy her body required.

They left the car slowly when they reached the Temple Orange Grove. Without saying a word, they were all on guard, watching for anyone else who might have arrived before them and be lying in wait. Senses primed for any sign that the escaped elementals were there. The smell of sulfur or of pine that Corvin had noticed.

But of course, the grove smelled instead of oranges. Reg breathed it into her lungs. It was a sweet, wholesome smell. Like the nourishing breakfast placed in front of her by a foster mom who hadn't given up on her yet.

They walked together, approaching the broken altar where the earth relic had been buried. Reg could feel the magic in the place. All the covens that had taken place there, weaving their rituals into a rich tapestry of community magic. The ancient geode with its power and the magic of the elemental that it had held. Even the violent, disruptive magic of October and his pack, confronting Corvin and smiting him with a curse so that he could no longer use the magic he had been exercising for hundreds of years.

Reg looked around carefully. She felt like they were being watched. Was there someone there ahead of them? Or was it Gideon's presence, his foot on the path, his statue standing over the broken altar? Maybe she was just feeling his presence there.

She touched the stone statue to reassure herself. She could barely feel him there anymore. Reg swallowed.

"It's a good thing we got here when we did. I don't think he has much longer."

She couldn't help but think about the young werewolf she had helped with October, who had been too weak after his transformation from werewolf into his human form to survive. What if she reanimated Gideon only to have him die? Maybe it was better to leave him petrified until someone with more power than she held came by to do it.

"Well, you know what to do," Sarah said quietly.

It was all up to Reg. She took a deep breath, hoping she would be able to do what she had come there to do. She started humming, and let the song swell in the back of her throat. The siren sisters did not seem to be as strong this time. She had a hard time hearing them and their voices did not harmonize with hers as they should.

Maybe it was too soon. Perhaps they, too, were drained from

the reanimation of Corvin. She didn't imagine that it was something that sirens were called upon to do very often. She had certainly never heard such a request from the other sirens in all the time she had been aware of them.

She was aware that Sarah and Davyn were looking at her with concern. She looked over at Davyn, her voice faltering.

Davyn took a step closer and raised his hands toward her. She felt the wave of warmth he shared with her and was instantly energized. Like a good jolt of high-test coffee in the morning, it stiffened her spine and gave her the will to carry on. She raised her voice and tried again.

Her voice was stronger, but still not joined by the siren sisters. Reg hoped that her voice alone would be enough. She still had the strength of a siren, the water and air affinity.

When she had nearly exhausted her voice, she transformed into her dragon form and blew fire at the statue of Gideon, trying to envelop him fully in the fire. If her song wasn't strong enough, she would make up for it with the intensity of her fire.

When she had done all she could, she sat back on her haunches and waited, watching Gideon carefully for changes.

It didn't happen as quickly as with Corvin. Maybe because he had been petrified for longer than Corvin or because her song had not been as strong. His face gradually took on color and, eventually, he started to move stiffly. Reg returned to her human form, thinking he would feel more comfortable dealing with humans than a dragon. As a human, she was tired and sore. Ready to go home and sleep for a day or two. It seemed like weeks since she had fought the forest fire. She sat on a flat rock, resting. It wasn't the altar stone or a gravestone or something with special significance.

Gideon's movements were infinitesimal, fractions of an inch. Davyn poured healing energy into him, hoping to speed his recovery.

Gideon took a slow, shuddering breath. "How long has it been?" he asked weakly.

"Four days," Davyn told him. "Or at least, four that we know of. How long you were here before that, we don't know."

Gideon rubbed his knuckles, then the back of his neck, and stretched his head this way and that, trying to relieve all the kinks and to stretch out cramped or atrophying muscles.

His gaze shifted toward Reg. "You were here before. I felt your presence."

Reg nodded. "We were all here before."

"It was you I felt. I did not think I would be able to come back. It felt like an eternity."

They all nodded sympathetically.

"Think how the elementals feel after being bound for hundreds of years," Sarah pointed out gently.

Gideon's eyebrows went up. "The elementals?" he repeated. "Elementals don't have *feelings*."

"How do you know that?"

He rolled his eyes and pulled his cloak close around him, seeking its warmth. "Everyone knows that elementals don't have feelings. They are pure energy and intelligence. Not emotion. Not reason. They have no concept of themselves or others, so whatever they do is instinct or reaction to their environment."

"How do you *know* that?" Reg asked, taking up Sarah's refrain. She wanted to know more about the elementals and how they might negotiate with them.

She feared that everything Corvin and Gideon had to say about the elementals was only rumor and conjecture. Rumor and conjecture would get them nowhere.

"Who are you?" Gideon asked. "How is it that you don't know anything about the elementals? You awakened me."

"Reg. Reg Rawlins." She wasn't sure how to introduce herself or explain who she was and how she had brought him back. "I'm… yes, I helped to reanimate you."

"Then you must know something of the elementals."

She shook her head. "Only what I have heard the last few days. It was my homunculus who suggested how we could revive you… wake you up. I wouldn't have known how without him."

"You have a homunculus?" He looked her over. "You seem very young."

"Yes… it used to belong to someone else. But it has since bonded to me."

"Indeed." His dark eyes glittered, and he didn't tell her that such a thing was impossible or ask to know how she had managed it. If he was a practitioner of questionable magical practices like binding free elementals, then perhaps he dabbled in darker arts too and knew things about homunculi that magicals who avoided that area of practice did not. "Well, you are indeed very skilled to have both a homunculus and the ability to reverse a petrifaction spell."

Reg shrugged modestly.

Gideon looked around the temple ruins. "We must make plans immediately to bind the earth elemental before it can do more damage. The others are still safe?"

Davyn cleared his throat. "The fire elemental is also free. It caused a forest fire not far from here. The earth elemental has petrified others as well." He looked at Davyn. "We will probably not be able to reanimate any others today. At least, I don't think Reg will be. Maybe the rest of us can put our heads together to find a way to complete the reanimation process that doesn't require Reg's powers. Each of us has affinities that might be beneficial. I am a firecaster. Sarah has an affinity for air."

Reg smiled, thinking of Sarah flying on the Roomba.

"Earth and fire are free," Gideon mused. "It will not be easy to bind them again. The water and air elementals are still bound safely?"

"We have them," Davyn said slowly. "But we are looking for a solution that will free all of them and have them living in harmony with the environment, not to bind them again."

Gideon stared at him. "Are you crazy?"

CHAPTER FORTY-SIX

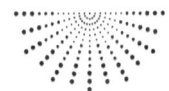

*G*ideon looked from one to the other, shaking his head in disbelief. "Don't you understand what is happening here? These rogue elementals wreaked havoc, caused all kinds of disasters, and took countless lives. The only solution is binding them to prevent that from happening again."

"We believe there may be alternatives," Sarah countered. "We have been doing research, and I think that there is the possibility of success if we—"

"You have been doing research? You have no idea what you are talking about. Research into what? You think that there is anything in your books and old scrolls that addresses this situation? We were the only ones who had any idea what to do to stop them. The only ones who were willing to act. Where were you before we bound them? Were you even born?"

Sarah drew herself up haughtily. "I was in this country long before you were even thought of, young man. Only youth would have the audacity to come up with a solution like this, sure that you know better than your elders." She stared him in the eye. "Youth and fools."

Gideon scoffed and switched arguments smoothly. "Excuses from the ancient. Your only solution was to let them run rampant.

You ruin our world with your neglect and then get upset when drastic measures are required to fix the mess you've left behind."

Reg thought it bizarre to hear complaints from such a wrinkled old man about the follies of Sarah's generation. To call him a youth when he looked a hundred years old and was actually even older was so incongruous that her brain refused to accept it.

"We reanimated you in hopes that you could tell us something about what happened and how to tame the elementals," Reg told Gideon. His discussion with Davyn and Sarah felt increasingly futile. "But since you don't know anything..." She shrugged and turned as if she planned to return to the car.

"I don't know anything?" Gideon growled. "I know more about these elementals and how to handle them than anyone in existence. Maybe in the entire history of man!"

What an ego! Reg couldn't help wondering if he was even sane. Who would make a claim like that? Maybe part of his brain was still petrified. She was wary of Gideon; it wasn't the first time she'd heard such a claim made by some warlock who intended to take over the world.

Maybe she should have left well enough alone and not reversed the petrifaction spell. Reg looked around, wondering if she would be able to sense the elemental if it were nearby. Despite the havoc they had apparently caused in the past, she was coming around to the idea that binding the elementals had been wrong and had only compounded the problem. Gideon's attitude alone told her he was covering something up.

"Why did you come here?" she asked Gideon, "You probably don't remember. I've heard that a spell like this addles the brain..."

Gideon sputtered and moved toward her. Maybe in his younger years, he would have attacked her. Maybe before his petrifaction, he'd still had the vigor to do so. But after being petrified for four days, his movements were slow and jerky. She watched his hands, knowing he was more likely to use magic than physical force. His aura was a dark, smoky red.

"I came here to strengthen the protection spells," he told her. "As soon as I heard of the attack on Corvin, I knew the spells he had maintained all these years would fail, making the relics vulnerable. But when I saw the broken altar stone, I feared the worst."

"You guessed that the earth elemental had escaped."

"It was the most vulnerable relic of the four. It was, perhaps, foolish of us to place it somewhere that was so freely visited by practitioners. The others were in more remote locations, not so easily accessed. The earth elemental was discoverable to anyone who chose to make a pilgrimage to the temple and had the power to sense it."

"The coven has met here for years," Davyn said, "It is a sacred place."

Gideon shrugged and nodded. "We hoped that the history of the place, the ley lines it was built upon, and magical energy that remained here would help to protect the Geode of Gaea. It would magnify the spiritual strength of the place, benefiting all who came here…"

"The temple is one of the reasons we have such a strong magical community here."

"That's right," Gideon agreed smugly. "And you wouldn't have that if not for the work that I and my fellows did here."

"You and Corvin."

Gideon narrowed his eyes at Davyn. "And others," he said sharply.

"Your shadow coven."

"A coven can be formed by any group of practitioners. We do not require sanction from some authority. A coven is a coven; it is not legitimate or a shadow organization."

Davyn and Sarah did not choose to argue the point. From what Reg understood of how things were organized in the community, Gideon was absolutely right. There was no central authority, but groups of practitioners organized themselves as they pleased.

There was, however, a department of magical investigations that looked into any reports that practitioners were doing something detrimental to the community or in violation of any of the treaties formed with other magical species. Or which caused harm to endangered magical species. That was the department Davyn's partner, Julian, was an investigator for.

There were numerous councils and organizations that tried to keep things running smoothly between different factions and species. Someone like Gideon, who had chosen to bind the elementals, would undoubtedly have run afoul of one of these organizations or tribunals if it had been broadly known.

"You knew when you saw the broken altar that the earth elemental had been freed?" Sarah asked.

"Yes. That was clear. But before I could do anything about it, as I attempted to ascertain the state of the geode and the elemental…"

"You were petrified."

Gideon nodded once. "I never felt anything like it before. I was not just unable to move, but unable to feel, to see or hear, and was only aware of the occasional being that moved through this place." He looked at Reg. "Like you. You have a strong psychic presence."

Reg shrugged, a bit embarrassed by his observation. She had reached out to him while he had been petrified; that was why he had felt her. Her presence couldn't be that much stronger than any other.

"You do yourself a disservice," Gideon said, reading her expression or possibly her thoughts. "You have great strength. Especially to be able to free me. I do not know why you would ally yourself with these practitioners." He flicked a glance to Davyn and Sarah. "You know that they will only hold you back. They are staid and traditional and, as you see, they will not accept innovation. Convincing an old witch to look at a new idea…" He shrugged expressively.

Reg thought about Sarah's and Davyn's opposition to Reg's rescue and use of Theodore. No matter what she said or how useful Theodore had already proven to them, they would not accept that Reg had done the right thing or had the right to do what she had done. Gideon was right about innovation. There were some things that the old guard, the traditional practitioners, would never accept.

"Like you binding the elementals. That was something you knew practitioners like Sarah would never accept."

Gideon nodded. "You can understand it when you look at history. Witches have been wrongly imprisoned or executed for their beliefs and spiritual practices. Many species have been enslaved and shown in freak shows and zoos. Any sentient creature being bound is anathema to them."

Sarah was nodding her agreement.

"But such thinking cannot be transferred to an elemental. They are not sentient creatures. They are not creatures at all. They have no bodily form. Whether they even have intelligence or whether it is only an energy force is up for debate. Not all powers within this sphere are wielded by intelligence. Some simply... exist. We have harnessed them with machines, exploited them for our own use, and there is nothing wrong with that because they are useful to us and they are not living, thinking things. Just forces."

He stared at her intently with glittering obsidian eyes. Shrewd and calculating.

"So it is with the elementals. You cannot view them as living, thinking beings, because they are not. They are just... sparks. Forces. And if those forces are not directed or harnessed, they can cause problems. Bring about dangerous imbalances and disasters."

Reg was almost convinced.

But she had learned a lot from Davyn and Sarah during her time living in Black Sands, and she trusted their viewpoints more than that of this stranger who had turned against the traditions of the community.

CHAPTER FORTY-SEVEN

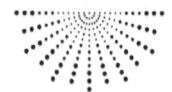

*T*here was a rumble of thunder in the distance. Reg looked up at the blue sky and wondered where it was coming from. She didn't see any threatening clouds. There was no wind, no sign at all of an incoming storm.

Gideon looked around, his face still pale as stone.

There was another rumble. This time, Reg felt it under her feet. Not thunder. An earthquake? She had never experienced an earthquake while in Florida. She wasn't sure if Florida ever got them. Sinkholes, yes, thunderstorms and hurricanes for sure, but an earthquake?

She caught a whiff of sulfur that was gone as quickly as it had come. Gideon held out his hands, looking around as if expecting an ambush, ready to use his magic to combat it no matter which direction it came from.

The ground shifted again. Reg looked at the spot where the broken altar stone lay, where Gideon had stood as a statue, and where she could still feel the power of the Geode of Gaea, surrounded by the protective ward stones. All clustered together in one place. She felt suddenly too close to them. Too much power was focused on that one place.

She was still tired from reanimating Gideon, as well as the rest of the adventures of the day. She felt the terrible weight of inertia. Trying to move from that place seemed like folly. But she had to do it. Reg crawled away from the altar and forced herself to rise.

Her injured leg buckled under her. It was like her body didn't want her to escape. But she did not wish to share Gideon's fate, whatever it was to be.

She gathered all her strength to take a few steps away, dragging her injured leg but managing to stay on her feet. Davyn watched and frowned, opening his mouth to ask her if she were okay. She could feel his concern.

The next rumble ended with a thunderous crack as if the bedrock beneath them had split. Reg reached out to steady herself on the wall of the temple but, of course, it was only an illusion. There was nothing for her to grasp, nothing for her to steady herself against, and she fell to her knees.

The ground under Gideon opened up, a tremendous black maw determined to consume him with a growl of grinding stone. He gave a yelp for help and tried too late to run. He was still too slow from his petrifaction, but he probably could not have escaped even if he were a young and vigorous sprinter. The earth was determined to have him.

Gideon disappeared from sight. The earth closed back up, pressing itself back together so that not even a crack showed. There was another rumble deep inside the earth that sounded remarkably like a belch, and then silence.

Reg stared for a long time at the spot where Gideon had disappeared. She swallowed, her mouth and throat very dry.

Davyn and Sarah looked at each other. Their eyes were wide and round. Reg didn't like to see her mentors frightened. What did it say for her own safety?

The ground could open up and swallow any of them at any time. What was to stop it?

"This is very disturbing," Sarah said finally, in a dry, cracked voice. She looked around her. "The earth elemental is clearly still here and has taken its revenge on the man—or one of the men—who held it bound for so many years. Now is the time for us to take action and make amends for what was done before it strikes again. It could turn all of us into stone at any moment."

Or...

Reg stared at the ground where Gideon had disappeared. She could no longer feel him, no matter how hard she tried. He was simply gone.

"How are we going to do that?" Reg asked. "What do any of us know about how to stop or control it? Gideon is the one who had that knowledge. And Corvin, but you know he isn't going to share. You saw how he reacted to Theodore reading what was in his library. He wants to keep all his knowledge a secret, to hoard it so that he is the only one who can understand what is happening."

"And Theodore."

Reg nodded. "Except for the locked books."

Sarah sighed. "It will have to do. What those boys chose to do was based on their interpretation of ancient texts, so perhaps those will inform us of our alternate path. We don't have the details of the exact spells Gideon and Corvin used or why they chose the places or relics they did. We will have to use what knowledge is available and guess at the rest."

"So now you *want* Theodore."

Sarah pressed her lips together. "I'm afraid I do," she admitted. "I fear that we are dabbling in arts that we should not, but it seems the only option at the moment. Will you summon him?"

Reg was already on her knees. She scooped up a handful of soil, wondering whether it was wise to summon her homunculus with earth when they were trying to avoid being killed by the earth elemental.

She threw the soil down in front of her, breathing the sweet scent of oranges in deeply.

"From soil and stone, by magic spin,
    Theodore reform, our work begin."

CHAPTER FORTY-EIGHT

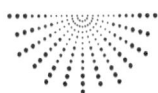

A small dust devil started to spin in front of Reg and, unlike at the Cyclone Tower, where it kept fizzling out, it worked this time. Reg was tired, but apparently that did not affect her ability to summon her homunculus.

Theodore stared at Reg with his flat black eyes, giving no indication of what he thought of being summoned there or the fact that she was kneeling on the ground. He looked around the ruins and observed Sarah's and Davyn's presence.

Knowing about all they had discussed so far, it was probably no surprise to him that they were all at the Temple Orange Grove.

"The warlock Gideon is here no longer," he observed.

"No," Reg agreed. "I managed to reverse the spell on him, but... apparently, the earth elemental wasn't too impressed by the fact, and..." Reg gestured helplessly at the place where Gideon had disappeared. "The ground just opened up and swallowed him."

Theodore nodded as if this were the most natural thing in the world. Maybe to him, it was. Maybe it was all expected after what he had read about the elementals and everything that had been happening in the ancient texts. Perhaps the whole thing had been prophesied a thousand years before.

Reg licked her lips and tried to figure out how to explain their dilemma to Theodore and find out if he had any knowledge that could help them succeed. It all seemed so convoluted that she was afraid he wouldn't understand or that he would give the wrong answer.

"The earth elemental is still here," she said slowly. She couldn't feel it like she had been able to feel the fire elemental, but then, her affinity was not for the earth. Everything but the earth. Sarah had said that the elemental was still there, and that was what had consumed Gideon, so she would go with that. "It took its revenge on Gideon. We want to... well, we don't want to be petrified or fall into the earth too. We just want... to help the elementals."

Theodore clicked and cocked his head at her, even though she hadn't asked a question yet.

"They were bound by Corvin and Gideon, like you said, and we want to free them. But we want to find a way to free them without them attacking us. And the big problem is, once we do that and they are free..." Reg looked at Sarah, trying to take any clues from her as to what to say. Sarah just nodded and looked reassuring. "Well, we want them to be free without causing any catastrophic events... Before when they were free, there were a lot of bad things going on... a lot of people were killed. That's why Corvin and Gideon bound them in the first place."

"They wanted the power."

Reg blinked. She looked at Davyn and Sarah to see if she had understood Theodore's words.

"What? What do you mean?"

"The elementals bound to the relics provide a powerful source of energy."

"Corvin harnessed them as a power source," Sarah said slowly, understanding spreading over her face. "Like having his own little nuclear generators. He would always have all the power he needed and more. Enough for several people, apparently."

Theodore nodded. His face betrayed no interest or concern in the matter. He was just the messenger. She had asked him to read all those books and scrolls, and he had done so and had come up with a theory. If it actually was a theory and not something that Corvin had explicitly detailed in an unlocked journal.

"I thought they bound the elementals to stop them from wreaking havoc in the community. They were dangerous. They had caused a lot of deaths."

Theodore shrugged. "There was much havoc and death," he agreed.

"So that part was true. They were causing a lot of chaos. *You* remember that, right?" Reg directed the question to Sarah. Sarah had been there. She could verify what Corvin and Gideon had said.

"Yes," Sarah confirmed again. "I remember all the stuff going on. It was a perilous time, with a lot of natural disasters as well as lawless people. The land had been through so much war, and people just wanted to... they wanted land and homes and a place where they could raise their families. But there were also many people who were there to hide from the law or make their fortunes by harming others. It was a difficult time to make your way." She sighed as if remembering how tiring it had been, then lifted her chin. "It was a lot of hard work, but we carved out an existence here. Clearing forests, draining swamps, cultivating the land for crops. It was a difficult life, but hard work won out."

"And in the middle of all that, the elementals were causing all kinds of problems," Reg suggested.

"Yes. Hurricanes, a huge tidal wave that wiped out all kinds of homes, malaria, yellow fever, crop failures. Just when you started to get a leg up, the next disaster would hit."

"So the elementals had to be bound. But how... how are we supposed to release them without having to face all of that again? There are already enough hurricanes and tropical storms, without adding to them."

"Heal the earth," Theodore told them. "The earth is not the domain of humans. It must be healed by one who knows it well."

Reg looked at Sarah, but she looked just as perplexed as Reg felt at the instruction. Davyn didn't look like he had any suggestions, either.

"How is the earth not the domain of humans?" Reg challenged.

"We live on the earth. We cultivate the earth. Everything we do... is connected with the earth."

It wasn't as if humans could survive in any of the other elements. They could not live in the air, water, or fire. Only on the earth.

"*Upon* the earth," Theodore pointed out, "not *in* the earth."

"*In* the earth? What, like actually burrowing in the dirt like animals?"

Theodore nodded at this. Reg rolled her eyes. Where were they going to find someone who lived in tunnels under the ground? Some hermit in a cave? Monks? They didn't even dig basements in Florida because of the high water table. No one lived underground. There were no mountains and no dwarfs building huge underground halls. Only pixies.

Reg frowned and thought about this. She had been to the pixie underground burrows soon after she had moved to Black Sands. Detective Marta Jessup had asked her to help with the case of a missing fairy girl, who had, as Reg had discovered, been kidnapped by pixies. They had gone into the underground burrows to rescue Calliopia, and Reg hoped never to go down there again. It was dark and damp and nasty. She had felt like the whole thing might cave in on her at any moment.

"What about pixies?" she suggested to Sarah. "They live in the earth."

"They believe anything in the earth belongs to them," Sarah said, nodding. "Precious stones and stones of power cannot belong to humans because anything under the earth is the pixies'."

"Right," Reg agreed, remembering more details as she thought it through. "So if there is anyone with an affinity to the earth and an earth elemental, it would be a pixie, right?"

"Yes," Sarah agreed reluctantly. "I don't suppose you are still in touch with any of those... people."

She said *people* like she really meant creatures or odious worms. Reg had to admit that she didn't see eye to eye with the pixies on very many things, but she had gotten accustomed to some of their ways as she dealt with Ruan, Calliopia's partner, and Karol, his sister.

All three were outcasts from both pixie and fairy society since the two peoples were mortal enemies, and pairings between fairies and pixies were forbidden. Despite Ruan's affinity for the earth and living underground, he now lived on the surface for his fairy mate. It was pretty amazing the two had stayed together, considering how opposite they were in so many ways.

"Ruan comes by every now and then," she told Sarah. "Brings a treat for Starlight and stays for a short visit. Calliopia likes the garden. She'll sit out there for a while in the sun while Ruan stays in the shade, and they are both… at peace. I think."

"You haven't let that pixie into the cottage?" Sarah demanded, aghast.

"No." Pixies did not have the same views on ownership as humans, and that tended to cause conflicts between them. Reg knew better now than to allow a pixie into her house where he might return later to help himself to something he had deemed his. "Just into the garden."

"Hmm." Sarah's expression told Reg clearly that she didn't like it, but now was not the time to argue about it, especially if they were going to try to get Ruan to help with their little problem.

"Do you think a pixie could help?" Reg asked Theodore. "Pixies live in the earth."

Theodore clicked and considered and nodded his head. "Pixies may have the knowledge and affinity needed to deal with the earth elemental," he agreed.

Reg took a deep breath and slowly let it out again. She didn't know where Ruan might be. He and Calliopia lived a nomadic life-style and didn't stay in one place for very long, since they might be targeted by either of their communities.

"Can you contact him?" Davyn asked.

Reg tried to reach out to Ruan, to envision where he was and what he was doing, but she didn't get very far. She was tired, and her head ached. When she tried to concentrate on Ruan, she felt like she should just lie down and go to sleep. She rubbed her forehead.

"I need... I don't know. I wish we could do this another day."

She knew that wasn't possible. The earth elemental had already proven it had no intention of waiting to see what they would do. It had swallowed Gideon and could do the same thing to any of them at any moment.

"You aren't looking so good," Sarah said, studying Reg.

"I'm not feeling so hot, to tell the truth."

"It has been a long day."

Reg nodded.

"Let me see if I can help," Davyn suggested. He walked over to Reg and sat down beside her. He took her hand and squeezed it, then released it and held his hands out toward her, warming her, again transferring strength and healing heat to her. Reg felt like a weakling for needing so much energy from him. She shouldn't have had to get energy from him so many times in one day.

But it had been a long, hard day.

"Don't resist, Reg," Davyn said. His eyes were kind and a little amused. "You need it, so take it."

"I just don't think..."

"You don't think transforming to and from a dragon, flying, swimming, fighting off sea monsters, flying monkeys, and unpetrifying two people should take that much energy? On what? Tea and Oreo cookies?"

"Well... yeah."

"Just relax and be open. We can't exactly go home and have a nap, but I can do this. I'm not the one who has been flying around doing all the work. Mostly, I've just been sitting in the car acting as your chauffeur."

"I always wanted a chauffeur."

"Well, there you go."

Reg closed her eyes and tried to do as Davyn had instructed and be open and accept what he had to give. It was the only way she would be able to carry on.

Her outlook improved as her energy grew and, after a few minutes, she tried reaching out to Ruan again.

She saw him sitting under a tree, his rosy round cheeks and curly brown mop making him look like a child rather than a grown man. He had on sunglasses which helped him tolerate the light above ground. He was talking to someone she couldn't see. Calliopia, no doubt. The two rarely separated, and none of their friends or family members would have anything to do with them, other than Karol.

"Ruan."

Ruan was startled and turned his head slightly. He smiled cheerily. "It is the great Reg Rawlins!"

"*Not* the great Reg Rawlins," she told him. "The very tired Reg Rawlins, asking for your help."

"My help?" he scoffed. "What can a piskie do for a great sorceress like thou?"

"I need you. Will you come?"

Ruan reached for Calliopia's hand to ensure that they were connected and would not go in different directions. He gripped it tightly.

"After all she has done, when Reg Rawlins calls, Ruan Rosdew will come."

"Come," Reg called, and pictured him there beside her. There was a jumble of images in her head as he tumbled across space to land beside her.

And then he was there, and she saw his dirt-smudged, rosy cheeks in person. The haughty fairy Calliopia was by his side as always, looking slightly discomfited at being brought across the country to sit in the midst of a human temple ruin.

"Why come we?" she demanded immediately. "Fairies do not help humans."

"Fairies have helped me more than once," Reg told her. "And I need a pixie's help, not a fairy's. Piskie's," she corrected herself, remembering to use the name Ruan used himself rather than the human corruption. "I need a piskie's help."

Ruan looked around at the stones of the ruin with interest.

"I have not been here before."

Reg nodded. She didn't imagine there was much there to interest him. But she was wrong.

He stopped where the Gideon had stood before the ground had swallowed him up. Reg raised her hand and started to warn him that it might not be a safe place to stand. But Ruan looked curiously at the earth beneath his feet; brows knitted together.

"What have you been doing here, Reg Rawlins?"

"That wasn't my doing. I just... I unpetrified someone, and it turned out that he wasn't very respectful of the earth elemental and wanted to bind it again, and it..." Reg shrugged with one shoulder. "I don't think it was very happy with him."

"You wish me to rescue him?" Ruan asked angrily, "He has gone the way of all the earth. He is beyond being rescued again. And Ruan would *not* rescue someone who had done such a thing."

"No. I'm not asking you to."

"I will do nothing to bind one of the fathers. Especially not the earth father!"

Reg continued to shake her head. "We want to free them, Ruan."

He looked at her, brows arced in query. He looked around at Davyn and Sarah and gave the homunculus a long, penetrating look. Then he looked back at Reg. "Tell me what has been done."

CHAPTER FORTY-NINE

*R*eg looked at Sarah and Davyn, then did her best to succinctly describe everything that had happened over the past few days and what they had discovered about what Corvin and Gideon had done centuries earlier.

Ruan's eyes were wide, and he listened with rapt attention. He shook his head in dismay at her description of how and why the elementals had been bound.

"Reg Rawlins tells the truth? You do not seek to bind the fathers?"

"No. We are trying to right the wrong that has been done. But we don't want a bunch of people to die because of it. We're hoping there is some way to... appease the elementals. If there is a way to achieve some kind of harmony."

Ruan nodded, thoughtful.

"There is much to be done. This will not be an easy task."

"What do you need us to do? We have the other elementals, still bound to the relics we want to release them from. The earth elemental is still close... I don't know about the fire elemental. It could be close by, maybe back toward the fort where it was bound. I don't know. Maybe it has gone farther afield. I haven't heard of any other forest fires."

"We must address the earth father first."

Reg shrugged. "I know it's the one that has been causing the petrifaction and... took Gideon, but I think the others are more powerful and dangerous. If we had the others all onside, maybe the earth elemental would just follow."

Ruan scowled. "Reg Rawlins knows nothing of this. The earth is the most powerful of all."

Earth was more powerful than fire, water, or air? When Reg thought of the devastation that could be caused by the other three elementals or how quickly they could kill, earth seemed undistinguished. Earth was just there. Other than when there was an earthquake, when did the earth cause mass casualties? And she didn't know when she had ever heard of an earthquake happening in Florida.

Most of the time, the earth just lay there under their feet. While it might provide stability and a surface to build on, it did not seem as important as the other elements.

Ruan could tell she didn't understand and shook his head sternly as if she were a student who wouldn't listen to the teacher, the expert who knew what he was talking about.

"Humans have no respect for the earth. What do humans do when they come to a place?" He looked around, glaring at all them. "They have to build their houses on top of the land. They cut down the trees, drain the swamps, break up the ground for their crops."

Sarah had just talked about how they had done all those things to tame the land in Florida. But Ruan spoke about it as if they had destroyed the earth rather than working it to provide the food and other crops they needed to survive.

"The earth dries out," Ruan pointed out. "It blows away in the wind. The animals die out. With the trees and the water gone, it gets too hot and dry, and the crops fail. Humans blame the land instead of themselves. There are no nutrients left in the soil. The fires start. The humans poison the land and water with their chemicals."

Reg looked at Sarah and Davyn, but they didn't dispute any of this.

"There are no trees or swamps to stop the storms that come in off the ocean, and more humans die." Ruan scoffed. "If they lived under the earth, so many would not die. But humans do not understand the earth. They fight the earth as if it is an enemy."

Reg felt embarrassed for the human race. She was not a farmer herself, having never even planted a garden. But she knew that they had poisoned the earth with pollutants and extinguished several animal species, probably plants, too. Instead of working in harmony with the earth, they thought they knew everything they needed to do to increase production.

Had all the chaos and devastation they had blamed on the elementals been their own fault for trying to change their environment and not understanding the consequences?

Ruan nodded his head sagely, studying her face. "Humans do not understand the power of the earth. You think the earth is weak, but it is the strongest of all."

Reg swallowed hard. She respected Sarah's garden gnome, Forst, for the work he did in the garden, and she knew that the food on her table had to come from somewhere. But she was disconnected from the earth. She walked and lived on top of it but didn't give it a single thought.

"So, what do we need to do?" she asked Ruan. "We can't fix how humans have changed the shape of the land. That would take years. We need to do something today. We don't want to keep the other elementals bound for another day." She appealed to Ruan's concern for the elementals rather than the people who could be petrified or killed by the earth and fire elements that had already been freed.

"Yes," Ruan agreed. "We must do what we can today."

Reg breathed a sigh of relief.

Ruan looked around, examining the ground and then his surroundings.

"We will remove the Geode of Gaea from this place, and make an offering to the earth father."

"Okay."

Ruan pointed to each of them in turn. To Davyn first, "You are fire." To Sarah, "Air." And to Reg, "And Reg Rawlins, water."

They each nodded solemnly.

"Each of you brings an offering to your element."

Davyn could bring fire. Reg was a little disappointed that she had not been assigned that element. But she had other affinities and Davyn did not. Reg wasn't sure what Sarah could bring for air. Maybe she could do an aerial show on her Roomba. Did elementals enjoy talent shows?

To begin with, Reg thought of offering a bottle of spring water from the cooler in the car. But she could do better than that.

Ruan approached the broken altar stone and knelt before it. He brushed the debris off the surface and ran his fingers over the runes carved in the stone, chanting in a low voice. He placed both palms on the earth in front of the stone. Reg felt a quiver go through the earth. She laid her palms flat on it as well, feeling the warmth of the soil, almost as if it were a living, breathing creature.

The earth boiled beneath Ruan, but he didn't seem alarmed by this development. He kept chanting quietly. Calliopia chose a better viewpoint to watch what he was doing, but said nothing that might distract him.

Several oval stones, almost like eggs, came to the surface of the soil. The ward stones. Ruan touched each of them, still chanting in pixie language. He removed each from the bed of soil in front of him and lined them up next to him.

He put his hands to the earth once more and closed his eyes. He stopped chanting and was silent, maybe communing with the earth elemental or feeling for the other stone that was buried deeply there.

The earth rumbled as it had before, and Reg's fingers curled into the grass and dirt beside her, as if by, holding on tightly, she could avoid sliding into the abyss where Gideon had disappeared.

Her heart beat hard and she felt sick to her stomach.

Was this it?

Were they all going to tumble into the earth and that would be the end of them? Would Marta Jessup investigate what had happened to them? Would someone look after Starlight and Ember?

She had never imagined her life ending this way. The thought of the weight of the earth piled on top of her was suffocating.

CHAPTER FIFTY

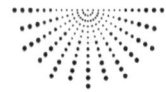

*T*he rumble trailed away. The earth had not opened up again. Perhaps it was just one last rumble of the earth's belly, satisfied with its last meal. Or having a difficult time digesting such a tough old bird.

The soil in front of Ruan did not boil this time. Only one stone came to the surface, cutting through the dirt as if it were water and rising, clean and sparkling, from the deep.

Ruan bowed down, his palms still on the surface. His face was almost in the dirt. His butt stuck up in the air, but Reg didn't think he looked comical or ridiculous. He paid obeisance to the geode that lay in front of him. One side of it was the round, rough shell of unfinished stone. The other side was as straight and smooth as a mirror and shone to a brilliant finish. The white and green crystals gleamed, laced with glittering gold. Reg was sure it must be incredibly valuable. But its true value did not lie in the money it could be sold for.

Ruan began chanting again, his voice breathless, as if he were overcome by the beauty of the earth relic. At long last, he pressed his face into the freshly turned earth like he might actually eat it, then sat back on his knees and slid his fingers under the geode.

"Follow thou me," he instructed, not looking at any of them, but at the stunning rock that lay in his hands.

Reg struggled to get to her feet. Davyn offered her a hand up and then a shoulder to help her over the uneven ground to the spot Ruan chose.

Ruan knelt on the ground again, gently laid the geode aside, and started to dig in the earth.

It was not the broken, loose soil of a tilled garden. The surface was overgrown with grasses and weeds. The ground was hard and filled with rocks of all sizes. Ruan's fingers ended in thick, claw-like nails, and these seemed to help him in his endeavor but, even so, it was not long before the skin of his fingers was torn and bleeding. He paid no attention to his injuries but continued to dig a hole for the geode.

Reg moved to help Ruan, but Davyn pressed her back. "You have already done too much today, and your role is not yet finished. Do not spend your strength."

No one else stepped forward to help Ruan. They all watched him dig his hole. Eventually, Ruan sat back.

"First the fire, to purify," he intoned.

Davyn stepped forward. He looked into the small hole. He glanced at Ruan, then crouched down and raised both hands to pour fire into the hole. It burned white hot for a moment, and then he gradually let it cool, then put it out. Reg almost expected the inside of the hole to be solid glass, melted by the heat of the fire, but it was not. Every blade of grass and tendril of root had been burned away, as well as any garbage or impurities left there by man.

"Water," Ruan commanded.

Davyn returned to Reg's side and helped her forward, lowering her to her knees where she was more comfortable and stable. Reg held her hands over the hole, much as Davyn had done, and closed her eyes.

She had been to the Temple Orange Grove a couple of times before and, on the way there, she had seen a small slough of water as they turned off the main road. She concentrated on it now, calling the water into her hands and letting it trickle through the cracks between her fingers into the hole until it was filled. It took a lot of water. The ground was very thirsty. But eventually, the hole was filled with water. Reg moved back out of the way and Davyn helped her to the side again to watch the ritual and wait.

Ruan put the geode into the rapidly disappearing water and, before the water all drained from the hole, he started to fill it with the earth he had initially removed. Before replacing it all, he flicked a glance toward Calliopia.

Reg had not anticipated that the fairy would have anything to do with the ceremony but, apparently, she knew her part without being told. She strode forward, her skirts billowing around her, and bent to add something small to the hole. Reg could not see what it was but could only guess.

Ruan nodded and filled in the rest of the dirt, pressing it down gently to make it smooth and level.

"And air," he whispered, as if afraid of waking a sleeping baby.

Sarah stepped forward. She seemed a little uncertain, but she didn't have her vacuum and didn't engage in any aerial acrobatics. She knelt before the filled-in hole and breathed gently on the surface of the dirt. She looked at Ruan questioningly, and he nodded. Sarah continued to blow on it gently until a leaf sprouted through the surface of the dirt.

Reg stared at it, mesmerized. She had seen many unbelievable things since moving to Black Sands, but this was a new one. The little green tendril grew and lengthened and sprouted more leaves until it had formed a small but perfect young sapling.

Ruan placed his hands on the tree trunk and repeated an incantation. Then, he returned to the temple foundations and picked up the six ward stones.

He set them in a circle around the tree, along the edge of the hole he had dug.

"This is the offering we have made," Ruan said aloud, speaking in English this time. "The beginning of the healing of this land. Trees provide strength, oxygen, shelter, protection, and sustenance. They hold the earth and keep it strong, retain moisture, and return nutrients to the soil. Without them, the land turns hot and dry."

He stroked the branches of the tree. "Grow strong and yet flexible, to stand up against the wind. Provide a break against fire, flood, and famine."

There was a rumble far distant, deep within the earth. This time, it did not scare Reg. She felt calm and soothed by Ruan's words.

He stood there for a moment in silence.

"Earth and fire be here already," he informed them. "Let us unite the four fathers. Bring water and air."

Davyn again motioned for Reg to stay while he and Sarah returned to the car to fetch the vial of the Tears of Poseidon and the Zephyr Pearl.

Instead of carrying the Zephyr Pearl casually under her arm, this time, Sarah held it reverently in both hands and walked with great care back to the sapling.

Davyn brought the vial with equal reverence. They both looked down at Ruan, then knelt, which brought them closer to his level. Sarah groaned and leaned on Davyn to get down to the ground again, but seemed fine once she was in place.

"Open the vial," Ruan instructed.

Davyn carefully unstopped the Tears of Poseidon. Ruan touched it and chanted. There was a rushing sound like the waves on the shore, and Reg caught a whiff of pungent sea air that hadn't been there a moment before. Her siren instincts were not triggered. *That* would have been awkward. She did not need to attack Davyn, or worse yet, Ruan, in the middle of the big reunification ceremony.

"And finally, air," Ruan said. He put both hands over the iridescent pearl and whispered to it. A long period of time seemed to pass. Reg opened her eyes. She was exhausted and was afraid she had missed something, falling asleep while waiting for the final step of the ritual. She rubbed her eyes and refocused her attention on Ruan.

"By fire's warmth and water's grace,
    By air's soft breath and earth's embrace,

We honor thee, our fathers old,
With hearts sincere and pledges told."

Ruan chanted the verse once, then led them through it, with each intoning the elemental they had represented, then all of them saying the whole thing together one more time.

There was no thunder or lightning, nor more rumblings from the earth, wind, or forest fire.

Reg feared that despite Ruan's careful work and chants, they would be caught in a maelstrom of wind and fire when they loosed the last of the elementals.

CHAPTER FIFTY-ONE

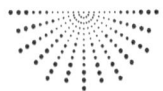

*B*ut there was no storm, nor were they swallowed up in the earth. Would the elementals stay quiet and calm in the coming days and weeks? Reg hoped they would not see a resurgence of the chaos that had plagued the area before the elementals had been bound. Healing the land would take years, and she wasn't sure whether the elementals would have the patience to wait or whether things would get unbalanced again and they would pay the consequences.

Ruan gave her an untroubled smile, again looking like a child rather than the serious man he had been while conducting the ceremony. "Reg Rawlins, we have done all in our power. There is naught to be worried about."

"But what will happen tomorrow?"

"None knows what will happen tomorrow. Perhaps thou, if you have the power of foresight. But not I. Tomorrow will bring what it will."

Reg sighed. She knew she couldn't predict the future. Sometimes, she had some prescience, but mostly, her power was in speaking with the dead, not predicting the future. Instead, she just worried about it.

"Come thou, Reg Rawlins," he told her, extending a hand as if to lift her up. "You have done much to be proud of today."

Reg didn't take his hand, not wanting to pull him over. Though she knew that his strength was at least equal to hers, probably more. Pixies, like insects, had considerably more strength than they ought to for their size.

When Reg didn't accept his proffered hand, Ruan reached under her arm and pulled her gently to her feet. He frowned, looking at the crumpled bandage on her leg. It had not fared well through her adventures and transformations.

"What injury has Reg Rawlins?"

"It was... a sea creature."

"Sea creature." The pixie shuddered. "Our kind should not be in the sea."

"Well, I am part siren, and how else was I to retrieve the water elemental?"

He nodded his agreement with this. "But thy companions should have treated this injury. Does the witch not know her potions? And the warlock has fire, like thee."

"Davyn helped me a couple of times. And Sarah did put a poultice on it. But... it's gotten worse. I didn't think it was anything to worry about, to begin with. It was just... I thought it was like poison ivy."

"Sit thou."

Even though Ruan had just helped her up, he now pushed her back to the ground. He stretched out her leg and moved Reg's skirt out of the way to better examine it.

He peeled the dressing back and reared back. Alarmed, Reg leaned over to look at the injury. The back of her calf was not easy for her to see, so she bent and rotated her leg, trying to get a better view. She could see that it was red and raw—much worse than it had been when Sarah had initially dressed it.

"It is poisoned," Ruan told her. He made her keep it still and leaned forward to examine it closely. He sniffed the injury and the dressing that had been on it.

"The sea monster must have been poisonous," Reg told him. "It wasn't that bad to start with. Is it like one of those spider bites? Should I go to the hospital?" She tried to look at it again, despite Ruan's attempts to hold her leg still. "Are they going to have to scrape it? I saw them do that on TV, and—"

"Hush, Reg Rawlins," he advised. He sniffed the bandage again, delicately. "Aconite. This is very dangerous."

"Aconite?" Reg repeated. She tried to remember what Sarah had put in the poultice and shook her head. "No, it was supposed to be aloe vera and... comfrey and echinacea and... candles."

"Calendula," Ruan corrected with a smile.

"That is what Theodore suggested," Reg indicated the homunculus. She had known that Theodore's answers were sometimes wrong, and she hadn't stopped to check whether the remedy he had suggested was safe. But she had thought that Sarah would know if it was not.

"This is not. It is aconite, not comfrey."

Reg swallowed. "All I wanted was some aloe. Is that what made it worse? Aconite?"

Ruan nodded. "Monk's hood must only be handled by those who know it well. All parts of the plant are poisonous."

"And that's what it did?"

Sarah and Davyn bent over Reg to see what was going on. Sarah saw the flaming red injury and covered her mouth. "What happened? The poultice should have reduced the pain and inflammation significantly by now!"

"It looks worse," Davyn contributed. "Maybe Reg had an allergic reaction."

"It is aconite," Ruan told Sarah, pointing to the used bandage. "Not comfrey."

"What? That can't be! I prepared it myself!"

"You should not prepare potions if you do not know your herbs," Ruan said flatly.

"Oh, Reg, I'm so sorry. I don't know how this happened. Are you okay? That looks very painful. And aconite poisoning... are you feeling all right? Your stomach and your head? Your heart?"

Sarah looked like she might faint herself. "Oh, how could I let such a thing happen? I could have killed you!"

"It's not that bad," Reg assured her, deciding that maybe it was best if she didn't let anyone treat the injury any further. "I think... I just need a nap. A rest. It's been a long day."

"Yes, yes, we must get you home and to bed as quickly as possible. Come, get in the car." Sarah started hurrying toward the car herself, looking back to ensure that Davyn and Reg followed. Davyn helped Reg back to her feet, and Ruan bravely tried to prop her up on the other side, despite his diminutive stature.

"Uh, do you have a way to get home?" Davyn asked Ruan, realizing they had not come with a car or any mode of transportation. "I don't know if you will be comfortable in the car..."

"We can share a seat," Ruan advised. "If you drop us in town, we can find our way from there."

"No, I brought you here," Reg protested. "I can send you back."

"Reg Rawlins must not tax herself," Ruan said firmly. "You need your strength. And more. Must not transport us."

When they reached the car, Davyn removed the cooler and other equipment from the back seat and placed them in the trunk. Sarah held the Zephyr Pearl and the vial of the Tears of Poseidon, which she had recorked, in her lap. Reg slid into her seat, trying in vain not to bump her leg on anything, but it kept touching and rubbing against everything.

Ruan squeezed into the middle seat, with Calliopia behind Davyn. Ruan sat up, straining to see the road ahead like a toddler without a booster seat.

"Let the smithy give thee strength and healing," he told Reg in a low voice as they rode back toward town. "But trust not the witch! Not to be able to tell the difference between comfrey and aconite!" He shook his head. "She could have killed thee."

Reg glanced at the back of Sarah's head, sure Sarah must be able to hear everything Ruan was saying.

"It was just an innocent mistake. Anyone can make a mistake."

"Anyone can kill their neighbor," Ruan intoned.

Reg smothered a laugh despite the way she was feeling. Pixies had no tact.

"She didn't kill me. I'm sure if we just leave it alone and wrap it in a clean bandage tonight, it will be much better tomorrow. And I'll…" Reg tried to think of what else she should do. How did one treat aconite poisoning? Just wait for it to leave her system?

"You must rest. And take healing from the smithy. But trust not the witch for remedies."

"I will have my mother send a potion." Calliopia offered. Reg had not even thought she was listening. Her mind appeared to be elsewhere as she stared out the window. "Milk thistle and licorice." She reached her arm across Ruan's face to put her hand boldly on Reg's chest. "Thy heart is steady," she said after the passage of several seconds. "I think foxglove be not required."

"That would be very kind," Reg said, feeling her cheeks warm. A gift from the fairies was unusual and unexpected. Though not always welcome, as fairy gifts tended to have both positive and negative aspects. "Are you in contact with your mother?"

They had cut off contact when Calliopia and Ruan had run away together, at least initially. Reg had returned Calliopia to them when she had suffered a dire injury, helped nurse her back to health, and participated in a quest to destroy the cursed blade that had injured the girl. But once Calliopia had returned to health, she had left home once again, and Reg hadn't known that they had remained in contact.

Calliopia gave Reg a sideways look, suggesting that maybe Reg was not supposed to know this. "Mothers and daughters sometimes know each other's thoughts without any formal communication."

"Oh, is that so?" Reg smiled. "Well, I'm glad to hear it. What about fathers and daughters?"

"It is harder," Calliopia admitted. "But… over time, it is possible."

"Will you ever be able to go back there?"

Calliopia shrugged. She gave Ruan a warning look, and he said nothing.

"The kin are not a forgiving people like humans," Calliopia said slowly. "It takes a very long time."

"But there is still hope?"

"Perhaps when those with longer memories are no longer part of our community."

That sounded like a very long time, indeed. Humans could live to be ninety or a hundred without any longevity spells. Fairies were longer-lived than that, easily racking up hundreds of years. If everybody who knew about Calliopia's rebellion had to die before she returned home, that could be centuries away.

CHAPTER FIFTY-TWO

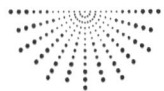

*R*eg was sorry to have to say goodbye to Ruan and Calliopia when they reached the town, but the two insisted that they had to go, and Reg could not invite them into the cottage for fear that they would steal from her. Or try to eat the cat.

As Calliopia climbed out of the car, Reg leaned over to whisper in Ruan's ear and ask how Calliopia was doing. She'd had a very hard time since her abduction, suffering from what Reg thought of as fairy PTSD. Such things were not spoken of among her people, and she was expected to just deal with it and not say anything, which did not sit well with Reg.

Ruan gave Reg's hand a squeeze. "She is not worse."

Reg knew better than to look into a pixie's eyes, but her eyes automatically met his in sympathy. Ruan nodded and turned away from her to join his mate.

Davyn then whisked Reg and Sarah the rest of the way home and insisted on helping Reg to the house. Sarah was beside herself over her part in Reg's poisoning. She kept apologizing and reiterating that she didn't know how it had happened.

When they reached the door of the cottage, a woman in a billowing white gown stood waiting, and Reg recognized her as

Lady Papillon, Calliopia's mother. For two people who were not supposed to be in communication, Calliopia had managed to let her mother know of Reg's need very quickly.

Lady Papillon handed Reg a vial. "Split this between tonight and tomorrow morning. Rest well. Put nothing else on the wound."

She bent over and lifted Reg's skirt to look at the injury herself. She shook her head. "I will send more over tomorrow. It may take a few doses to heal."

"Thank you, my lady," Reg said, bowing low. Davyn grabbed at her, perhaps thinking she was about to faint, and looked relieved when she straightened again. "You are very kind."

"You restored our daughter," Lady Papillon reminded her. "No payment could suffice."

They had already paid Reg a king's ransom for what she had done. Though a ransom in cursed gems was worth nothing until they could be cleansed of the curse, which proved to be a lengthy and sometimes dangerous prospect.

Reg hoped there would be no negative consequences from the healing potion. Hopefully, it wouldn't turn her into a cat, make her lose her voice, or anything else unexpected.

Lady Papillon nodded very slightly in acknowledgment, then swept regally away. Sarah unlocked the cottage door, and she and Davyn accompanied Reg inside.

The interior of the cottage looked like it had been ransacked.

Reg always laughed at the old TV shows that showed furniture being overturned and destroyed, evidencing someone had been searching for something while the homeowner was gone. If someone were searching for a paper, a USB drive, or even illegal drugs, why would they cut open all the couch cushions, overturn all the furniture, rake out the contents of the fridge and drawers, and do all the other things seen on such shows?

Any thief worth his salt would not waste his time. He would look in drawers, safes, or common stash spots and would be careful to put everything back and leave the room undisturbed. The longer it took for the victim to discover the theft, the better the chances of getting clean away.

The interior of Reg's cottage looked like the scene from one of those old cop shows. Furniture tipped over, several cushions torn to shreds, boxes of dry goods from the cupboards scattered all over the floor, and just about every delicate ornament pushed off the shelves or tables where they resided, several of them broken.

Starlight sat on his haunches, watching Reg come in with Sarah and Davyn. Sarah gave a dramatic gasp, looking around in horror.

"What happened here?" Davyn asked, also surprised by the destruction.

Reg looked around in dismay, bone tired. She didn't have time to clean up and see to the feeding of the savage beast.

"Starlight," she said.

"What?" Sarah demanded. "Starlight did this? Why would he do such a thing?"

"Because I wasn't home all day, and neither were you. He doesn't like to be alone with nothing but dry kibble to eat."

"Well, to be fair, I wouldn't either," Davyn chuckled.

Sarah glared at him. "Well, now you see why I don't like cats," she said icily, turning to look back at Starlight.

Sarah normally doted on Starlight despite her dislike of cats in general. With her affinity for birds, it was understandable that she would not take kindly to cats, especially those who lurked around her garden, but she had come to like Starlight. He stayed in the cottage so she didn't have to worry about his chasing the birds that came to her feeder or her gray parrot familiar in the house. She gave him little treats, spoiling him even when Reg told her that he'd already had enough to eat. *Just one more morsel wouldn't do any harm.*

Starlight, who had been looking at Reg with an aura of superiority and self-satisfaction at expressing his dissatisfaction, looked cowed by Sarah's words. He put his ears back and crouched slightly.

"You are a bad cat," Sarah scolded. "You had what you needed. Reg has been out on very important business, saving this town from ruin and destruction, and was injured in the process, and this is the way you repay her?"

Starlight's ears lay flat against his head, and he crouched even lower. Reg bent to pick up a chair that had fallen over, but Sarah motioned her away.

"You need to save your energy. In fact, if Davyn still has any to spare…?"

Davyn nodded. "Of course," he agreed. "And if we light a few candles in the bedroom, that would also help."

"But I can't just leave this mess," Reg protested.

"It will be dealt with. You don't need to worry about it," Sarah assured her. "If you do not take care of yourself, you will end up in hospital, or worse. Indeed, with aconite poisoning, we should be taking you straight to the hospital anyway, but I know how little they will do for you, and they will keep you awake all night with their checking and their PA announcements and the constant noise and commotion. You need to take the fairy potion, take healing power from Davyn and the fire, and sleep as much as possible. The rest will be dealt with."

Reg didn't want Sarah to have to do all the cleaning and repairing, but she could see that neither she nor Davyn would allow Reg to do anything but go straight to bed. Sarah probably deemed having to clean up a suitable penalty for poisoning Reg.

"Starlight needs to be fed," Reg told Sarah as Davyn escorted her toward the bedroom.

"Oh, he does, does he?" Sarah challenged. "We'll see about that."

Of course Starlight could go one evening without food, but seeing what he had already done when Reg had stayed away all day, who knew what he would do if left the night without anything but crunchies in his bowl? But she was not allowed to stay and argue with Sarah about it.

The bedroom was the scene of more destruction. Everything knocked off the top of the dresser, which had not been very tidy to begin with. Another pillow savaged. Several scarves and necklaces strewn about the floor where Starlight had been playing with them or deliberately making a bigger mess. Reg was embarrassed that Davyn had seen her room like that. He would think she was a bigger slob than she actually was, leaving her room in such a state.

"Don't worry about it," Davyn soothed. He pushed her toward the bed. "Lie down. Do you want to change first?"

Reg shook her head. She didn't think she had the strength to do it herself and didn't want Davyn's help stripping down and pulling on her usual sleep shorts and ratty t-shirt. She obediently went to the bed, pulled back the blankets, and lay down, pulling one of the extra pillows over to sleep on. Starlight had known which was her favorite and destroyed it. Darn cat.

"Take the potion," Davyn guided her hands. She didn't know whether she was still holding the potion or whether he had put it back into her grasp. "Only half now. The other half in the morning."

He helped Reg dribble half of the potion into her mouth. She'd had one of Lady Papillon's medicines before, so she didn't dread the taste. It was sweet with honey and had a faint licorice taste, mixed with fruit juices, perhaps peach and cherry. She would have drunk the whole thing if Davyn had not stayed her hand.

"Good. Rest for a moment while I light the candles."

She closed her eyes and listened to Davyn moving around the bedroom, picking up candles from the debris on the floor and lighting them without matches. When she opened her eyes again after a few minutes, at least a dozen candles of different sizes and shapes spread their cheery light. It was twilight outside, and they brightened the room considerably. Even when the sun was down completely they would keep the room well-lit.

Reg felt the strength from the tiny flames. They would regenerate Davyn as well, and he could go home once he was finished and light a big fire in his fireplace. Or have Ember do it.

She missed Ember. He was too big for her little cottage, and he and Starlight were rivals, but Reg would have liked to see him again. Her eyes closed drowsily.

Davyn moved close to her. He spoke softly so that he would not startle her and hovered over her injured leg, pouring heat from his fire into it. Reg could tolerate a lot more than a non-firecaster would have been able to. That would help it to heal much faster. Maybe she would be better in the morning and not even need the additional doses of Lady Papillon's medicine. Though it was so tasty, she would take it anyway.

CHAPTER FIFTY-THREE

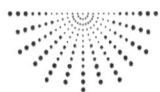

*W*hen Reg woke the next morning, she was still too tired and nauseated to get up and take care of herself and her disaster area of a cottage. Sarah was there to give her the rest of the fairy potion, and Reg went back to sleep.

She thought that Sarah had stayed the night. There had, perhaps, been several awakenings in the night when Sarah had seen to her needs and calmed any fears. But the memories were dark and murky and Reg could not have described them with any detail.

It was early afternoon before she started to waken enough to consider getting out of bed. But it wasn't that much later than her usual waking time, so maybe she would be fine by the end of the day.

Reg slipped out of bed and shuffled to the bathroom. There were no piteous meows for attention and feeding from Starlight. Sarah had probably dealt with him earlier despite her scolding.

Reg took care of her immediate needs in the bathroom, splashed water on her face, and probed at the inflamed spot on her calf to evaluate whether it was better. It seemed less painful than it had been the day before. It was not any worse. And the nausea and exhaustion that she had been feeling the night before had definitely improved.

Reg exited the bathroom, blinking away sleep and heading directly for the coffee maker. A good jolt of caffeine to get her engine running, and she was sure she would be fine for the day. She would probably be able to meet her obligations to see the clients written into her planner and not have to reschedule any of them.

Her mug was already positioned under the nozzle of the coffee maker, so Reg hit the button to start the coffee brewing and rested against the counter with her eyes mostly closed to wait for it.

Starlight gave a quiet meow from the kitchen island in front of her. Reg opened her eyes to look at him seated on the counter.

"Well, I guess it's time for the two of us to have a little chat," Reg told him.

She looked around the cottage and saw that it was spick-and-span, everything back in its proper place, the broken knickknacks repaired or disposed of. Reg smothered a yawn.

"Wow, this place looks great. Much better than it did after your little temper tantrum. It probably took Sarah hours."

"Not me," Sarah said, arising from the chair where she had been sitting out of Reg's sight.

"You didn't make Davyn do it, did you? I could have done it, you know. If you'd just left it for me today."

"No, I sent Davyn home to regenerate himself in case he needed to give you more strength and healing today."

Reg frowned and shook her head, not getting it. Who had cleaned the house, then? Had Sarah called in a crew of brownies to do the job?

"If a cat can make such a mess, a cat can clean it up," Sarah told her.

Reg looked with surprise at Starlight, who seemed very penitent and contrite now. He made a little trill, encouraging her to pet him, and Reg did so. She looked around the cottage. "How did he do all that? A cat can't clean the house."

"You know Starlight has other forms," Sarah pointed out.

In several emergency situations in the past, Starlight had transformed into an ancient Egyptian warrior in order to help Reg. And while an ancient Egyptian warrior might not want to clean Sarah's guest cottage, he was certainly capable of it. Reg scratched Starlight's ears.

"So you had to clean up everything you had made a mess of?" she asked him in her *good kitty* voice. "It's not quite so much fun to make a mess like that when you have to clean it up again afterward, is it?"

He rubbed against her until the coffee maker beeped that it was done. Reg had a few sips of her first cup of coffee, then checked the fridge to see what Starlight might like for his dinner.

* * *

While Reg didn't feel like going out to run errands after her brush with death, Sarah insisted that they needed to take care of a few items as soon as possible to try to keep the balance and harmony in Black Sands. She promised that she would do the driving and Reg could just rest and relax in the car as much as she needed to. But Reg knew Sarah's driving and there was no way she would be able to rest and relax in the car with a speed demon behind the wheel.

"I need to do something," she told Sarah. "You've already done so much. I've just been sleeping for the last twenty-four hours."

"Not quite twenty-four," Sarah said, though she allowed that it had been a long time.

The first stop was Corvin's house. Reg wasn't sure whether they were going to check on how Corvin was recovering from his petrifaction or something else. The warlock had not been eager to leave the house or have visitors since the werewolf attack, and Reg didn't imagine his spirits had been improved by the elemental attack.

Corvin looked none too pleased to find them on his doorstep. But at least he was able to answer his door this time and was not standing frozen in his study. It was hard for Reg to believe that she had been able to free him and Gideon from their petrifaction spells. The previous day felt like a dream. Looking back, it felt like she had watched it on TV, not that she had participated in it herself.

"Come in," Corvin invited tersely, his teeth apparently clenched and his lips pressing tightly together after he spoke.

They stopped in the entrance hall, not following Corvin to the study or the living room. Corvin looked back, irritated.

"Do you mind if I check the kitchen?" Sarah asked, pointing in that direction.

Corvin shook his head. "Why?"

"I need to figure out what happened. What went wrong with the healing poultice I made for Reg while you were still indisposed."

"What went wrong?" Corvin looked at Reg, eyebrows lifted.

Sarah held her head high, maintaining her dignity. It would be hard for her to admit her mistake, especially to Corvin.

"It would seem that... I somehow put aconite in the poultice instead of comfrey."

Corvin rubbed the whiskers of his short beard. "Good heavens. Are you all right, Reg?"

Reg nodded. "It was pretty sore, and I didn't feel good. But I had a good sleep, a healing potion, and an energy infusion from Davyn, so now... I'm doing a lot better."

"You are still pale. You should stay at home for a few days after such a thing. Sarah, you really shouldn't be dragging her around town."

"There are issues that need to be dealt with," Sarah told him, in much the same tone she had used the night before to scold Starlight for his shenanigans. "And as it seems that you are determined to closet yourself up here for the rest of your life and not accept responsibility for your part in it, someone else has had to step in."

Corvin stared at her, blinking owlishly.

"Now, if I could just take a quick peek around your kitchen to see if I can figure out how things went so wrong with the poultice, that would ease my mind. At this point, I wonder if I am going senile! I don't know how I could have made such a mistake, even in the urgency of the moment."

Corvin stepped to the side and motioned toward the kitchen. Sarah strode forward with authority as if it were her own home and started going through the cupboards. She pulled out a glass jar filled with dried, crushed leaves and purple flowers. It looked like any of the many spice jars in Sarah's kitchen, or Reg's own for that matter, even though she didn't cook.

Sarah held it up and tapped a label pasted to the side. It was an old, faded label that looked a hundred years old but was still recognizable as "Comfrey."

"This is what I used," she remembered. She unscrewed the lid and poked her nose inside, taking a deep sniff. She put it down on the counter with a bang. "Aconite."

Corvin's face grew gray. He approached Sarah and the cupboard in which the herb had been stored. He brushed his fingers along the edge of the shelf Sarah had pulled it from until he found a small slip of paper that he drew out and held between his fingers. A label that had apparently been glued over the original Comfrey label, but had dried out and come loose. He showed the label to Sarah.

Wolfsbane.

Reg stared at it. "Wolfsbane?" she repeated. "You said... aconite."

"Like many herbs," Sarah explained, "aconite goes by a lot of different names. Monkshood, wolfsbane, devil's helmet, queen of poisons. This is what you were poisoned with. I am sorry I did not pay close enough attention to the fact that it was actually what it was labeled. We were in a hurry to get on with our mission. I saw purple flowers and didn't even stop to smell them or examine them closely. I just measured out what I needed and dumped it into the poultice."

"This is one of the reasons it is better to use fresh herbs," Corvin said with a sigh. "They are much easier to identify when fresh. Sarah would never misidentify fresh monkshood as comfrey. But we can't always have fresh herbs when we need them. I had just recently refilled the jar. The wolfsbane label was on it when I refilled it... but it must have flaked off after I put it back in the cupboard."

"Why do you have wolfsbane?" Reg asked.

The back of her leg was throbbing. She was sure it was just because she was thinking about it and had been on her feet for a few minutes, and not because she was in such close proximity to the poison. Even though she felt much better than the day before, she knew she had not fully recovered.

Corvin looked at Reg; then his gaze slid over to Sarah. Sarah didn't make any suggestions as to the use of wolfsbane in healing potions. Reg only knew of one use for wolfsbane. She wasn't well-versed in herbology, so there might have been a dozen other legitimate uses.

"Do you not think," Corvin said carefully, "that having been attacked by werewolves once, I would not protect myself against a future attack? Wolfsbane, as I'm sure you well know, is used to repel wolves."

Reg nodded slowly. "So... you're going to use it against October?"

"I am going to use it against any wolf who dares to hunt me. I may not be able to use my powers, but the curse does not stop me from using herbs or other physical means to stop them. I do not intend to be taken off guard or unable to defend myself against another attack."

"But why would they attack you again? They've already prevented you from doing anything that might harm them."

"I do not expect another to think the same way as I do. The wolves, October in particular, have shown themselves to be without honor. A sneak attack in the middle of a spring equinox ritual, their attempt not only to disrupt our ritual and prevent me from sharing powers with the coven, but to punish me when I had done nothing wrong, and to continue to punish me whenever I try to use my powers again, even with something as minor as sensing your mood."

"You think there is going to be more trouble?"

"How could I know it?"

"But you're not going to... hunt them."

Corvin folded his arms across his chest. "I would be well within my rights to do so after they attacked me unprovoked and cursed me."

Reg stared him down. Corvin looked away from her.

"I am not going to hunt him."

Reg did not have powers like Damon Knight, who could immediately sense when someone was lying. But she had a feeling that, once more, Corvin was not telling her the full truth.

"Corvin has barely left his house since being attacked," Sarah pointed out. "I hardly think that he will be out hunting were-wolves. Well, Reg, you and I have more work to do. We will leave Corvin to his brooding while we continue to set things to rights."

Corvin shifted, looking uncomfortable with Sarah's evaluation. "What happened yesterday?" he asked. "Am I to assume... that you were able to bind the elementals that had escaped and to secure the ones who had not?"

"No, you should not assume that," Sarah said acidly. "I never told you that was our course of action. The elementals have been released. You no longer hold any power over them and you will no longer be able to use the energy they produce to sate your hunger. They are free."

His jaw dropped. "How could you do that? Do you have any idea how dangerous that was? The elementals must be secured, or they will wreak havoc on the population."

"So we have heard," Sarah agreed. "But we have released them. It is done. Since you cannot use your powers, you cannot re-bind them. Nor will Gideon Darkwood, who has passed beyond the veil. Your imprisonment of those entities is over."

"You will live to regret this action."

"Is that a threat?"

Corvin shook his head. "It is a prediction. I know what will happen. Maybe not today, but soon. I know what will happen when those rogue elementals are allowed to roam free."

"They are in harmony," Reg told Corvin. "They were only a danger while they were out of harmony with humans, because of all that had been done to the land here."

"All that had been done to the land?"

Reg tried to think of how to tell him everything she had come to understand about how important balance with the land was for the smooth functioning of the environment and climate of the region.

"All the things the settlers did, and the city builders. All the ways that they took from the land and caused the environmental disasters."

"You think the environmental disasters were caused by human activity rather than the elementals? You weren't paying very close attention. I was there, Reg. I know."

Reg looked at Sarah. Sarah patted her on the shoulder. "Let's go, Reg. You're looking rather piqued and should rest."

CHAPTER FIFTY-FOUR

*R*eg was not particularly happy to find herself at the Cyclone Tower once more.

Sarah had agreed to Reg using her powers to return the Tears of Poseidon home to the Oceanids' keep by simply sending the vial back to where she had gotten it. Having been to the underwater cavern in person initially, she could simply envision the place where the water relic had rested, and cause it to be transported through space to return there.

That saved a lot of time and energy and saved Reg the trouble of trying to explain to the Oceanids why she had stolen it from them in the first place and why the water elemental no longer dwelt in the relic. They would just be happy to have the relic back and would, presumably, eventually understand that the water elemental being freed was a good thing.

But Sarah would not allow Reg to simply transport the Zephyr Pearl back to the Cyclone Tower. She insisted that it needed to be returned in person.

The last thing Reg wanted to do was meet the flying monkeys again. Or to have to face Skippy the troll, which Sarah insisted upon.

This time, they were written in on the schedule Skippy had

clipped to his clipboard. He met them in a clean, pleasant reception area at the bottom of the tower where there was no sign of flying monkeys. The woman at the reception desk looked human to Reg's eyes. She tapped her computer keys to verify their appointment with the supervisor and asked them politely to have a seat.

A few minutes later, a tall man in a blue uniform stepped off the elevator, clipboard held firmly in his left hand. He looked at the entry and checked it off with his pen.

"Sarah Bishop and Reg Rawlins." He looked at them, then his eyes went to the Pearl. "It took longer than expected to clean the Pearl," he said in a slightly accusatory tone.

"Yes, it did," Sarah agreed. "You can't rush these things."

Skippy nodded and sighed. "Indeed. They seem to have minds of their own, don't they?" He held out his hands for it, tucking the clipboard under his arm.

"No Spanner today?" Sarah asked, handing it over. "I thought he would be the one who would be taking it back and reinstalling it."

Skippy snorted. "Whoever thought that a gremlin would be a good mechanic should be fired. You wouldn't believe the number of problems we have had since he took over. I will be glad to be training someone else for the position."

"He's gone then? Fired?"

"Better than that," Skippy told them, polishing the Pearl on his uniform shirt. "He was promoted."

"That's better?"

"I don't have to worry about him anymore. He's someone else's problem."

"Well, that's good, then. You'll be reinstalling the Pearl?"

"Yes."

"You might notice that... it has changed a little," Reg told him tentatively.

Skippy polished it some more. "It has been purified. With all impurities purged, it should function better and meet all specifications."

Sarah nodded her agreement. "I think you will be pleased."

"They should have had that done a couple of hundred years ago." Skippy shook his head. "You just can't find good help these days."

"Well... good luck."

"When will you be back?" Skippy asked, shifting everything around so he could again write on his clipboard. "When is the next scheduled maintenance period?"

"Oh... a hundred years or so," Sarah offered.

Skippy wrote it down. He pulled out an appointment card like the dentist used and wrote a date one hundred years in the future. "Do you want a reminder call?"

"No." Sarah took the card and tucked it into her purse. "This will be fine."

Sarah and Reg walked back to the car. "He's wound just a little bit tightly," Reg observed.

"Well, he has a reputation to keep up," Sarah allowed. "After all, he is the world's best troll."

* * *

Continue Reg's journey in:
Fur and Fury, Book #24 of the *Reg Rawlins, Psychic Investigator* series by P.D. Workman.
You can find it at pdworkman.com

Did you enjoy this book? Reviews and recommendations are vital to making a book successful.

Please leave a review at your favorite book store or review site and share it with your friends.

Don't miss the following bonus material:
Sign up for mailing list to get a free ebook
Read a sneak preview chapter
Other books by P.D. Workman
Learn more about the author

DON'T MISS A THING! GET THE LATEST NEWS AND A FREE EBOOK

PDWORKMAN.COM/SIGNUP

PREVIEW OF FUR AND FURY

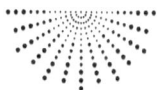

PREVIEW CHAPTER 1

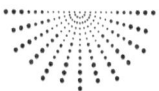

*R*eg had not expected to have to pose for the camera when she arrived at City Hall. Several of the attendees had encouraged her to go to the summit meeting between the warlocks and the werewolves, though she didn't exactly feel qualified to be there. Who was she? She didn't have any standing in the negotiations between the two factions.

"But don't you see, that's just the point?" Sarah asked. She was Reg's landlord and one of the witches who would be attending the so-called peace talks. "We need people there who are impartial third parties who can help to come to an acceptable solution for both sides. We must find some way to de-escalate the violence between the coven and the pack before further harm is done."

Eventually, Reg had let herself be talked into attending. She had to admit that she was curious to listen in on what was being done. She could go and just keep quiet and listen to what everyone else had to say. Attending didn't mean she had to stand up in front of everyone and give them her opinion or try to personally mediate peace between the two sides. She would just go and watch.

She had pictured a room full of chairs, maybe forty or fifty of them, with all kinds of people from around town who wanted to sit in and hear what was going on. She was not expecting the security check she had to go through when she got to City Hall. She needed to show her identification and have her picture taken for the security badge she was issued before entering the community room where the debate would occur.

She tried to tidy herself up for the picture. She gathered up her skinny red box braids and pushed them all behind her shoulders, made sure that her blouse and headscarf were straight, and smoothed her colorful, voluminous skirts, even though she knew that they probably wouldn't make it into the picture. It was a lot more attention than she had expected to get.

"What is your position?" the security guard asked her after taking her picture.

Reg wondered if he was a troll. He was quite tall, and his face did not show what he was thinking. She was clearly just another person to be processed, not of any real interest to him. He wanted to classify her, put her into the system, and get onto the next person. The rigidity of his process reminded her of Skippy, the supervisor at the Cyclone Tower.

"I don't have a position," Reg explained, shaking her head. "I'm a psychic here in Black Sands."

"You are part of the coven?"

"No. I'm not—"

Reg stopped herself from saying that she wasn't a witch. She had never seen herself that way, even though Sarah and others had repeatedly told her that her powers were very well-developed and she had a number of gifts that were quite rare. Even more surprising was that she had learned to exercise them as she had when she had been forced to repress them for her entire childhood. She hadn't even been aware of them until she had moved to Black Sands just a couple of years before.

Reg still didn't consider herself a witch. She had chosen to be known as a psychic, back when she thought she was just really good at cold-reading people and didn't know that she could read thoughts or auras and hear the actual voices of the dead. She had been told that the voices in her head were not real and she needed to shut them out and pretend that they didn't exist if she didn't want people to think that she was crazy.

She might also be part siren and part immortal, but she chose not to spread those tidbits around. They made her a target of the people who feared those races and she preferred not to find more smashed eggs on her car or door, mystical graffiti, or remnants of curses in the yard.

The guard looked at her, scowling. "Are you a member of the pack?"

"No, I'm not a wolf."

"So you're just… independent."

Reg nodded. "Yeah. I just wanted to see what was going on, what everybody has to say…"

He tapped whatever information he needed into the computer and printed her security badge onto a white plastic card, which he attached a lanyard to and handed her. Reg looked at the unflattering picture on the badge and shook her head. She didn't think she looked that bad. Somehow, the government always seemed to produce the ugliest identity pictures. It was like they did it on purpose.

Reg hung the lanyard around her neck and adjusted the length, trying to center the badge and position it so that it didn't sit in such an awkward position. She wished it had been on a pin instead of a lanyard.

"Move along," the security man encouraged, "I need to get everyone processed."

It wasn't like there were a lot of people behind Reg, and they had three officers checking people in.

The halls had wood paneling and tile floors. Smudgy beige paintings hung at intervals down the corridor.

The room was much smaller than Reg had expected. A large boardroom table with chairs around it rather than a podium at the front of the room and mostly anonymous people observing from rows of chairs.

Sarah was talking to Davyn and turned around when Reg walked in.

"Oh, Reg, I'm glad you made it!"

She made it sound like she hadn't just talked to Reg about it a couple of hours earlier and might have thought Reg was still in bed, even though it was afternoon, and Reg was always up by noon.

Almost always.

"I thought there would be more people," Reg said. There was a quiet murmur of voices. Reg looked around at the people who had assembled so far. She recognized most of them. Davyn was her mentor in helping her to hone her firecasting ability. Letticia, the old crone who led the witches' coven. Mayor Nichols, whom Reg had only ever seen on TV and never in person. Jake, Reg's ex-boyfriend who had accidentally been transformed into a werewolf while he had been conducting heinous experiments on them.

John, the son of Corvin, the absent leader of the warlock coven. Reg had not seen Julian, initially. Julian Sabat was an investigator with the Magical Investigations Endangered Species Division. Reg supposed he was there because of the involvement of the werewolves.

And Aleph, the alpha of the werewolf pack was there. Reg had rarely encountered him in his human guise. He had a rugged appearance, with shaggy blond hair and a gaunt, wary expression.

Aleph saw Reg examining him and frowned. But his eyes did not linger on her for long. She was clearly not a person he needed to be worried about.

"We would like to call the meeting to order," the mayor said pompously. "If everyone would please take their seats."

Reg looked for the chair where she would be the least visible. She was regretting that she had listened to Sarah. She didn't belong there with the community leaders.

"Come sit over here," Sarah tugged on Reg's arm and guided her toward a seat. There wasn't really anywhere for Reg to hide around the oval table. Everyone had the same visibility. It wasn't Arthur's round table, where everyone had an equal place, but it was pretty close. Reg sat down as instructed. The poofy seat squeaked as she settled in. The rest of the attendees sat down. Bending down to talk in his ear, the mayor's PA asked in a loud whisper whether he needed anything else. He motioned her away, and she drifted out of the room, pulling the door shut quietly behind her.

As soon as it closed, Aleph shot out of his seat. He wrenched the door back open, startling the PA so that she shrieked and jumped back.

"This door is not to be closed," Aleph said fiercely. "There will be no closed doors."

"I'm sorry!" The woman looked past him, through the doorway to her boss, for confirmation.

Mayor Nichols gave a little wave. "It's fine, Chelsea."

She put a hand over her heart, trying to calm herself. "I'm sorry, Mr. Aleph, I didn't know."

He looked around, alert for the approach of any enemy. Eventually, he gave a nod and retreated to his seat in the meeting room.

PREVIEW CHAPTER 2

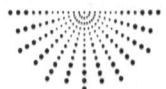

*M*ayor Nichols looked around the table as everyone settled in. He repositioned the yellow legal pad on the table in front of him, and his eyes moved slowly around the table, evaluating each person present.

"Should we start with introductions?"

"I think everyone here knows everyone else," Letticia observed. "I suggest we get right into it."

There were a couple of faces that Reg did not know, but she was not going to argue Letticia's suggestion. She preferred not to introduce herself to everyone when she knew she had no standing there and should have just stayed home. Sarah and Davyn could have filled her in on anything she needed to know.

The mayor looked around the table. "Is everyone okay with that?"

There were no objections. The mayor didn't have a gavel, but he gave a brisk, official nod. "Moved by Letticia Adams, I will second. No objections."

He looked at the scrawny, ferret-like man seated to his right, who scribbled something in the thick, hardcover black book that must be the official minutes of such meetings.

"I don't see the need for your human rules of order," Aleph

barked. "We do not follow them in our gatherings. They're just the humans' way of trying to assert dominance."

The mayor raised his eyebrows. He looked at his recorder as if he didn't know whether a change in procedure was even allowed.

The recorder shrugged his narrow shoulders. The mayor looked around the table. "Are there any objections?"

Aleph's expression was a snarl. If anyone had thought to object, they were probably dissuaded by his long canines. Reg swallowed. She was on good terms with the werewolves, but even as a friend of the pack, she would not want to argue with that snarl. No one in the room raised any objections.

"Fine, then," the mayor said slowly, "I'm not sure how to proceed without our usual order of functions... the purpose of this meeting is an open discussion of... the tensions between the were-wolves and other practitioners. There are concerns about an escala-tion in violence. As various community leaders, we wanted to gather together to discuss possible solutions."

"There is no need for any outside interference," Jake asserted. "There is no need for the municipal government or anyone else to get involved in something that is none of their business."

"If our citizens are being targeted by these attacks, the munici-pality can't just look the other way," the mayor disagreed. "We need to deal with it before it escalates and more people are hurt."

"The reason for attacks on humans is that they have been targeting wolves," Aleph said. His voice was a low growl. "They will soon learn that doing so is a dangerous proposition, and they will stop." He gave a cold smile. "It is what we call a natural conse-quence. Wolves find using natural consequences to be a very effec-tive way to train our cubs."

"Why are the wolves even coming into Black Sands?" John challenged. "After their unprovoked attack on the coven in the midst of our spring equinox ritual, they are not welcome here. I thought they had agreed to move out of the area. Maybe even out of Florida."

"The attack was perpetrated by a small number of wolves," Aleph pointed out, "not the entire pack. They have moved on.

There is still talk about moving the full pack, but this is a big decision when we have just gotten established here. We have one litter of cubs only half-grown, and two more expected in the next couple of weeks. Even humans can understand the difficulty of disrupting so many infants. Such a move would put both the mothers and the pups at considerable risk."

"Maybe the wolves should have considered that before attacking the coven," John shot back.

"The actions of a few rogue wolves do not constitute a decision of the pack."

"We all know about the attack at the Temple Orange Grove," Sarah interposed, "and if October and the other wolves involved in that attack have left, then that doesn't enter into today's discussion."

There were a few nods from around the table.

"What we are talking about today is something quite different. There is ongoing friction between the warlocks and the wolves even though the wolves involved in the attack have left," Sarah went on. "That is what we need to address."

Reg had heard only rumors and half stories about what had been happening around town. She listened with interest, wanting to get all the details of what had happened.

"There have been more unprovoked werewolf attacks," John spoke up. He absently rubbed a long, red scar on his forearm that he had sustained in the equinox attack, his movement drawing it to everybody's attention. "The attack at the temple was not the only one. Either the perpetrators of that attack have not left the area, or more are willing to take up the cause."

"There have been no unprovoked attacks," Aleph argued. "Not since the one October led. You have been misinformed."

"There have been attacks," John repeated, raising his voice to a shout. "Why do you think we are fighting back? We have been living in peace for decades. Why would that suddenly change? You need to leave here and take all of the pack with you. You say that October is gone, but he is obviously still here, being hidden and protected by the pack, or else others have taken up his cause."

Jake stood up. While he had some of the wildness of Aleph, he still retained the beauty that he'd had before his transformation. Even without the spell that Jake had used to bind Reg to him, she found herself irresistibly drawn to him, yearning for the closeness they once shared. The spark in his blue eyes and the chiseled contours of his biceps and pecs, reminiscent of a statue carved from marble, made her heart race. His strong jawline, framed by either a short beard or a rugged stubble, only added to his allure.

"The warlocks have been harassing the wolves," he accused. "Every time someone from the pack comes into town, they are bullied and harassed until they are goaded into taking action or have to return to the pack without completing their errands. Does it amuse you to tease and taunt women and children? To keep up a constant stream of pressure until we are all forced to either fight back or leave?"

"It's not that long since you were a warlock yourself," John said with a smirk. "You're pretty new to the shifter scene. Exactly how did *you* treat the wolves before you were turned?"

Jake reddened at the accusation. Reg was sure he did not like to be reminded of how he had caged the wolves, keeping them in tiny kennels in deplorable conditions while he performed his abominable experiments on them. Not only on adult wolves but also on embryos. Things that were forbidden by the human authorities, not just by unwritten moral or ethical standards. He had not cared about the wolves' human characteristics, claiming that they were not sentient. He had told many other lies to justify what he had done.

In the end, it had been a blessing that he had been bitten and turned by one of the newborn werewolves he was tormenting. It had been a kind of justice that no one had expected. Now, it would appear he was a full member of the pack with no sentimental ties to the warlocks he had once been aligned with.

"There must be some independent reports of what has been going on," Reg murmured to Sarah. "Have the wolves been harassed and provoked? Where are they now?"

John heard Reg, even though she was speaking quietly. "Whether they have been confronted or not doesn't make any difference. There is no excuse for the werewolves attacking humans in the town. They are in human territory. They are expected to abide by human laws."

"Wolves are an endangered magical species," Julian spoke up. "All of Florida is their territory. Any violence toward wolves, any kind of harassment, is punishable by fines and possible jail sentences."

"Nobody wants to hear from you," John snapped. "Who invited you here, anyway?"

"Magical investigations has every right to be present at this meeting. We must do everything within our power to preserve this endangered species." His eyes flicked toward Aleph. "Especially when there are actively breeding pairs in the area. One litter of cubs already born and two more on the way! They cannot be moved now. They must remain here."

"You think that because they're pregnant they can't be moved? Women move while they're pregnant all the time. Are the werewolves so delicate that their women drop their litters at the least disturbance? Are they like other animals that will eat their young if the babies have been touched by humans?"

Aleph leaped to his feet with a roar. His chair crashed to the floor. There was chaos for a few minutes while everyone tried to keep Aleph and Jake away from John and the others. Eventually, everyone was seated again, and when Reg looked around the room, it didn't appear that anyone had sustained any injuries. No bloody noses or split lips. It was a good thing no one was drinking, or it would have been a good old barroom brawl.

"Everyone sit," the mayor said belatedly. "Everyone must remain in their seats. Keep your hands to yourselves. This is a discussion; there will be no physical contact."

He looked around at everybody, pausing on each person individually until he got a nod or word of acknowledgment from them.

* * *

Fur and Fury, Book #24 of the *Reg Rawlins, Psychic Investigator*
series by P.D. Workman
can be purchased at pdworkman.com

* * *

ABOUT THE AUTHOR

P.D. Workman is a USA Today Bestselling author and multi-award winner, renowned for her prolific output of over 100 published works that span various genres. With a knack for crafting page-turners, Workman captivates readers with everything from cozy mysteries like the Auntie Clem's Bakery series to gripping young adult and suspense novels.

Her stories resonate deeply as she masterfully weaves sensitive themes—such as childhood trauma, mental illness, and addiction—into compelling narratives that evoke a powerful emotional response. Readers are drawn to her unique voice and empathetic portrayal of complex issues.

With each new release, fans eagerly anticipate another thrilling blend of thought-provoking storytelling and relatable characters that define P.D. Workman's brand as an author of unforgettable page-turners—gripping tales that leave a lasting impact long after the last page is turned.

> P. D. Workman, does not shy from probing the deep psychological scars of childhood trauma, mental illness, and addiction. Also characteristic of this author, these extremely sensitive issues are explored with extensive empathy, described with incredible clarity, and portrayed with profound insight.
>
> — —KIM, GOODREADS REVIEWER

Some of Workman's titles have been translated into Spanish, French, Portuguese, German, and Italian.

Workman began writing at an early age and is a prolific reader as well as writer. She is also passionate about teaching and learning, expresses her creativity through art and cooking, and loves exploring the Calgary parks and green spaces where the Parks Pat Mysteries are set. She was a legal assistant for many years and has done extensive charitable work.

Workman was born and raised in Alberta, Canada, and is married with one adult son.

Please visit P.D. Workman at pdworkman.com to see what else she is working on, to join her mailing list, and to link to her social networks.

If you enjoyed this book, please take the time to recommend it to other purchasers with a review or star rating and share it with your friends!

tiktok.com/@pdworkmanauthor

facebook.com/pdworkmanauthor

x.com/pdworkmanauthor

instagram.com/pdworkmanauthor

amazon.com/author/pdworkman

bookbub.com/authors/p-d-workman

goodreads.com/pdworkman

linkedin.com/in/pdworkman

pinterest.com/pdworkmanauthor

youtube.com/pdworkman

Find P.D. Workman's books at

PDWORKMAN.COM

Scan the QR code below

www.ingramcontent.com/pod-product-compliance
Lightning Source LLC
Chambersburg PA
CBHW030934260626
47169CB00002B/469